"That's enough, Mr. Adran," she said. "I'm not going to allow you to poke through my personal things."

He glanced at her computer, no doubt itching to check for signs that she herself was behind the lascivious e-mails. However, the police had already searched it, which he must know from reading the report.

On the office floor sat a wastebasket containing a crumpled envelope. Zahad frowned. "They should have emptied that. Or if that item was tossed there by the police, they contaminated the scene."

Jenny bent to get a closer look.

"Allow me." The sheikh knelt beside her, so close that an edge of his leather jacket draped across her knee. Warmth moved through her.

Using tweezers, Zahad held the bit of paper up to the light. "Do you recognize this pattern?"

"There's a pattern?" At an angle, she saw that he was right. There was a watermark in the paper, part of a logo.

Jenny recognized it, and almost wished she hadn't.

Br

Ch

Dear Harlequin Intrigue Reader,

At Harlequin Intrigue we have much to look forward to as we ring in a brand-new year. Case in point—all of our romantic suspense selections this month are fraught with edge-of-your-seat danger, electrifying romance and thrilling excitement. So hang on!

Reader favorite Debra Webb spins the next installment in her popular series COLBY AGENCY. *Cries in the Night* spotlights a mother so desperate to track down her missing child that she joins forces with the unforgettable man from her past.

Unsanctioned Memories by Julie Miller—the next offering in THE TAYLOR CLAN—packs a powerful punch as a vengeance-seeking FBI agent opens his heart to the achingly vulnerable lone witness who can lead him to a cold-blooded killer.... Looking for a provocative mystery with a royal twist? Then expect to be seduced by Jacqueline Diamond in *Sheikh Surrender*.

We welcome two talented debut authors to Harlequin Intrigue this month. Tracy Montoya weaves a chilling mystery in *Maximum Security,* and the gripping *Concealed Weapon* by Susan Peterson is part of our BACHELORS AT LARGE promotion.

Finally this month, Kasi Blake returns to Harlequin Intrigue with *Borrowed Identity.* This gothic mystery will keep you guessing when a groggy bride stumbles upon a grisly murder on her wedding night. But are her eyes deceiving her when her "slain" groom appears alive and well in a flash of lightning?

It promises to be quite a year at Harlequin Intrigue....

Enjoy!

Denise O'Sullivan
Senior Editor
Harlequin Intrigue

SHEIKH SURRENDER
JACQUELINE DIAMOND

TORONTO • NEW YORK • LONDON
AMSTERDAM • PARIS • SYDNEY • HAMBURG
STOCKHOLM • ATHENS • TOKYO • MILAN • MADRID
PRAGUE • WARSAW • BUDAPEST • AUCKLAND

ISBN 0-373-22749-3

SHEIKH SURRENDER

Copyright © 2004 by Jackie Hyman

Visit us at www.eHarlequin.com

Printed in U.S.A.

ABOUT THE AUTHOR

A former Associated Press reporter, Jacqueline Diamond has written more than sixty novels and received a Career Achievement Award from *Romantic Times* magazine. One of her previous three Intrigue novels, *Captured by a Sheikh*, introduced the hero of *Sheikh Surrender* as a supporting character. Jackie lives in Southern California with her husband, two sons and two cats. You can write to her at P.O. Box 1315, Brea, CA 92822, or e-mail her at jdiamondfriends@aol.com. Keep up-to-date online with her new releases at www.eHarlequin.com or www.jacquelinediamond.com.

JENNY'S NEIGHBORHOOD

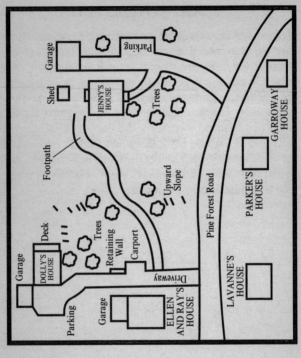

THE SUSPECTS

Zahad Adran—Only his half brother Fario stands between him and the sheikhdom he should have inherited.

Hashim Bin Salem—This political rival has much to gain by killing Fario and framing Zahad.

Al Garroway—If greed drives him to become a contract killer, who is he targeting—Fario or Jenny?

Dolly Blankenship—The retired policewoman always seems to be first at a murder scene.

Bill Blankenship—Did his bad temper turn murderous?

Grant Sanger—His ex-wife's death will give him custody of their daughter.

Lew Blackwell—Does he want Jenny's job enough to try to kill her?

Ellen Rivas—Formerly a friend of Jenny's, she's become intensely jealous of her.

Ray Rivas—A clue from a murder scene leads to the bank where he works.

Sergeant Parker Finley—His fascination with Jenny may have sent the detective over the edge.

In memory of Jane Jordan Browne

Prologue

Sheikh Fario Adran, governor of the country of Alqedar's Yazir Province, halted his sports car in the small parking bay. He swayed rhythmically to the closing bars of a rap piece on his CD player before killing the engine.

Late-afternoon sunlight slanted across the windshield. Crisp mountain air, tangy with the scent of autumn leaves, filled his lungs. What a strange land, he thought, where a man could drive a couple of hours from Los Angeles and enter an entirely different climate.

And, in a few minutes, meet an entirely different sort of woman.

From the bucket seat beside him, Fario lifted the picture he'd printed out of his Internet sweetheart, Jenny Sanger. Her dark blond hair color looked natural, although you could never tell, and those moss-green eyes gazed at him alluringly. It was the delicacy of her bone structure and a hint of uncertainty in her face that particularly drew him.

She was a woman meant to be dominated by a man like him. Young, too, although with the Internet, he supposed he ought not to assume she was exactly as she appeared. Her skin couldn't be that perfect, could it?

He'd been skeptical at first when a friend at UCLA graduate school suggested trolling the Web for women. Fario had never had any trouble in that department while attending school in Switzerland and university in England. American women, however, were too assertive for his tastes, and a bit suspicious of Middle Easterners as well, although Alqedar was a U.S. ally.

Jenny seemed different: warm and enthusiastic. She wanted a strong man, she'd told him, someone to fulfill her sexual fantasies.

At first, she'd questioned Fario's claim of being a sheikh. He'd e-mailed her a shot of himself and suggested she compare it with his portrait on the Web site his older half brother and chief adviser, Zahad, had set up as part of his campaign to modernize the province of Yazir. That had done the trick.

Zahad was always doing things like that since their father had died two years ago, after a long and debilitating illness. In addition to establishing a Web site, he'd sought international funding and hired an economic consultant. Fario appreciated this, since he preferred to spend as little time as possible in their dusty, backward province.

He would not like to have Zahad as an enemy. There was something hard and dangerous about his half brother. But his loyalty, Fario believed, was beyond reproach.

From the seat, he lifted the red-and-white checked headdress he seldom wore in America, except when he made the rare diplomatic appearance, and fitted it over his head. Jenny would love this, although it went oddly with his tailored jacket and designer jeans.

She'd promised to be waiting for him. As for her wardrobe, she wasn't going to be wearing a stitch.

Collecting the bottle of French champagne he'd brought as a gift, Fario slid out of the sports car and took stock of his surroundings. The land here was rugged, and from where he stood, he could see peaks rising to the north. On one side, a ravine filled with tangled brush bordered Jenny's property. On the other, a downward slope led to a couple of small houses tucked behind a screen of trees. There was no sign of anyone around and not even a hum of traffic from the narrow road.

The one-story home had a quaint roughness typical of the mountain residences he'd passed on the way, and utterly different from the mud-brick houses back in Alqedar. Fario liked the privacy. If all went well, he planned to visit here often.

Zahad had drilled him with warnings about potential assassins and insisted he exercise caution everywhere he went. To Fario, this seemed unnecessary. It had been a dozen years since Zahad and his comrades had freed Alqedar from its dictator. No one was going to attack a sheikh in the placid ski community of Mountain Lake, California.

Fario's Italian leather shoes whispered along the walkway from the parking area to the front steps. Perfume drifted from a flowering bush that defied the early-December chill.

Fario pressed the doorbell and heard the chimes peal within. He saw no movement at the window, although he'd expected Jenny to be watching through the blinds. Nor could he hear footsteps inside.

Growing impatient, he pressed the bell again. It was true that he'd given Jenny only an approximate arrival time, but she'd been so eager to meet him that he'd assumed she would be waiting. He didn't see any other cars around, but hers must be parked in the garage set past the house at the end of the long driveway.

Suddenly he smiled. The door appeared to open outward; if she answered it in the nude, someone might see her. Even in such a remote setting, it paid to be discreet.

He tried the knob. It turned easily.

"Hello, Jenny," he called and opened the door.

A blast destroyed the peace of the afternoon. A crushing pain spread through Fario's chest as the gunshot sent him sprawling backward down the steps. The bottle hit the walkway and shattered, spraying him with glass and champagne.

As darkness closed in, he formed one last fierce wish. "Avenge me, Zahad," he whispered, and then he spoke no more.

Chapter One

Three days later.

There was a man in her toolshed.

As Jenny Sanger emerged from the garage, she saw the shed door standing open. An instant later, she glimpsed a masculine figure moving inside the rough-hewn structure less than twenty feet away.

Tools had been stolen from that shed to rig a murder weapon. Had the killer come back?

Behind her, the heavy garage door clunked shut, cutting off her retreat. No doubt it also alerted him to her presence, in case he hadn't already heard her drive up.

Inside her oversize purse, Jenny's hand searched for the clicker or for her cell phone. Her fingers scrabbled in vain through a sheaf of reports from the elementary school where she worked as principal.

Maybe it was the police, she thought frantically. But detectives had searched the property thoroughly and given the all clear. Besides, the only vehicle she'd seen nearby was an unfamiliar car parked a short distance down the road.

Under the papers, her fingers identified her lipstick, a tin of breath mints and a bottle of Tylenol. Why couldn't she find what she needed? The man would come out any second now.

At least her keys were still in her other hand. Jenny edged

toward the back of the house and winced when her pumps crunched on the fallen leaves.

The late-afternoon sun cast a shadow across the man as he stepped out of the shed. Even in silhouette, she could see that he was tall and solidly muscled. Although she stood five foot eight and had taken self-defense classes, Jenny knew she'd be no match for this guy.

Inside the purse, her hand closed over a tube of pepper spray. She jerked it out, heedless of the tissues and mints scattering onto the walkway, and took aim.

The man lunged. He was so fast that the tube vanished from her hand before she could press the button.

He stopped a few feet away, the spray canister engulfed by his large hand. They stared at each other in a frozen tableau.

The glare of sunlight revealed a sharp-featured man with white scars vivid against his tanned skin. He stood almost six feet tall, with dark, shaggy hair straggling across his forehead and his temples. In his black leather jacket, he put her in mind of a warrior.

He broke the silence first. "Miss Sanger, I presume?" It didn't surprise her that he had a deep voice, but she hadn't expected a British accent mixed with a trace of something exotic.

"It's Mrs. Sanger." Although divorced for three years, Jenny had retained her married name.

"My name is Zahad Adran," the man said. "My brother, Fario, was murdered here three days ago."

His introduction made her only marginally less alarmed. Fario Adran, she had learned, was a sheikh from the small country of Alqedar. There was no telling what notions of honor or revenge his brother harbored.

Jenny zeroed in on a little scar on the right side of Zahad's face. It was balanced by a jagged slash bisecting his left eyebrow, further evidence that a lot of people apparently disliked this man. Irreverently, she wondered what other scars he hid from view, until she realized what she was speculating about and banished those thoughts.

The best defense was a good offense. "I'm sorry about your brother," Jenny said. "But you have no business trespassing."

Zahad ducked his head. "I apologize for startling you. You startled me, also. I will return your property." He tossed her the tube.

Jenny's hand came up instinctively and snatched the small container from midair. She wondered if it would be a violation of etiquette to spray him with it. Not a good idea, she supposed, given the speed of his reflexes. Besides, its return implied that the sheikh had no immediate hostile intentions.

He picked up the items she'd dropped and handed them to her as well. "I came to bring my brother's body home, but the coroner has not released him. I took the liberty of examining your shed because I understand the tools were used to position the murder weapon."

A couple of deep breaths gave her courage. "Let me bring you up to speed on a few things," Jenny said. "Number one, this is not public property. It's my home. Number two, believe it or not, we have a police department in Mountain Lake. They already did all those high-tech things like check for fingerprints and collect DNA evidence."

"I am aware of that, Mrs. Sanger," he replied mildly. "Because of my connection to the deceased, they allowed me to read their report. I attempted to speak with the detective but he was out investigating a carjacking at the ski lodge. They have a small robbery-homicide detail, apparently."

"I still don't see why you're prowling around duplicating their work. I don't need any more footprints messing up my yard."

His mouth twisted in what might have passed for a smile in other circumstances. "I can see that no one bullies you."

"I spent too much of my life being bullied," Jenny said,

although she wasn't certain why she chose to reveal that to a stranger. "I refuse to let it happen anymore."

"Nor should you. Let me be honest. I want to find the killer for my brother's sake, but I am also acting out of self-interest. Because of the situation in my home country, there are those who suspect that I may have had a hand in his assassination."

"Assassination?" No one had referred to the murder that way before.

"Our father chose Fario to succeed him as sheikh and governor of our province, although I am the elder son by my father's first wife," he explained. "The position carries with it a certain amount of power and access to hereditary wealth."

She didn't need him to fill in the blanks. "So your brother's death makes you a rich sheikh. Or is there a third brother lurking around the oasis?"

Again, the man favored her with a ghost of a smile. "Just me, although I am certain my stepmother wishes she had another son."

"So you want to clear your name." It made sense, but Jenny wasn't about to take his problems to heart when she had more than enough of her own. "I apologize if I sound cold, but I really don't care what's going on between you and your stepmother. Someone's been cyber-stalking me, sending out photos from years ago when I used to model, and luring men here by promising them sex. As far as I'm concerned, that bullet probably had my name on it, not your brother's."

After a long pause, the sheikh said, "You believe someone was trying to kill *you?*"

"Someone hates me. The gun was in my house and it was almost time for me to come home from work. That makes it a logical assumption. Speaking of which, I just put in a long day and I haven't been able to get inside my house since Monday except to pack a suitcase. The police just gave me permission to reenter and I've got a lot of cleaning to do.''

Today was Thursday, and her five-year-old daughter, Beth, would be returning on Sunday from a two-week visit with her father and stepmother in Missouri. By then, Jenny wanted everything as normal as possible.

"If someone is trying to kill you, how do you know there isn't another gun ready to fire when you walk in?" the man asked.

She'd been trying to reassure herself about that all day. "Because I had an alarm system installed and the locks rekeyed."

"According to the report, it is not certain the killer used a key," he said.

"That's true, but there was no forced entry." Several keys were probably floating around from the days when her great-aunt had owned the house. However, Jenny may simply have forgotten to lock the door.

"I would be pleased to enter the house ahead of you and ensure that it is safe," the sheikh offered. "I hope you do not interpret this as bullying. I assure you, Mrs. Sanger, if I wished to bully you, there would be no need to interpret it."

She didn't know whether to admire his gall or order him off her property again. She also wasn't sure she wanted to allow this man to look around inside, which was obviously what he sought. On the other hand, Jenny had been dreading the moment when she would have to step into the house.

Also, a part of her couldn't help hoping Zahad might find some piece of overlooked evidence. Much as she respected the local police, they were understaffed and possibly overmatched. Even after weeks of investigating, they still couldn't zero in on her cyber-stalker. What were the odds of their solving this murder quickly?

"I'll need to see some ID," she said.

From a pocket, he withdrew a gray-green passport stamped Republic of Alqedar. Inside, she found writing in both Arabic and English, along with a photo showing a younger Zahad.

In a flowing white robe and a checked headdress banded with dark cord, he projected an air of authority and, from the forward thrust of his jaw, impatience. "You don't like having your picture taken," she remarked.

"I loathe it."

The passport contained visa stamps from numerous countries, including more than one from the United States. "You've been to America before."

"I occasionally travel in the service of my country." He accepted the document back without further comment.

She could hardly refuse to let him help now that he'd cooperated with her request. "All right. But you can't stay."

"I only wish to take a look around."

"Do you really think you can find anything the police missed?" Jenny asked as she led him to the front. Although the back door was closer, it would make her uncomfortable to take him inside through her living quarters.

"I underwent special training in England. My goal was to become a security expert, not an investigator, but to be thorough I took several forensics courses."

When she reached the front, Jenny tried not to shudder at the bloodstains fading to brown on the concrete steps. "Watch out for glass. I doubt the police caught all the slivers."

"Ah, yes. The champagne bottle. Imported from France, no doubt, although the report did not specify the label."

"Your brother had expensive tastes?" She fitted her key into the new lock.

"Indeed." Zahad stepped forward quickly and covered her hand with his. His calluses brushed her skin, making her feel oddly protected. "Allow me."

"Okay." She retrieved her hand from beneath his. Jenny's gratitude at his apparent willingness to put himself in danger warred with a hard-won resistance to letting a man—any man—look after her.

"Stand aside, please," said the sheikh.

She moved away and braced herself as he opened the door. There was a pause, and then she heard the beeped warning that gave her one minute to disable the alarm.

As soon as Zahad cleared the doorway, Jenny input the code. She felt his eyes following her movements and reminded herself to change the code as soon as he left.

Indoors, a faint chemical scent lingered in the cool air. She hadn't been inside since Monday, when she'd arrived home to find police cars outside along with a fire truck and paramedic unit. She'd glimpsed a covered body on the sidewalk and smelled champagne and musky, unpleasant odors she hoped never to smell again.

Now Jenny took one look around her living room and wished she could twitch her nose and make the mess go away. Detective Finley had assured her the police were taking care not to damage things, but she'd be lucky if she could move back from the cabin she'd borrowed by the weekend.

All the furnishings had been pulled away from their usual resting places and the colored glassware in the china cabinet was disarrayed. Books sprawled across low shelves and some had tumbled onto the floor.

On the walls, painted china plates and framed reproductions of *Saturday Evening Post* covers hung askew. Dirt and black powder streaked the carpet and there were ashes around the fireplace. Some of the powder had drifted onto the skirted covers with which she'd updated the old sofa.

Seeing her home torn apart this way made Jenny feel personally violated. Until this point, she'd simply been terrified by the possibility that someone was trying to kill her. Now she felt angry, too.

"What on earth did they do in here?" She reached to right a vase that lay on its side atop the coffee table. "What's all that black stuff?"

"Fingerprint powder." Zahad's hand closed over her wrist before she could pick up the vase. "Do not touch anything."

"Why not? They're done here." She didn't think she could bear to leave this mess for one more second.

"*I* am not done," he said.

Jenny wanted to grab some rags and start righting this affront to her home. "The police have obviously gone over this house with a fine-tooth comb and maybe a sledgehammer for good measure."

"Yes, but they do not know my brother and I do."

"Your brother got shot on the porch."

"That's the way it looks, but looks can deceive."

Could the murder victim actually have come into the living room? Could other terrible things have happened in her home? If so, Jenny didn't want to know about them.

Zahad stared at a heavy chair upended directly ahead of them. "Would that be the one to which the gun was attached?"

"I guess so." Jenny didn't know how it had been done. She'd only heard that the killer had used wire from the toolshed to connect the trigger to the door.

Zahad indicated a couple of small holes in the wall. "That must be where he inserted the eye hooks."

"Maybe." She was reluctant to admit she hadn't known the killer had run the wire through eye hooks. The holes leered at her, yet another reminder of the violation that had occurred here.

"The gun belonged to you?" Despite his offhand tone, she knew this was no minor matter.

"I inherited it from my great-aunt, along with the house," Jenny said. "I fired it a few times at a target under Dolly's supervision. She's a retired policewoman who lives next door."

"She is the one who found my brother's body?"

"Right." That fact had been in the police report, of course.

"You kept the gun loaded?" Zahad asked.

"No. Unloaded and high up in a cabinet," Jenny replied. "The bullets were in a separate drawer." For good measure, she added, "This is an isolated place. My great-aunt once shot a rabid raccoon in the backyard."

"Surely you considered a gun good insurance against these unwanted suitors," the sheikh said. "Did you not even consider the possibility of rigging it as a form of self-defense in case one of them broke in?"

The suggestion that she'd set up the gun was ludicrous. "First of all, if I had, I'd have been more likely to shoot myself than anyone else because I'm about as mechanically gifted as a bunny rabbit. Second, if Dolly had checked the door to see if it was locked, she might have been the one who got killed. And third—wait a minute, I'm sure I've got a third point—"

"Perhaps you knew it was illegal to create such a deadly trap," Zahad offered.

"Well, I might have guessed that, if I'd thought of doing something like that, but I didn't," Jenny said. "Oh, I know. The guys showing up at my door weren't the real threat. Why would I want to kill someone who got suckered into coming here? It doesn't solve anything."

The sheikh lifted a hand to stop the flow of words. "You have persuaded me. Since I assume the police kept the gun as evidence, have you bought a replacement? It might not be a bad idea, if you are being targeted by a murderer."

One thing Jenny knew: She wasn't going to allow anyone to force her into taking steps that felt wrong. In retrospect, she should never have kept a gun, even unloaded, in a house with a child.

"No, and I don't plan to," she said. "I've never liked guns. My father was a military man, and he wanted my brother, Jeff, and me to learn how to shoot. I refused." She didn't add that it was one of the few times she'd defied her father.

Zahad studied the room. "What kind of music do you listen to?"

"Show tunes and pop," she replied puzzled. "Linda Eder, Audra MacDonald, Tony Bennett."

Releasing her, Zahad clasped his hands behind his back, crossed to her CD rack—which sat, displaced, on the floor by the coat closet—and made a cursory examination. "Very good."

"What were you looking for?"

"Rap CDs. If my brother visited often, he would have deposited some. I do not see any." He straightened.

"You mean, you thought I was having an affair with him?" Jenny retorted. "While I presumably stashed my five-year-old daughter in a closet?"

"Many women with children have affairs. Where is your daughter now?"

"She's out of state with my ex-husband." Jenny hadn't been happy about taking Beth out of kindergarten in the middle of the school year, but Grant had claimed those were the only weeks when both he and his wife, Shelley, could get vacation.

"It is fortunate that she was away when this happened."

"You're not kidding." Jenny was deeply grateful for this coincidence, and for the fact that she hadn't come home early that day.

She hated feeling glad that Fario had taken the bullet instead of her. She didn't want anyone to die. But, oh, she was glad that she hadn't been the one, for Beth's sake as much as for her own.

In her nightmares, the scenario played itself out repeatedly, with variations. Sometimes she arrived home in time to see Fario on the porch but too late to stop him. Other times she got here first, vaguely sensing danger but unable to prevent herself from reaching for the knob. Always, just as the door opened, she woke up on the verge of screaming and lay gasping for breath.

Zahad prowled through the front room. "The report indicated my brother carried several suggestive e-mails."

"That was the word the police used—'suggestive?'" She expected more direct language after reading a few brought by her previous unwanted visitors.

"I believe the term they used was 'explicit.'"

"That's more like it. I don't understand why someone wants to lure men here, but they didn't have any trouble doing it," she said. "It's amazing how gullible guys are."

"Your photograph obviously makes quite an impression." With one oblique glance, the sheikh let Jenny know that her features, from her high cheekbones down to her long legs, hadn't escaped his notice, either. To her dismay, she felt herself blush.

Although she considered herself on the thin side, with breasts barely large enough to fill an A cup, Jenny had been aware of her effect on men since her early teen years. It was the blond hair and green eyes, she supposed.

Usually, she wanted nothing more than to keep them at arm's length, but it was difficult to imagine any woman not reacting to this lean, restless man. Still, she didn't want anything from him except to be left alone.

"The kind of impression my appearance made on these men is something I could happily live without," she informed him.

"Tell me about them, these men."

When the first cyber-suitor had arrived six weeks earlier with a photo and expected to have sex with her, Jenny told him she must be the victim of a prank. Then she had to persuade a second visitor to leave. Worried, she'd called the police.

"They speculated that it might be a student's revenge for being disciplined," she explained. "They contacted an officer with a larger department who specializes in cyber-crimes."

He'd learned that someone was visiting various Internet chat rooms pretending to be Jenny and claiming to seek lovers. Whoever the cyber-stalker was, he'd covered his tracks by changing names and leaving false addresses. So far, four men had turned up at Jenny's home.

"At first, I figured someone just wanted to pester me," she said. "Then I began to worry that he wanted to harm me. Now I'm certain of it."

"It sounds like the behavior of an ex-husband." Keeping his hands at his sides, the sheikh shouldered through a swinging door into the kitchen.

There was more mess in there, Jenny discovered unhappily, although not as bad as in the living room.

"How do matters stand between you?"

"Grant and I were getting along fine until his wife discovered she can't have children," she admitted. "He started making noises a few months ago about wanting custody of Beth." Jenny had been stunned and furious. Every day since then, she'd expected to be served with papers.

So far, Grant hadn't taken any steps in this direction, although she had the impression he considered this two-week visit with Beth a trial run. Some women, she supposed, might have been tempted to coach their daughter on how to drive a stepmother crazy, but it would be cruel to treat Beth as a pawn.

"Sending these men here might give him leverage in court," Zahad said.

She'd considered that possibility. "Maybe. But I don't think he set it up. A couple of them confronted me when I was with Beth. Grant would never have endangered her that way."

"Does he have an alibi?"

"For Monday? I'm sure the police have checked. Besides, he lives in St. Louis."

"Perhaps so, but he may have some involvement." After removing a plastic bag from his pocket, he put it on, as if it were a mitt. The fact that he'd brought his own bag both impressed Jenny and made her uneasy.

If this man ever put his mind to committing a crime, he

would know how to avoid getting caught. She could see why some of his countrymen believed him capable of murder.

Yet she'd allowed him to come in here alone, even after he'd admitted he was under suspicion. That said something about Zahad's powers of persuasion. Jenny wasn't so sure what it said about her judgment.

He opened the refrigerator and inspected the contents. During Beth's absence, she hadn't done much cooking, and, of course, she hadn't been home in days. The sparse pickings included yogurt, pickles and a salad wilting under its plastic wrap.

"Is this necessary?" Jenny asked.

"It helps to substantiate your story," the sheikh replied.

"Because there's nothing in here your brother would eat?"

He closed the door. "The lack of wine and caviar speaks for itself."

Jenny recalled reading that many Middle Easterners avoided alcohol. "Is a sheikh allowed to drink?"

"My brother was raised in Germany, Switzerland and England." Zahad led the way into the guest room at the back of the house. "He chose which customs he wished to obey. He would have outgrown such notions in time." Beneath the critical tone, she detected a note of gruff fondness.

In the room, which doubled as a home office, the sheikh started toward her desk. She tried not to focus on the clutter of papers and computer disks the police had left in view. "That's enough searching, Mr. Adran," Jenny said. "I'm not going to allow you to poke through my personal things."

He glanced at her computer, no doubt itching to check for signs that she herself was behind the lascivious e-mails. However, the police had already searched it, which he must know from reading the report.

"Very well." He turned toward the door that led to the

hallway. "I understand the killer entered through the back. He must have come down this way."

"I suppose so."

On the office floor close to the hall sat a wastebasket containing a crumpled envelope. Zahad frowned. "They should have emptied this. Or, if that item was tossed there by the police, they contaminated the scene."

Jenny bent to take a closer look. "It's from a utility bill I got on Saturday."

"Allow me." The sheikh knelt beside her, so close that an edge of his leather jacket draped across Jenny's stocking-clad knee. Warmth fleeted through her.

Using the plastic bag, he moved the wastebasket to reveal a previously hidden scrap of paper on the dark beige carpet. "This is why the police should have emptied the waste-basket."

"It's just a piece of the envelope, isn't it?" she queried.

"I do not think so."

From a pocket, the sheikh took tweezers. By this time, Jenny wouldn't have been surprised if he'd produced a fingerprint kit and a test tube for DNA.

Using the tweezers, Zahad held the bit of paper up to the light from a window. "Do you recognize this pattern?"

"There's a pattern?" At an angle, she saw that he was right. There was a watermark in the paper, part of a logo.

Jenny recognized it, and almost wished she hadn't.

Chapter Two

"It's part of a crystal," Jenny said. "It looks like the logo of the First National Bank of Crystal Point. That's a town about five miles from here."

"Do you bank there?" Zahad kept a tight grip on the tweezers as he deposited the scrap into the bag.

"No." She hesitated. "I'm sure it doesn't mean anything."

"Who banks there?" he pressed.

"Lots of people. They offer free services that other banks charge for, including safe-deposit boxes." This wasn't a straight answer and they both knew it. Reluctantly, she finished, "One of my neighbors, Ray Rivas, started work there a couple of weeks ago."

Ray was no stalker and no killer, either. The affable man, who'd been glad to help Jenny with everything from plumbing problems to rototilling her garden, was married and had a four-year-old daughter. Most importantly, although he occasionally joked about her movie-star looks, she'd never felt any romantic interest or sexual pressure from him.

"A woman can tell if a man's trying to manipulate her," she explained to Zahad. "Believe me, I've got my radar permanently on alert."

"The fact remains that this bit of paper came into your house, possibly stuck to someone's pants cuff. And the police believe the killer walked down that hallway, although he apparently covered his shoes.''

"If Ray was smart enough not to leave muddy footprints on the carpet, how likely is it he stupidly dropped something that indicates where he works?" she retorted. "Besides, he might have left it before Beth went on her trip. His daughter, Cindy, is Beth's best friend."

Silently, she admitted that she didn't want to think someone she trusted could betray her this way. Was it possible she could misjudge a friend to such an extent?

"Beth left nearly two weeks ago, correct?" Zahad's eyes took on a hooded appearance that told her he was far from convinced. "You must have emptied your wastebasket since then."

"I might not have noticed a little scrap like that on the carpet," Jenny said. "I'm afraid I don't vacuum as often as I should."

This wasn't enough evidence to implicate Ray, to her relief. She could see, however, that in the sheikh's estimation her neighbor had just become a suspect.

"Where does this man live?" he asked.

"Next door." She gestured.

"I thought the woman who found Fario—what is her name? Dolly?—lived there." He pronounced "Dolly" with a hint of disdain, as if it were too frivolous a name for a grown woman. "What is their relationship?"

"Her name is Dorothy Blankenship, although everybody calls her Dolly. She's his mother-in-law." Jenny trailed Zahad along the hallway as he examined the carpet and moldings. "There are two houses on the property."

"They do not live together?"

"No, but Dolly owns both houses. She rents the front one to her daughter."

Jenny sometimes envied the close family grouping. Her own mother, who lived in Connecticut, had become absorbed in her husband and stepchildren after remarrying.

By contrast, Dolly was always there for friends and loved

ones. A dynamo at sixty-two, she tended to her ailing husband, Bill, and baby-sat for her daughter, Ellen. Since the cyber-stalking began, she'd also begun patrolling Jenny's property while she was at work.

Zahad peered into the master bedroom. Jenny saw the police had been here, too. Not only had they pulled aside her flowered coverlet, they'd also opened drawers and left black powder on the surfaces. She quailed at the thought of strangers pawing through her things.

Everything needed to be laundered. She wanted to scrub the whole house with Lysol and take a shower so hot it scalded.

"Do any of your neighbors have extensive knowledge of the Internet?" Mercifully, the sheikh's question pulled her away from her inner turmoil.

"Ellen designs Web sites at home. Everyone else uses it, too, I'm sure, except maybe Bill," she said. "He used to be a truck driver, but he's in poor health now and kind of forgetful. He might play video games."

"Who else lives close by?" He glanced into Beth's room but made no attempt to enter.

"The lot on the other side is undeveloped." As they returned to the living room, she filled him in on the people across the street. They included an elderly widow and a young married couple who'd moved in six months before. Directly across from her lived the police detective, Sergeant Parker Finley, along with his ten-year-old son, Ralph, and his housekeeper. His wife had died about five years earlier.

"Are you good friends with him?" the sheikh asked.

"Am I what?" She raised an eyebrow. It was the same expression with which she would greet a student's explanation that the cribbed test notes in his hand had fallen out of another student's pocket.

Zahad made a placating gesture with his hands. "I do not mean to insult you, Mrs. Sanger."

"It may come as a surprise, but I don't jump into bed with every male I meet," she snapped, and felt doubly annoyed when she recognized the note of hysteria in her voice. Jenny knew unflattering rumors about her had been circulating ever since the cyber-stalking began.

"That was not my implication. You may be completely blameless."

"Well, that's a relief." Her words dripped with sarcasm.

Frustration tightened his jaw. "I should have sent my cousin Amy to talk to you. You would love Amy. She is a rabid feminist who can never bear to lose an argument."

"Not with you, anyway," Jenny ventured.

He shrugged. "Yes, why me? I will never understand women and their prickliness. I am simply going about investigating this case in a rational manner. I had no intention of offending you."

"Oh, really?" She couldn't resist baiting him.

"It is not your fault if men react to your appearance. There. Have I apologized enough?"

"You haven't apologized at all." However, Jenny didn't feel angry anymore. She was beginning to find this man's clueless behavior around women almost appealing. He might be a male chauvinist, but at least he wasn't a smooth playboy. "You aren't exactly overloaded with social graces, are you?"

"I have had more important things on my mind." As Zahad spoke, his white scars stood out against his olive complexion. "I was forced to become a freedom fighter when I was young. Even after we liberated my country, assassination attempts were made against my cousin Sharif, an important leader for whom I served as chief of security. Now my brother is dead. I am sorry if I tread upon your delicate sensibilities, Mrs. Sanger, but it is in the pure interest of finding the truth."

The country of Alqedar, which had once been just a name on a map, began to seem more real to Jenny as the sheikh spoke, and so did the man himself. He had not merely led a colorful existence but a proud and distinguished one, which involved risking his life to protect his people.

It was hardly fair to expect him to behave like a politically correct Californian. Besides, she needed to find out who was stalking her, and he might be able to help.

"All right," she said, "let's make a pact. You treat me with respect and I'll do the same for you. That doesn't sound hard, does it?"

His bunched shoulders relaxed. "I can see that you must make a good school principal. Yes, that seems acceptable. May I continue?"

"Please do."

"If I may ask this without raising your hackles, I would like to know whether you have had any romantic entanglements with a man who might behave jealously. Any man."

"Okay, I'll answer that," Jenny said. "But I'm going to start cleaning up while we talk."

"Allow me to assist you," he offered. Despite some reservations, she agreed.

The sheikh not only helped move furniture, he volunteered to vacuum, although it took him a few minutes to get the hang of guiding the device over the carpet. When his longish hair flopped onto his forehead, he pushed it away impatiently.

As they worked, Jenny explained that she hadn't dated seriously since her divorce from Grant. Nor had she grown up in Mountain Lake, so there were no old boyfriends hanging around. With her father in the military, the family had moved frequently. They had lived in several countries, including Japan.

"I came here three years ago, after my divorce," she said. "Since I'd inherited a place to live, I applied for an opening as assistant principal at the local junior high." She'd been hired and remained there for two years before being promoted to elementary-school principal a year ago.

When the vacuuming was finished, Zahad borrowed her bottle of cleanser and a rag and tackled the fingerprint powder that had drifted to the dining table. "You have no inkling of anyone who wishes you ill?"

"Not aside from Grant and his wife," she admitted.

"Does your ex-husband have any friends in Mountain Lake?"

"He has no connections here that I know of." She paused in the middle of straightening her glassware to observe Zahad with mingled amusement and dismay. He was swirling the rag around the tabletop, smearing the powder rather than removing it. "I take it you don't do much cleaning at your palace. I suppose that's your wife's job."

"At the palace, the servants handle such matters. I have no wife. I have never taken the time to look for one." He frowned at his handiwork. "Why does this not look clean?"

Jenny started to laugh but changed her smile to a cough when she saw his mouth tighten. She *had* promised to treat him with respect. "Your technique could use some improvement."

"I believe I have assisted you sufficiently." With a grimace, he set down the cloth and went into the kitchen. She heard the water running as he washed his hands.

When he came out, Zahad said, "The detective is expected at his office by now. I believe he will want to see what I found."

"Do you plan to stay in town long?" she asked.

"A few more days, until Fario's body is released. I have taken a room at the Mountain Lake Inn."

Jenny felt a twinge of disappointment that he was leaving so soon. Despite his high-handed manner, there was something reassuring about the sheikh's confidence, not to mention his background in security.

No, she was being naive. This man was not her cyberstalker, but he might be the killer. He could have visited Fario in Los Angeles and seen an e-mail with her address and the date of the rendezvous. Zahad certainly knew enough to have set up the gun, and he had benefited from his brother's death.

She didn't really think he would have done something

so dishonorable. But she didn't intend to let down her guard with him.

"Well, have a safe trip back to Alqedar," she said.

The sheikh looked into Jenny's eyes as he extended his hand. When they touched, his strength enveloped her. At one time, she would have found it easy to yield to such a man.

And that kind of weak-mindedness, she told herself sharply, *is how you ended up being a thirty-two-year-old divorcée with a daughter to support and an arrogant ex-husband at your throat.*

She felt vulnerable, that was all. Shaky and scared and longing to turn back to childhood, when she had always had someone to protect her. But she couldn't and wouldn't turn to a man that way.

The sheikh held on to her hand a moment longer than necessary. "It is you who must be careful. You should hire a bodyguard."

"That's way beyond my budget." If Grant filed for custody, attorneys' fees would quickly deplete Jenny's modest savings.

"Then let us hope my brother was the intended target and you are in no further danger." Zahad released her hand. "Still, I am troubled about this cyber-stalker."

"Why do you care?" she asked.

"That is a question I cannot answer," he replied gravely, "except that I despise those who attack women and children. Also, you and I were brought together by a tragedy that will always haunt me and perhaps you as well. Such connections are not to be dismissed lightly."

Jenny had never given much credence to the idea of fate shaping someone's future. If there was a code of beliefs in California, it was that people made their own choices and determined their own futures. Yet the strength of Zahad's conviction made her less certain of that.

"I promise to watch my step," she said. "Good luck talking to Parker. I mean, to Sergeant Finley."

"Thank you. One more thing."

"Yes?"

"I suggest you lock your toolshed. If someone decides to do any further mischief, at least make him bring his own tools."

"Good idea," she said.

With a nod, he took himself away. The room seemed to shrink, as if adjusting itself to his absence.

Jenny waited until she heard the hum of an engine starting out on the street. Then she went to the alarm box and reset the code.

THE WOMAN WAS even more beautiful than she appeared in the photograph Zahad had seen at the police station. The passage of a few years since the picture was taken had given her an air of wisdom and maturity without diminishing the vulnerable look in her eyes.

She clearly had become cautious about sharing herself. The more he thought about her, the less able he was to consider her as the immoral temptress he had expected. Had he not read it in the police report, he still would have guessed that her ex-husband had been abusive.

Even if a woman infuriated him, Zahad would never strike her. That was the act of a coward.

Focusing his attention on the four-mile drive to town, he noted the way Pine Forest Road snaked between wooded rises and set-back, rustic homes. To those primarily concerned with aesthetics, Jenny's property would seem an ideal setting. To one concerned with safety, its isolation made it a poor bet.

Mountain Lake itself was a small town, distinct both from the dusty, ancient, spice-scented towns of Alqedar and from the medieval solidity of England, where Zahad had attended university. The buildings along its main street, Lake Avenue, blended frontier vitality and ersatz Swiss coziness with, at present, a garish overlay of Christmas lights and Santa Claus decorations.

He parked his rental car on the main street rather than tucking it out of sight at his nearby motel. It was harder for someone to tamper with a car in open view.

Across the street, the blandly modern building that housed the police department sat in a cluster of municipal structures beside an outdoor mall. Visible through a break between shops, Crystal Mountain Lake failed to live up to its name. In the dusky light, its surface appeared flat and leaden.

Nor was Zahad lulled by the apparent placidity of the town. Someone had committed a heinous crime here, and the list of suspects forming in his mind included the man he was about to meet.

In the glass-fronted lobby of the station, the desk sergeant called someone in the detective bureau and spoke in a low tone. The only other person there was a young man farther down the counter, filling out what appeared to be a theft report.

Thefts, traffic accidents and domestic disputes composed the majority of crimes in almost any jurisdiction. Zahad wondered how much experience Detective Finley had solving murders.

A middle-aged woman opened the door from a hallway. "Sheikh Adran?" She surveyed his leather jacket and slacks with a trace of disappointment. Apparently she'd been hoping for Lawrence of Arabia. "This way, please."

She led him past Traffic and Records to Detectives. An unoccupied desk in front bore a placard reading Mrs. Altoona. This, he presumed, was his escort.

The partitions that subdivided the large space failed to reach the ceiling and to dampen the clamor of ringing phones and beeping computers. Scuffed linoleum underfoot and acoustic tiles overhead, along with the uninspired ceiling fixtures, did nothing to soften the utilitarian planes.

Mrs. Altoona pointed the way to a corner office. "Sergeant Finley is expecting you."

"Thank you," he said, and took a moment to gird himself for the interview. Competent or incompetent, dedicated or corrupt, the detective he was about to meet would play a significant role in determining whether Fario received justice.

As Zahad entered, a man in a conservative business suit rose from behind his desk. Jenny's neighbor had regular features, a muscular build and the permanently tanned skin of an outdoorsman. From the touch of silver in the man's brown hair, the sheikh estimated him to be in his mid-forties.

"Sergeant Parker Finley," he said, thrusting out his hand.

The sheikh introduced himself and shook it firmly. At the detective's invitation, he took the only free seat, a straight wooden chair. A file cabinet loomed to his right, while a window behind the sergeant offered a view of a leafless tree and the municipal library.

"Sorry I wasn't available when you came in earlier." Finley resumed his seat behind the desk. "I understand you were allowed to read our preliminary report. It's not our custom to share the details of our investigations with the public, not even the families of victims. The desk sergeant shouldn't have shown it to you."

"I believe he consulted one of the captains before doing so." Zahad had no patience for bureaucratic stonewalling.

"I'm just letting you know that we won't be sharing our information from here on out," the man said.

"I, however, am willing to share whatever I come across," Zahad answered. "I think you will be interested in what I found at Mrs. Sanger's residence."

The sergeant's expression hardened. "You went poking around the house?"

"With Mrs. Sanger's permission, of course." He struggled to keep his tone even. He preferred not to get locked into a testosterone-fueled battle over territory, unless it was unavoidable.

"Please don't bother Jenny in the future."

"It is Mrs. Sanger's right to decide who enters her property."

The sergeant folded his arms. "You may be some kind of high official in your country, Mr. Adran, but you're in my jurisdiction now."

"Yes, and therefore I turn over to you the evidence that you overlooked." Zahad handed the plastic bag across the desk. "This lay underneath a wastebasket adjacent to the rear hall. It appears to bear the logo of the First Bank of Crystal Point. Mrs. Sanger will confirm that I discovered it in her presence."

The sergeant inspected the contents through the plastic. "Damn. I can't believe we missed this."

"Jenny—Mrs. Sanger—said she does not keep an account at this bank. A neighbor named Ray works there," Zahad added.

"A lot of people use that bank," Finley said. "Including me." He clamped his jaw shut as if he wished he hadn't volunteered the information.

"I'm sure a number of people could have accidentally contaminated the scene."

The detective's mouth worked angrily. But he replied with a terse, "We'll check it out." He retrieved an evidence envelope from his drawer and placed the Baggie inside.

"I will, of course, provide you with any other evidence I come across." Zahad waited for the explosion. He didn't have to wait long.

"Mr. Adran, you have my condolences about your brother," the detective retorted. "But if I find you interfering with my investigation, I won't hesitate to bring charges against you."

"As Fario's elder brother, it is my responsibility to uphold his honor."

"Not everyone in your country sees your relationship with your brother in such a benevolent light. I received a phone call this morning from a Mrs. Adran, whom I gather is your stepmother. She thinks you're behind his death."

That didn't surprise him. "Numa is distraught about losing her son."

"Apparently you should have inherited the—what do you call it?—sheikhdom from your father, but your half brother displaced you," the sergeant pressed on. "Now it's all yours."

"And you consider that to be a motive for killing him?"

"Wouldn't you?"

Zahad didn't bother to point out that what he had inherited was the lifetime burden of rescuing a province from the neglect incurred during his father's exile and subsequent long illness. Nor that, although he'd inherited substantial personal wealth, he intended to spend most of it on his compatriots. "Many people have motives."

"Did your brother have other enemies?" Finley asked.

"I was not his enemy. As to anyone else, there are people in my country who would prefer me as their sheikh in place of my brother. Others might wish to frame me and get rid of us both. But for any of them to have learned about Fario's infatuation with Mrs. Sanger and to take advantage of it in such a roundabout way stretches credibility."

The detective regarded him coolly. "Fortunately for you, even your stepmother admits you were in your country on Monday. That doesn't preclude the possibility of an accomplice."

"The same is true for Mrs. Sanger's ex-husband. I assume you have verified his whereabouts on the day of my brother's death," he said.

"We have."

"And where were you?" Zahad asked, in the slight hope that surprise would make the detective reveal something unintended.

Cold fury replaced the man's wariness. "This meeting is at an end." Finley got to his feet. "I don't want to see you around here again, Mr. Adran, and I don't want to hear about you bothering Jenny, either."

Zahad also stood. "When the coroner releases my

brother's body, I will leave town. Until then, I reserve the right to make my own inquiries. Particularly seeing that your department is not as thorough as it might be.''

Before the choleric redness could finish infusing the detective's face, the sheikh strode out of the office and past Mrs. Altoona's desk. Engrossed in reading a paperback with a knight and a large-bosomed maiden on the cover, she barely glanced at him.

He could almost hear his cousin Sharif chiding him for making an unnecessary enemy. *You shouldn't keep pointing out other people's incompetence. You make your life harder than it needs to be.*

It was true, Zahad reflected. When it came to diplomacy, he had a lot to learn.

But he didn't regret one word of what he'd said.

Chapter Three

By the time Jenny left her office on Friday, the secretary and the teachers had already departed. She checked the exits from the school's classroom wings and went out, locking the main door behind her.

In the field behind the school, a group of students was playing a pickup game of baseball despite fading light and a soft swirl of falling snow. Standing by her sport-utility vehicle in the adjacent parking lot, Jenny watched them for a few minutes. Although the forecast called for a storm and she wanted to put in another hour cleaning her house before heading off to the cabin, she enjoyed the chance to observe the students.

The boys, along with a couple of girls, appeared comfortable with themselves except for one undersize fifth-grader, a new transfer with the unfortunate name Elmer. When an opposing player struck out, he cheered so enthusiastically he tripped and fell, drawing catcalls from the rivals and smirks from his teammates.

"Some kids have a hard time fitting in, don't they?" Lew Blackwell, a fourth-grade teacher, said from a nearby space where he'd just unlocked his pickup truck. Reed-thin and balding on top, Lew was one of only two men on the teaching staff.

"He doesn't trust himself." Jenny's heart went out to the boy. "He's trying too hard."

"He'll learn," the teacher said.

"I suppose so." Jenny knew the boy had to find his own way of fitting in with his peers. Yet it went against the grain to leave him struggling.

"How's the cabin?" Lew asked.

"It's great. I really appreciate it." Lew, who lived in town, had loaned Jenny the cabin, which he'd bought as an investment and rented out to skiers and summer tourists. It had been a kind gesture, particularly considering that, as a longtime teacher who'd applied for the job of principal himself, he might have resented her winning the post.

Their relationship had been strained at first, after Jenny's promotion the previous year. It hadn't helped that Lew had asked her on a date while she was still assistant principal at the junior high. She'd declined, citing her recent divorce and the fact that she was in no emotional shape to start dating.

At forty-two, he seemed a bit old for her, and their personalities simply didn't click in romantic terms. Jenny felt glad she'd had an excuse not to go out with him. Nevertheless, he was a good teacher and had been courteous to her.

On the field, Elmer came to bat. He shivered as a cold wind hit him.

"Maybe we should go home," somebody said. "My butt's freezing."

"Let me strike him out first," called the pitcher.

"Don't count on it!" Elmer posed awkwardly with the bat.

"You couldn't hit a piece of cake." To demonstrate, the pitcher threw the ball right over the plate.

Elmer swung late and missed. The pitcher grinned. "See?"

The batter's team members grumbled among themselves. "He's going to blow it again," one of them complained.

Elmer's face crumpled. When the next pitch came in, he didn't even try to swing. Fortunately for him, it was high.

"If I were his coach, I'd tell him to let the ball hit him so he can walk," Lew said.

"Well, I wouldn't." Rummaging in the back of the SUV, Jenny found a pair of canvas slip-ons and exchanged them for her pumps. After tossing in her purse, she hurried to the field, heedless of the strange picture she must make in her tailored coat, suit skirt, stockings and incongruous shoes.

Elmer was grimly facing the batter as she trotted up. "Hold on!" she called.

"It's okay for us to play here, Mrs. Sanger," one of the boys said. "We do it all the time."

"I know." She smiled. "I'm an old baseball player from way back. Just thought I'd pass on a few tips." Her father had insisted his daughter spend her free time on the ball field, although she'd much rather have hung out at the mall with friends. Some of her most painful memories of her father involved their baseball games.

The children regarded her skeptically. It was too bad she hadn't had time to work with them during P.E., Jenny thought, because, willingly or not, she'd acquired a certain expertise.

"Elmer, pull the bat back like you're going to swing," she instructed.

Dubiously, the boy obeyed.

She could see him making the same mistake he'd made before. "You're locking your arm. That's going to slow you down and make your wrist roll." She sensed the others coming to attention as they realized she knew what she was talking about. "Keep your front elbow bent." She tugged on Elmer's arm until he achieved a more effective position. "That's it. Hands together, close to your body. No, not so far back. You'll lose the flexibility in your front arm." She stepped aside and nodded to the pitcher.

He threw another easy one over the plate. Elmer tensed as if about to swing, then got cold feet.

"Strike two!" shouted the umpire. One of the opposing players made a snorting noise.

"Here's another pointer," Jenny told Elmer. "Think yes! Every time, every pitch. Get ready to hit it. Don't second-guess yourself. It's yes, yes, yes. Track the ball with your eyes. Get ready to hit it right until the moment when you see that it's too far from the plate. Okay?"

"Okay!" He shifted as if getting a grip on himself.

The pitcher winked at the catcher. "He's going to throw it way off," one of Elmer's teammates said.

"Think yes!" Jenny hoped she wasn't going to screw this one up for the kid.

The pitcher sneered, wound up—and threw the ball straight over the plate. Teeth gritted, Elmer swung hard. With a *crack!* the ball went flying over the outfield. Two boys gave chase.

"Run, you idiot!" screamed a teammate. Recovering from his shock, Elmer raced around the bases and made it to third.

"Wow." His teammates shook their heads and grinned. "Way to go, Mrs. Sanger," one of them said.

"Way to go, Elmer," she corrected. "Okay, guys, don't play too long. If your fingers get numb, go home. I don't want to come back on Monday and have to dig your frozen bodies out of the snow."

A scattering of laughter followed her back to the parking lot. Her breath caught when she saw a man in a black leather jacket standing near Lew, his broad shoulders and masculine stance instantly recognizable. The sheikh's over-grown mane gave him a fierce air compared with the teacher's sparse thatch.

An unwanted shimmer of pleasure ran through Jenny. Zahad was the first man she'd met in Mountain Lake who made her think of tumbled bedsheets and late-night laughter. It was just her luck that a guy who probably thought women belonged in a harem made her knees wobbly and gave her the urge to check her lipstick.

"Hello, Mr. Adran," she said.

"You know this guy?" Lew asked.

She made introductions. "The sheikh's brother was the man killed at my house," she explained.

Lew blinked at the word *sheikh,* then caught up with the rest of the sentence. "I'm sorry for what happened. So you're only in town for a few days?"

"Correct," Zahad replied. Lew looked relieved.

"Is there something I can do for you?" Jenny asked the sheikh.

"I did not realize you would still be on the grounds. I wanted to familiarize myself with the town, and this place was on the list." To Lew, he explained, "As Fario's brother, I have a responsibility to make inquiries."

The teacher's eyes narrowed. "Jenny has enough to deal with. She doesn't need anyone hassling her."

"Your protectiveness is commendable," said Zahad. "Although unusual for a member of her staff. She is your boss, is she not?"

Tact really wasn't his strong point, Jenny thought. "Lew's also a friend. Now, if you don't mind, I want to do some more cleaning at home before the snow hits in earnest. So if you gentlemen will excuse me?"

They nodded stiffly. In her vehicle, when she glanced in the rearview mirror, she half expected to see them hissing and circling each other like tomcats. What was it about men that made them behave so possessively around a woman who was perfectly capable of taking care of herself?

Lew stood his ground. Zahad began strolling across the grounds, studying the one-story stucco building as if he might actually learn something from it. Most likely, he just wanted to provoke Lew.

With a sigh, Jenny headed home.

ZAHAD WASN'T CERTAIN what he'd expected to learn by visiting the elementary school. Despite what he'd said, he'd hoped to see Jenny, and in that he'd succeeded. The fact that she would sacrifice her dignity in order to coach her students in athletics impressed him. It showed real dedication.

He'd expected a very different sort of woman when he first saw her photograph. In person, too, Jenny gave an impression of soft femininity that went oddly with baseballs and canvas shoes, but she was also a serious professional. Her contrasts intrigued him.

Apparently they intrigued several other men, as well. The detective, for one. And now that teacher, the one glowering at Zahad as he pulled out of the lot—yet another potential jealous stalker.

This town was full of them. So was the Internet.

Last night, Zahad had e-mailed Viktor, a Russian programmer who worked under contract for the provincial government of Yazir, from his home base in central Russia. Viktor had promised to check chat rooms and see what he could come up with.

This morning, he'd forwarded some disturbing information. In the wee hours, California time, he'd found someone prowling the chat rooms pretending to be Jenny Sanger. The impostor had attached the same photo and urged the programmer to come visit her if he ever traveled to the United States.

Viktor hadn't succeeded in tracking down the sender's identity, but he had sent Zahad a copy of their conversation. The chat dialogue itself proved salacious but not very informative. A couple of misspellings might rule out a teacher as the perpetrator. On the other hand, one never knew.

At midmorning, Zahad had driven five miles to Crystal Point to look at the bank, which turned out to be a small, free-standing building with drive-up windows, ATM machines and a glass front. He'd ventured inside and spotted a desk whose placard bore the name Ray Rivas.

Jenny's neighbor was a stocky Hispanic man who'd been discussing loan terms with a young couple. When the man's gaze flicked upward, he'd fixed on Zahad with a glint of curiosity.

Withdrawing, Zahad had cursed under his breath. He should never have risked attracting attention.

So far today, he was batting zero, to use terminology those baseball players would understand. This made him wonder whether most American women were as knowledgeable about sports as Jenny. It seemed unlikely.

He found himself seeking an excuse to swing by her house. A poor idea, since she would no doubt insist that he work while they talked. Zahad could still smell the lemon scent of the furniture spray on his hands, despite repeated washings. Give him blood and guts over lemony freshness any day.

His cell phone rang. Since only key people had this number, he pulled into a petrol station—gas station, he corrected himself—and responded.

It was his cousin Amy Haroun. Although she had a knack for irritating Zahad, he'd hired her six months ago, with Fario's consent, as Yazir's director of economic development.

Together, she and Zahad had drawn up a master plan for revitalizing the economy of the province and bringing the infrastructure into the twenty-first century. Not only did she boast a business degree and an international background, she also understood the politics and the needs of their people. She worked hard, too, as evinced by the fact that she was telephoning in what was the middle of the night back home.

Amy went right to the point. "Numa's asked President Dourad to appoint her nephew governor of Yazir until you're cleared of suspicion in Fario's death."

Zahad uttered a few colorful phrases. Although the president couldn't take away the title of sheikh, he could reassign power. The tangle that would result from conflicting loyalties and arguments over who controlled what aspects of the provincial government would only harm its much-needed reforms.

"This must be stopped, but I cannot come back yet to

defend myself. Which nephew does Numa want appointed?''

"Hashim Bin Salem."

At twenty-four, Hashim was a playboy who'd been a close friend of Fario's. "Someone she can control," Zahad noted. "Or perhaps he has ambitions of his own."

"Could be."

It didn't surprise Zahad that his stepmother wanted to solidify her position as well as get revenge against him. He was sure she blamed him for Fario's death not only because she thought he'd arranged it, but because he'd encouraged Fario to attend graduate school in America. In addition, she must fear that once Zahad solidified his position, he would take revenge against her for persuading his father to disenfranchise him.

He had no such intention. To him, Numa was simply a nuisance that he wished to move aside.

"I require an advocate," he said. Since Amy worked for him, she was already compromised in the eyes of their countrymen. "Perhaps Sharif would be willing." Their cousin was a powerful sheikh who headed a larger province.

"He already called and offered to speak out on your behalf," she explained. "He wishes he could go to the capital in person, but Holly is expecting a baby any day."

Sharif had lost his first wife in childbirth while he was away fighting in the revolution. He would never leave his second wife at such a time.

However, President Dourad held Sharif in such high regard that his help would be valuable even at a distance. "I know he will do his utmost," Zahad replied. "Please ask him to point out that I am awaiting the release of my brother's body so I may escort it home. Surely there is no reason for hasty action during this time of mourning."

"I'll do what I can, but Numa's being a real pain in the butt," Amy said. "She has friends at court, so to speak." His stepmother was known for cultivating political friendships.

"I hope she is not treating you disrespectfully." The two women lived in the same palace complex.

"She doesn't dare. I've hinted that Harry's stockpiling bombs in his lab."

Amy's husband, Harry Haroun, a chemist, had moved to Yazir with her and their two children when she accepted the post from Zahad. In the laboratory furnished for him on the palace grounds, he was developing an improved fertilizer suited to the desert climate. Although bombs could be made from fertilizer, Harry had the heart of a kitten. But Numa didn't know that.

"Good thinking," he said.

"You know, I'm on your side in this one," Amy reminded him.

Although it pained Zahad to make a concession, he could see that he must. "I rely on you utterly."

"That must have hurt."

"More than you can imagine."

After he rang off, he sat in his car, seething at his stepmother. He hated it when people acted for petty personal gain, particularly when they got in his way. Why must he fight Numa and that callow nephew of hers simply for the right to improve his province's living conditions?

Perhaps it was a good thing that circumstances prevented him from flying back to Alqedar and giving the president a piece of his mind. Although he respected Abdul Dourad, he knew the country's leader must juggle competing interests. Zahad's take-no-prisoners approach to negotiating was unlikely to win him allies.

He wanted to get on with this investigation, and he wasn't making any progress sitting here watching people pump petrol into their tanks. Dropping by the elementary school and indulging himself in making conversation with Jenny hadn't helped his case, either.

Let the other men in town prostrate themselves at her canvas-covered feet. Zahad had better things to do.

JENNY GREW TENSE as she neared her house. In the aftermath of the murder she'd lost the sense of security she'd always associated with the place.

When she was a child, the house on Pine Forest Road had become a haven to return to as her parents moved around the globe. Whenever possible, she had visited her maternal great-aunt, Brigitte Ostergaard, a childless widow who'd operated a Swedish smorgasbord restaurant in town. After Brigitte died five years ago, Jenny had been deeply touched to learn she'd been named as heir.

For two years, as her marriage crumbled, she'd rented out the property. It had been wonderful to land a job in town after her divorce and to move here permanently.

Now she wondered if she would ever look at that front porch and walkway again without picturing the flash of emergency lights and the huddled shape she'd seen on Monday. If not for Beth, she might consider selling the place.

But what good would it do? The stalker would likely continue the harassment as long as she stayed in the area, and Jenny refused to be driven from her job. Besides, there was no guarantee she'd be safe anywhere else, either.

Resolutely, she pulled in to her driveway. Instead of proceeding to the garage, she halted in the parking bay. Given the rapid rate at which snow was accumulating, she'd only be staying a short while.

Her mind leaped ahead. She ought to change into jeans, and she also wanted to retrieve a pair of boots to take to the cabin. Absorbed in these thoughts, Jenny didn't see the man until he emerged directly in front of her.

"Jenny! It's me, Oliver." That broad, lascivious smile was all too familiar, although she'd never seen this bald, tattooed man before and didn't know anyone named Oliver. Her heart sank when she spotted the computer-printed photograph he held.

"Oh, for Pete's sake!" she snapped, silently rebuking herself for not paying more attention to her surroundings.

A quick glance told her the intruder had passed the parking bay and stashed his red sports car behind a tree near the garage. That's where he must have been lurking while he waited for her to come home.

She reached into her purse, but before she could find the cell phone or pepper spray, Oliver's beefy hand closed over her wrist. At close range, he smelled of alcohol. "No games, baby," he said, stuffing the photograph into his pocket and reaching for the front of her coat. "You promised me a good time and I want it."

The prospect of being pawed set off waves of fury and disgust. "Let go!" Jenny tried to twist away, but she couldn't get a firm foothold on the snowy concrete and the man was too strong. "Someone's played a trick on you. I never sent you that picture. I'm being cyber-stalked."

"Quit messing around," Oliver panted. "I didn't drive all the way from Nevada for nothing."

"Let go or I'll have you arrested!" Why couldn't he get it through his thick head that she hadn't invited him?

"I ain't letting you call no cops. I violated my parole to get here because *you* told me to," he growled.

Wonderful. Her cyber-stalker had found an ex-con to do his dirty work. "Just go away," she said.

"I don't think so." His lip curled.

Up close, she read Live Free or Die! on the tattoo snaking up his neck. As snow formed a curtain around them, Jenny realized how isolated they were. No matter how loud she screamed, none of her neighbors was likely to hear.

Who despised her enough to keep setting her up? And how was she going to get out of this?

Chapter Four

Almost subliminally, Jenny registered the buzz of a car approaching on Pine Forest Road. Even if the motorist could see them through the trees, however, there was no guarantee of help.

Oliver's head jerked toward the house. "Inside. Now!"

"No!" Although she was so frightened she could hardly breathe, Jenny tried to break away. "Leave me alone!"

"Shut up!" His grip like a vise, the man began hauling her up the walk. She felt as if her arm were being pulled from its socket.

Jenny tried to scream, but nothing came out. Although the sound of the engine grew louder as the car turned in to her driveway, it remained largely hidden from view.

Oliver halted. After an indecisive moment, he released her. "If you know what's good for you, you'll send them away."

Despite Jenny's desire to put as much distance as possible between herself and her attacker, her knees had turned to mush. She hated this paralyzing fear. What was wrong with her?

Then she caught sight of the car and its infuriated driver. Behind the wheel, Zahad had realized what was happening.

Barely taking time to brake, he came flying out and dodged across the snowy walkway as if expecting a bullet to whiz by. Jenny felt the shock of air as he slammed into

Oliver. The next thing she knew, the ex-con lay on the ground, facedown with his arms yanked back and Zahad straddling him.

"Are there any more of them?" the sheikh demanded as he patted the man down for weapons.

"I don't think so." The quaver in Jenny's voice embarrassed her.

Oliver struggled for breath. "Hey, man!" he rasped. "She sent for me!"

Zahad caught sight of the crumpled photo lying in the snow. "Count yourself lucky. The last man who showed up here caught a shotgun blast in the chest."

"Yeah?" the ex-con said. "Who the hell are you?"

"The victim's brother."

"Then you oughta hate this witch as much as I do."

Jenny's fists tightened with rage. The only problem was, she wasn't sure who or what made her angriest—this creep, her stalker or her own inability to act a few minutes earlier.

"Did he hurt you?" Ignoring Oliver's crude remark, the sheikh shook a wing of dark hair from his forehead.

She rubbed her wrist. "Just a bruise." Her shoulder was going to ache later, too, she thought.

"It ain't my fault," Oliver whined. "She made me mad."

"Do you want to press charges against this scum?"

"Who're you calling scum?" Oliver tried to twist around. Zahad drove one knee into his ribs and the man collapsed.

Furious as she was, Jenny had to face facts. Once the intruder showed the authorities the e-mails to prove he'd believed his advances were welcome, he would at the most simply be sent back to prison for a parole violation. He looked like the type to hold a grudge, and she didn't need any more people holding grudges against her, especially one who would likely soon be back on the street.

"Let him go," she said. "He's not the real enemy."

That wasn't entirely true, she thought, her teeth clench-

ing. Any man who believed he had the right to subdue a
woman by force was the enemy. Still, sending this creep to
jail for a few months wasn't going to knock a sense of
decency into him.

Zahad swung off the man. As Oliver staggered to his feet,
the sheikh spoke in a low, menacing tone. "If I ever see
you again, anywhere, anytime, you will be dead. I have
killed more men than I can count. No dogs yet, but I am
willing to start with you."

"Don't worry. I don't want nothing to do with you crazy
people." The ex-con headed for his car. The engine turned
over twice. Just as Jenny began to fear he might be stuck
here for repairs, the guy took off so fast he nearly clipped
Zahad's vehicle.

She took a wobbly step toward the house. Thinking the
better of her bravado, she grabbed the porch railing for
support. "Thank you," she whispered.

"You should let the police know what happened," the
sheikh said. "He may hang around."

Jenny nodded. "I'll give him time to leave, then file a
report in case he comes back."

She and Zahad regarded each other through the falling
snow. He was breathing harder than usual, she noted, and
then realized she was, too.

The world had just turned dark, and Zahad's watchful
figure shone like a beacon. If he hadn't been here…

She refused to dwell on what-ifs. "Your timing was perfect. I'm grateful you came by."

"It is my intention to interview the neighbors." He
glanced up and caught a snowflake right on his well-formed
nose.

"Be careful you don't get stuck out here. There's a big
storm forecast." On the point of fitting her key in the lock,
Jenny felt a wave of aversion. After what had just happened, she couldn't face the sense of violation in her house.
"Actually, I think I'll go straight to the cabin where I've
been staying. I'll call the police after I get there."

"Are you well enough to drive?" Zahad asked.

Jenny could handle an automobile, but approaching the remote cabin alone in her current state of mind was another matter. "I'd appreciate it if you'd follow me."

"Of course." She felt glad he didn't fuss or insist on driving for her.

Zahad's car fell into place behind her vehicle along the curving two-lane highway, heading away from town. In the thickening storm, only two other cars went by. She kept checking her rearview mirror to reassure herself that he was still there.

Jenny reached the turnoff three miles down the road before it occurred to her that the sheikh didn't have four-wheel drive. She ought to send him away rather than let him risk driving an additional mile on a side road already dusted with snow.

But the prospect of arriving alone in the rapidly falling darkness stopped her. Although three or four other vacation cabins lay near the one where she was staying, she didn't know whether any of them were occupied at the moment.

There was no reason the cyber-stalker couldn't have found out her temporary address. He might direct someone here, too.

Shivers racked her, almost erasing the hard-won self-control. For once, Jenny didn't even try to give herself a pep talk. She just made the turn and let Zahad follow her to Lew's cabin.

Built of timber and glass, the A-frame structure was smaller than her house but more distinguished architecturally. Jenny halted in a double carport beneath the faint glow of a safety light.

On the approach, Zahad's wheels spun briefly in the snow before catching purchase. He pulled in beside her, shut off the engine and got out.

Yesterday, this lean, scarred man had been a complete stranger. But now, his presence was so welcome Jenny had to fight the urge to throw her arms around him.

"Do you mind waiting until I get inside?" Despite her determination, the words came out shaky.

"Does this place have an alarm?" he asked.

She shook her head.

"Then I will go in first." His gaze swept the wooded lot and the darkened houses nearby. "The owner should install one."

"I don't think Lew wants to go to the expense for a rental."

The sheikh finished inspecting their surroundings. "This cabin belongs to the teacher I met at your school?"

"Yes. He was kind enough to lend it to me for the week."

"How generous," the sheikh said dryly. "I presume he has a duplicate key?"

"I'm sure he does, but Lew isn't a threat." He'd only dropped by the cabin the first day to make sure she had everything she needed.

"How do you know this?" Zahad's shoes sank into the snow as they approached the porch. He wasn't exactly dressed for winter weather, Jenny noted.

"Instinct, I guess," she admitted.

"If your instincts about dangerous men are so trustworthy, why didn't they warn you about your husband?"

Jenny's temper flared. Although she'd mentioned Grant's abusive behavior in her statement to the police, it was nobody else's business. "My relationship with him doesn't concern you!"

"Except that he may be responsible for my brother's murder," Zahad said levelly.

He had a point, but he'd just pushed one of her buttons. "The fact that I made one mistake doesn't make me an idiot. Marriage is complicated, but I don't suppose you'd know about that, would you?" As soon as she heard the words slice through the air, Jenny regretted them. "I'm sorry. You just saved me from that creep. I didn't mean to be rude."

Although it seemed to pain him, Zahad said, "I am the one who should apologize. Tact is not my strong suit."

"Today, it doesn't seem to be mine, either." Much as the sheikh annoyed her at times, Jenny reflected, there were worse things than a man who blurted out what he was thinking.

"I will stick to the areas in which I have some expertise. Such as security." He removed the key from her hand. "Stand back, please."

She moved aside. When Zahad opened the door, Jenny braced herself. She wondered how long it would take before she stopped expecting the crack of a gun.

Inside, a trace of warmth greeted them. She turned up the thermostat and switched on the soft overhead illumination.

"Please remain here while I inspect the premises." The sheikh moved swiftly between the spare Scandinavian-style furnishings and climbed the stairs to the loft.

While she waited, Jenny put in the promised call to Parker, who as usual was working late. She felt sorry for his son, Ralph, although the housekeeper, Magda, appeared genuinely fond of the boy.

After Jenny described the incident, Finley promised to alert the patrol officers about Oliver. "What about Sheikh Adran?" he asked. "Has he left?"

"He's checking the cabin for me."

"You're there alone with him? I'll come and get you," Parker offered. "You can stay at my house tonight."

The detective hadn't asked whether she wanted his help, Jenny noticed, and the truth was, she didn't. The prospect of sleeping in his house made her feel smothered, not secure. "I'm fine here."

"How much do you know about Mr. Adran?" he demanded.

She recalled Zahad's statement that he'd killed a lot of people. "Not much." *Except that, no matter what he's done in the past, he protects me without trying to take over my life.*

"I don't consider him trustworthy. I certainly wouldn't want him spending time around you." Jenny pictured the detective's cool gray eyes narrowing as he spoke.

She'd found those same eyes assessing her from the day she moved into the neighborhood. Since then, Parker had occasionally dropped by to discuss matters ranging from his son's schoolwork to improving snow removal on their street. They'd attended a couple of community events together with their children, but Jenny had declined further invitations, and the detective appeared to have taken the hint.

He'd never entirely given up, though. Sometimes she got the impression he was just biding his time.

"Give me one good reason why I shouldn't trust him," she said.

"This guy was part of a rebel army that overthrew the government of his country about a dozen years ago," he replied. "We're talking violent revolutionaries here."

That must be when he'd killed people, Jenny reflected. "I thought Alqedar was a democracy."

"That I don't know," Parker admitted.

"Well, if he overthrew some other form of government to install a democracy, doesn't that make him a freedom fighter?"

"Maybe." The detective sounded gruff. "That isn't all."

"Let's cut to the chase," Jenny said. "Has he been charged with any crimes?"

"Not that I know of."

"End of story." She already knew Zahad had lived a rough life, one far outside her own experience. Since she had no intention of getting involved with him beyond her present predicament, none of that mattered. "Don't come and get me. What you ought to do, Parker, is go spend more time with your little boy before he grows up."

"I can take care of my own business," he snapped.

"I'm speaking as an education professional. It's good advice. Don't ignore it."

Coolly, he said, "I'll make a report about the intruder. Thanks for letting me know."

"You're welcome." If she'd thought it would do any good, Jenny would have added that it was going to be difficult to keep the police informed of developments if, every time she called, Parker became overbearing.

The sheikh descended the stairs, his dark clothing stark against the light decor. "Everything appears secure."

"That's all you have to say?" Jenny couldn't resist teasing.

"What more would you like?" He remained standing, making no move to take off the leather jacket he wore over a turtleneck sweater. As his unassuming virility filled the room, Jenny clenched her hands against the temptation to reach out and unbutton his coat.

"It's just that everyone else feels compelled to give me instructions, whether I want them or not," she said. "Parker Finley wants to carry me off to his house for safekeeping. A couple of my colleagues keep nagging me to stay at a motel."

"People can get killed in motels, too," Zahad replied.

"Well, that's comforting!"

"I am not here to comfort you. I am happy to help where I can, but you know my purpose."

To solve Fario's murder. Beyond that, he took no interest in anyone or anything in Mountain Lake. To Jenny, that was a mark in his favor.

In movies and on TV, beautiful women seemed to have all the advantages. There definitely were some, as Jenny knew from having helped pay for college by modeling. But after spending much of her life fending off unwanted attention, and now assailants, as well, she could see the disadvantages, too.

The funny thing was that she wouldn't have minded a

little more concern on Zahad's part. Just enough so that he would linger for another half hour or so until her nervous system returned to normal.

"We both want this case solved," she said impulsively. "Some mutual cooperation might be in order."

"You are offering to work with me?" He sounded dubious.

"You did find that piece of paper the police missed," she noted. "And it doesn't sound like Parker plans to take advantage of your abilities."

"I would be pleased to accept your input. The question is whether you have anything to contribute beyond your goodwill."

No one could accuse the sheikh of currying favor, Jenny thought with a touch of amusement. "You may have the security training, but I'm the one with an inside track," she retorted.

"Please explain."

"My neighbors are more likely to talk freely if I introduce you."

"And you will do that?"

Until now, she'd had no intention of it, but she doubted he'd get far without her. "Sure. Except maybe to Tish Garroway, the young woman who lives across the street. She doesn't like me."

"Why not?" Zahad asked.

"I honestly don't know." Tish, a waitress at the ski lodge, and her husband, Al, a ski instructor, had moved in six months ago. Although she'd made friends with Ellen, Tish was frosty to the point of rudeness toward Jenny.

"Introductions would be helpful," Zahad conceded. "Also, since this killer may be the same person who is stalking you, it would help me to gather more information about your life."

Jenny started to bristle, until she realized that guarding her privacy too jealously might cost her dearly. "All right.

We can compare notes over dinner.'' That would give her time to regain her equanimity—if he agreed.

Zahad's gaze had shifted to the upper windows in the A-frame. Unlike the curtained lower windows, they provided an unobstructed view of a rapidly descending wall of whiteness. Jenny could already hear the conventional demurral: If he stayed any longer tonight, he might get snowed in.

But she didn't feel ready to be left alone yet. The chafing of her wrist and an ache in her arm reminded her of how she'd been brutalized.

Zahad startled her by removing his jacket and hanging it on a rack. His turtleneck jersey clung to his broad chest. ''Very well. I presume you have food.''

''I'll rustle something up.'' She retreated into the small kitchen, separated from the front room only by a counter. ''How about omelettes?''

''What we eat does not matter.''

''Not at all?''

''Not as long as it does not violate my people's dietary customs,'' he added. ''Despite my brother's fondness for wine, I do not drink alcohol. I also do not eat pork.''

''I don't put wine in my omelettes. And the last time I looked, pigs didn't lay eggs,'' Jenny said.

A smile transformed Zahad, for the space of a heartbeat, into the handsomest man she'd ever seen. It vanished almost instantly. ''An omelette will be suitable.''

She preheated the oven for French bread and began fixing salads. Leaning against the counter, the sheikh watched without speaking. It was like having a puma in her kitchen, Jenny thought, but one that didn't appear likely to pounce, at least not at the moment.

''Tell me about the police report,'' she said. ''If they identified any suspects, they haven't told me.''

''There were no fingerprints other than yours on the gun or the chair. The killer was careful.''

''What about DNA evidence?''

"That has not come back from the laboratory. I believe it takes several weeks. However, if the killer had legitimately visited your house in the past, his or her residue would indicate nothing."

"Only if it comes from a stranger?" she asked. "Someone from your country, perhaps?"

"They would have to know who to test." Zahad drummed his fingers on the counter. "I doubt we will solve my brother's murder through physical evidence. Whoever set this up was clever and possibly knowledgeable about police procedure."

The implication chilled her. "You suspect Parker?"

"He must be considered, although many people know about police procedure from television. Your neighbor Mrs. Blankenship is also a former police officer," Zahad pointed out. "In any case, I doubt I am as suspicious of Sergeant Finley as he is of me."

"What makes you say that?"

"I met with him." The sheikh released a short breath that was almost a laugh. "He became insulted when I asked his whereabouts at the time of the murder."

Jenny popped a loaf of refrigerated bread dough into the oven. "No, I don't imagine Parker was pleased. But disliking you isn't the same as suspecting you." She set the salads and dressing on the counter.

"He pointed out, with reason, that I benefit most from Fario's death. Even my stepmother concedes that I was in Alqedar at the time, but the murder could have been carried out by a hit man."

Jenny shuddered. A hired killer in her house? "You think that's who did this?"

"I find it unlikely. The method was imprecise. It posed too high a risk of killing the wrong person."

"Don't remind me." She deliberately changed the subject. "Tell me, why did your father choose Fario over you? You seem like you'd have been a better leader."

"He did not choose my brother because of his superior

abilities,'' Zahad said with no apparent rancor. ''Still, I grant that he was more sociable than I am. That is not difficult.''

Jenny liked the fact that he was as uncompromising with himself as with the rest of the world. Still, he'd dodged the point. ''You didn't answer my question.''

''There were several reasons why my father elevated Fario. Of course, it pleased my stepmother, Numa.''

While she waited for him to continue, Jenny cracked eggs into a bowl and stirred them. Perhaps if she refrained from asking questions, the sheikh wouldn't keep getting side-tracked.

His tone became reminiscent. ''Seventeen years ago, when I was nineteen, a dictator named Maimun Gozen overthrew the legitimate government of Alqedar. We chose different paths, my father and I. I joined the forces training to fight Maimun. My father sought to appease him and to keep a low profile.''

Vaguely, Jenny recalled reading about the troubles in the small Arabian country. But at the time she'd been a high-school student more concerned with grades and her overly strict father than with foreign affairs.

''My activities created serious difficulties for my father. He and Numa were forced into exile in Europe for nearly five years. Even after we overthrew Maimun, my father never forgave me. With Numa's encouragement, he blamed me for his continuing health problems and the economic troubles of our province.''

''When did your father die?'' she asked as she chopped onions and tomatoes, then sautéed them.

''Two years ago. I admit, I was as stiff-necked as he. After he rebuffed my first attempts, I never again asked for his forgiveness. Sadly, I was not called to his bedside and we never said goodbye.''

''What kind of relationship did you have with your brother?'' Jenny sprayed oil into an omelette pan.

''We got along well, considering that Numa and others

did their best to create ill will. Although with the title came the position of governor, Fario had no interest in improving the lot of our people. He asked me to serve as his lieutenant. Unfortunately, he wasted part of our family's personal fortune, which I believe should be invested in our province. He did allow me to make certain improvements and to hire a minister for economic development. We have been working to encourage foreign investment, but a tremendous amount remains to be done.''

Jenny finished cooking while he talked. She divided the omelette between two plates and retrieved the bread from the oven. ''Dinner's ready.''

Instead of remaining seated, the sheikh approached one of the front windows and pulled back the curtain. Jenny thought he was checking for intruders until he said, ''My car will not be able to negotiate this level of snow. I assume you sleep upstairs. I will take the couch.''

''Wait a minute.'' She hadn't planned on his staying all night. Since the loft opened directly over the downstairs, the cabin lacked privacy. Unless she decided to sleep in the bathroom, she wouldn't be able to close a door between them. ''That wasn't part of the arrangement.''

''It is now.'' Releasing the curtain, the sheikh returned to the counter. ''Believe me, it is with great reluctance that I expose myself to this awkwardness.''

''*You're* reluctant?'' She didn't know whether to be offended or amused. ''What exactly do you think will happen?''

Zahad downed a bite of his food before noticing that she wasn't seated. After swallowing, he said, ''Excuse my rough manners. Please join me.''

Jenny perched on a stool opposite him. ''Okay, I'm sitting. Now, what's your great reluctance?''

''The last thing I need is for anyone in Alqedar to learn that I have stayed at the home of the temptress who lured Fario to his destruction.''

Jenny stared at him in outrage. It embarrassed her to

realize that at some level she'd been attracted to this man, because he'd just thrown her vulnerability in her face. "I don't know how I'm going to control my irresistible urge to rip your clothes off, but I guess I'll manage."

The sheikh stopped with his fork halfway to his mouth, his startled expression almost comical. "That is not what I meant."

"And in case you've forgotten, I didn't lure anybody," she said. "Look, in the interest of protecting your precious reputation, you can take my four-wheel drive and get the heck out of here. You'd better hurry before the snow gets any thicker and you're really stuck. We wouldn't want the good people of Alqedar to question your maidenly virtue."

Zahad set down the fork. "We have not finished discussing the case."

"Yes, we have."

He leaned back and folded his arms. "I see I have given offense."

"You think?"

"I see also that I have been foolish. It is not my custom to allow the prejudices and suspicions of others to influence my behavior. If I leave you here with only my pathetic rental car for transportation, you will be at the mercy of anyone who comes along."

He might be right, but she felt so angry she didn't care. "That's not your problem."

"I think it is. As you pointed out earlier, I require your help to clear my name and win justice for my brother. As I suggested, you need a bodyguard, and you will never be able to find one better qualified than I."

"A bodyguard?" How had she gone from being a despised temptress to a damsel in distress? "Look, if you want to stay here tonight, fine. I'm sure both our reputations will recover. Beyond that, forget it."

"We will leave the matter for now." He tore off a hunk of bread. "By the way, you are a very good cook."

"Thanks, I guess." Obviously, neither her outrage nor

her sarcasm would have any effect on this man, Jenny re-flected. Like it or not, she was stuck with him for the night.

She only wished that, deep inside, she didn't feel just a little bit glad.

Chapter Five

"Why don't you heave a hunk of that stuff at me, too?" Jenny said.

"I beg your pardon?" asked the sheikh.

She allowed her gaze to rest meaningfully on the serrated knife sitting untouched on the decorative cutting board she'd used to serve the bread. "Since we seem to be ripping it apart with our bare hands, please tear off a chunk for me as well."

Zahad glanced ruefully at the piece he was holding. "Sometimes I forget I am not camped out with the rebels. I will try to do better." He lifted the knife and sliced the French loaf neatly.

Jenny decided to press her luck. "While you're at it, you might consider getting a decent haircut."

Her guest studied her from beneath a lock that had, as usual, fallen across his forehead. With a subtle shake of the head, he dismissed the remark and handed her the cutting board. "As I said, we have not finished discussing the case. The list of suspects will be longer if the stalker and the murderer are not the same person."

"You think they might be different?"

"It is possible we are dealing with an opportunist."

"That would be kind of a relief," Jenny conceded as she buttered her bread more generously than usual. She felt in need of sustenance. "I mean, I'm sorry about your brother, but I've been terrified that whoever's stalking me may have progressed to trying to kill me. Can you think of anyone from Alqedar who could have taken advantage of the situation?''

Zahad's mouth twisted. ''Yes.''

''Who?''

''A young man named Hashim Bin Salem. He is Numa's nephew. She is proposing that the president of our country appoint him governor of our province in my stead. That would be a great step for Hashim.''

''Do you really think he could have managed it? How would he have found out about me?''

''He and Fario were friends. Fario might have told him of your intended meeting.'' The sheikh frowned at his salad as if uncertain what those shreds of vegetation were doing on the table. Or perhaps he was simply lost in thought. ''Removing my brother has presented him with a great opportunity.''

''Wouldn't he try to remove you as well?''

''I am not as easily led into a trap as my brother. Perhaps he wished only to frame me. Or I might be in danger. I am always on my guard. Still, we must not dismiss the possibility that you are the target.''

At his use of the present tense, Jenny set down her fork. Although she hadn't finished her omelette, she'd lost her appetite. Still, this discussion seemed unavoidable. ''Who's on your list?''

''The possessive Sergeant Finley. Your neighbor Ray, because he works at the bank. Also Dolly. She found my brother. And as a former policewoman, she should know how to cover her tracks.''

''Dolly has a key to my house,'' Jenny agreed. ''But there's no motive.''

She explained that Dolly, who'd bought the adjacent cabins as an investment and vacation getaway before her retirement, had become good friends with Jenny's great-aunt, Brigitte. Four years ago, Dolly had retired and moved in, bringing her husband and her daughter's family. She'd been delighted when Jenny arrived a year later. "She and I get along fine."

"In any case, we are blowing smoke," Zahad said. "The main suspect is obvious."

Although Jenny didn't like to think about it, he was right. "Grant."

"For motive, there is the custody issue. The police report states that he is a computer consultant, so he is capable of cyber-stalking. Also, he was a wife beater."

A wife beater. Jenny hated the way Grant had reduced them both to a cliché. She hated even more remembering the downward spiral of their marriage and the way she, conditioned to appeasing her domineering father, had tried to make peace until the night her husband crossed the line.

These memories had been haunting her all week, revived and intensified by Fario's murder. Today, she'd tried to shrug off the encounter with Oliver, but now a twinge in her arm brought that back full force as well.

Jenny started to shake. Embarrassed, she wrapped her arms around herself, fighting for steadiness.

All along, she'd believed that Grant couldn't be the cyber-stalker because he would never endanger his child. Well, even if he wasn't, that didn't mean he hadn't taken advantage of the situation.

Knowing their daughter would be safe at his home these past two weeks, he could have paid someone to eliminate Jenny. *A hired killer, in my house.*

"Are you ill?" Zahad leaned across the counter.

"No, I'm…" Her teeth chattered so hard she couldn't finish the sentence.

"It is a delayed reaction." The sheikh came around and helped her to her feet. "We must get you warm. You suffer from shock."

It had been a long time since anyone had taken care of Jenny, settled her on a couch, wrapped her in a blanket, talked to her soothingly. The sheikh even found a packet of hot-chocolate mix in the cabinet and made some for her. She didn't mind that it clumped together because he'd failed to stir it enough. At least it was warm and sweet.

After she finished drinking, he sat beside her and chafed her hands. The hard angles of his face softened as he worked. "Your family should be with you at such a time."

"My father died years ago," Jenny said. "My mom's remarried and lives in Connecticut. Her husband doesn't like her to travel."

"You should go and stay with your mother."

"I can't leave my job." Anyway, although she didn't like to talk about such personal matters, she didn't feel comfortable staying at her stepfather's. He was too possessive of her mother and seemed to resent her love for Jenny.

"There is no one else?"

"My brother's in the air force. He lives in Texas." He and his wife were wrapped up in their two children and their busy lives.

"This country is too large," Zahad remarked. "Families should stay close."

She refrained from pointing out that his family didn't appear to be very close. But at least he'd flown halfway around the world to claim his brother's body and try to solve his murder.

"I'd better turn in." She gathered the blanket around her. "This sofa folds out, and there are sheets in the linen closet."

"I require no such luxuries," he said.

"You have to stretch out or you'll get a cramp. I don't want my bodyguard getting a charley horse and falling on his face at the first sign of trouble." She managed a smile.

"Very well." He glanced with a touch of apprehension toward the kitchen. "Also, I will wash the dishes."

"Thank you." Gripping the arm of the sofa, Jenny got to her feet. At least, she intended to. Halfway up, her knees started shaking.

Zahad's powerful arms lifted her. Unsure how to respond, she lay pressed to his chest, the faintly exotic scent of his jersey intensifying her light-headedness. ''You didn't put anything in the hot chocolate, did you?'' she joked feebly.

''If I had, it would have been to make you stronger, not weaker.'' Carrying her easily, the sheikh mounted the steps to the loft. He scarcely seemed to register her weight, although at five foot eight Jenny was no trifle.

The upstairs room held a queen-size bed, a pine bureau and a desk. After lowering her onto the covers, the sheikh removed her shoes. ''Can you finish undressing unaided?''

''Yes.'' She would sleep in her clothes if necessary.

''If you need anything, you have only to call. I will hear you.'' His dark eyes lingered on her.

''I'm glad you're here,'' Jenny said.

He nodded. ''It is as it should be.'' When he stood up, the bed released him with a sigh.

After he went downstairs, Jenny listened to the clink of dishes being washed and, later, the creaks as the couch was transformed into a bed. Feeling more secure than she had in a long time, she fell asleep.

TEMPTRESS. He'd been wrong to use that word to Jenny's face, Zahad mused as he lay trying to ignore the lumps in the thin mattress. Yet that's exactly what she was. Not in the way he had once assumed, however.

He understood why men became fascinated with her. Superficial beauty was commonplace, but intelligence and wariness tempered by vulnerability were not. A man wanted to explore this woman and the sweetness beneath the peppery surface.

Not him, of course. Although possessed of normal drives, he had never been susceptible to feminine allure. As a soldier and fighter, he sublimated the needs of his body.

There had been women, of course. While a student in England, Zahad had dated a girl who considered his background romantic. She had not considered it romantic when he left to train at a military camp, however, and had soon found someone else.

His only other involvement had been with a French photographer who covered the revolution that restored democracy to Alqedar. She had seemed a kindred spirit, reveling in hardship and danger. But once peace broke out, she lost interest in Zahad and in Alqedar. The last time he'd seen her byline on a photograph, it had been from another war-torn country.

Until he became sheikh, Zahad had not considered marriage a desirable goal. Now that the title was thrust upon him, he supposed he would have to do so. He intended to choose a woman from his own background who cared about his people as he did. In the meantime, he took no interest in casual liaisons.

He smiled at the absurdity of contemplating a casual liaison. Jenny would slap his face if she even suspected him of harboring such intentions.

Amused in spite of himself, he finally found a comfortable position on the bed.

JENNY AWOKE IN BLUE-BLACK STILLNESS. Through the tall windows, she could see scattered stars against the deep sky. The storm must be clearing.

The hum of the refrigerator and the ticking of a clock reverberated from downstairs. These sounds were not yet familiar enough for her to ignore.

She'd been dreaming again. Certain images haunted her: a shadow moving in her yard, a hand clamping her wrist. When she moved her arm, her shoulder ached. Like some ugly burned thing, fear hissed and shriveled inside her.

Jenny craved reassurance. Was Zahad still here? Surely he was, yet she needed to be sure.

As she slid her feet into her slippers, she pulled on a robe. At the railing that overlooked the lower floor, she studied the angular shapes of the furnishings. It was impossible to see whether anyone lay on the pull-out couch.

He wouldn't have left. She should go back to bed.

It was impossible to sleep, though, in the aftermath of that dream. The tension in her lungs seemed to gain strength the more she tried to subdue it.

Perhaps she could fix a cup of tea without disturbing him. After a moment's internal debate, Jenny eased her way down the stairs. At the bottom, she decided to make a quick pass by the bed to satisfy her curiosity.

When she came close, she made out Zahad's solid shape sprawled across the mattress, a thin blanket bunched around him. Jenny listened with satisfaction to the regularity of his breathing.

Earlier, he'd said that she ought to be with family at such a time. Ironically, Jenny felt more at ease with this stranger than she ever had with relatives.

She'd grown up half-afraid of her rigid father. Despite an occasional show of tenderness, there'd been no predicting when his temper would flare and he'd lash out at her.

Only once had he physically hurt her: she'd messed up during a softball game and he'd become so incensed he'd deliberately thrown a ball, hard, into her arm. She'd wanted to take after him with the bat, but she hadn't been able to stir, just clutch her aching arm and stare at him in disbelief.

She hadn't fought back. Maybe that was why she still felt angry about it.

No matter what the provocation, Zahad would never vent his fury on a woman or a child. Jenny sank onto the edge of the bed and let his presence soothe her. If she sat here for a while, she might be able to sleep again.

Her eyelids drooped. Overcome by weariness, she lay down, just for a moment.

ZAHAD AWOKE with his arms around a woman. Sweet-smelling blond hair tumbled across his face and his body hardened with desire where it pressed into her back.

Although she was clothed, he wore nothing beneath the blanket. His instincts urged him to rearrange her garment and, with a few short strokes, unite them. Then he remembered where he was and who he held in his arms.

Instantly, he released her. She half turned and blinked in the morning light.

He sat up, adjusting the blanket to keep himself covered. "Why are you here?" he asked.

"I'm sorry." Jenny rubbed her eyes. "I had a bad dream. I just sat down here for a minute."

Zahad had no wish for her to guess his state of arousal. It was merely an instinctive response, after all. "It appears the storm is over." After pulling on the cloth robe that he'd left by the bed, he slid from beneath the covers and went to the window.

Outside, sunlight refracted off snowy branches and thick whiteness. Zahad wasted no time on sentiment. He had looked with some appreciation at the snowy landscapes in Europe as he passed by on a train, but he'd never had to drive through the stuff. On the positive side, the pristine surface gave no sign of any visitors.

Jenny joined him at the window. In her flowered robe, the woman was a rainbow of soft colors, Zahad reflected grumpily. He did not wish to have rainbows and gardens inflicted on him first thing in the morning.

"We should not delay," he said. "I may have only a few days, if that long, to conduct my investigation."

"And I have to get the house ready for Beth. Grant's bringing her home tomorrow," Jenny replied. "You use the bathroom and I'll make breakfast."

"Very good." Zahad marched across the room to retrieve his clothes.

IT WAS APPARENT TO JENNY the moment they stepped outside that the rental car would not be able to negotiate snow of this depth. She offered the sheikh a lift as well as an introduction to her neighbors.

"I'll be coming back here later to collect my things,"

she said. "It's warm enough, so the snow should start to melt and maybe you can get out then."

"You plan to stay at your own home tonight?"

"I think so."

As she unlocked her vehicle, Jenny hoped she would feel less spooked by the evening. She had to pull herself together before Beth arrived tomorrow, both for her daughter's sake and so she could stand up to any attempt by Grant to keep her. She was a little surprised her ex-husband hadn't called and demanded this already, since he must have learned about the murder from Parker.

Perhaps he realized she would never consent. And if he violated his visitation agreement by holding on to Beth longer than agreed, he'd hurt his potential custody case.

"I accept your offer," Zahad said, interrupting her train of thought. "It will help me make the most of my time." He took the passenger seat in the SUV.

He hadn't mentioned anything about her waking up in his bed this morning, Jenny reflected as she slid behind the wheel. She had a hazy memory of him holding her close, then pushing her away. She appreciated his self-control.

She tried not to think about the muscular body she'd glimpsed in nearly all its glory. A long white scar that zagged across one shoulder emphasized the sheikh's ferocity. His leanness, the absence of any wasted bulk, made even the athletes she saw on television seem soft in comparison.

Last night, she'd hotly denied any suggestion of being a temptress, and then crawled into his bed. Despite his rough manners, Zahad was more of a gentleman than most men would have been.

Her own response had been far from demure. The close contact and his tantalizing scent had filled her with longings she did *not* intend to act on.

As she backed out of the carport, Jenny noticed a stubble of beard darkening Zahad's jaw. He hadn't asked to borrow a razor and didn't seem to care that he lacked one. The man was obviously untroubled by vanity. She felt a bit alarmed by how much she was starting to like his raffish side.

Several inches of snow had fallen, with deeper drifts. No one had broken the surface on the side street, so it was slow going. Once she reached Pine Forest Road, where traffic had turned the snow to slush, she began to make better time.

Jenny rounded a corner near her home and slowed, her throat tightening at the sight of a group of neighbors standing across the street from her house. There were no emergency vehicles, but half a dozen people didn't stand around talking in the snow for no reason.

"Something's wrong," she said.

Although what she could see of her home through the trees looked undisturbed, frightening possibilities raced through her mind: Oliver had come back; another unwanted visitor had arrived; someone had broken into the house.

Jenny wished for one crazy moment that she could retrace their path to the cabin. She wished it were last night again and she lay curled against the sheikh, sheltered by his warmth.

Zahad studied the assemblage as Jenny halted in the entrance to her driveway. "Who is who?"

"I'll give you the short course." She pointed out widowed Louanne Welford, who lived on the far side of Parker Finley's house, and Tish and Al Garroway, the young couple in front of whose home the group stood. Dolly and Ellen, both stocky with short, reddish brown hair and freckles, were unmistakably mother and daughter.

Everyone turned to look at Jenny and Zahad, but only Dolly and Al Garroway waved. She saw no sign of Ray, who was probably working on his car as usual.

Jenny made her way across the street. "What's going on?"

"You know those carjackings near the ski lodge?" Dolly replied. "Someone jumped Tish last night. Got away with her Accord and her purse."

"Were you hurt?" Jenny was willing to set aside personal differences, even though she knew her neighbor had taken a dislike to her.

"I'm fine," Tish answered curtly. Of medium height, she had a bony build and blond hair with dark roots. Parker had said that, from a distance, she looked a little like Jenny.

Seeing everyone's attention fix on her companion, Jenny said, "I'd like you all to meet Sheikh Zahad Adran. It was his brother who was killed on Monday."

Ellen paled. "I'm so sorry." She'd taken the news hard, Dolly had told Jenny a few days ago. They'd all been shaken to realize that, had Dolly tried the door during one of her patrols, she rather than Fario would have caught a gunshot in the chest.

"I'm just glad my wife wasn't hurt last night." Al slipped an arm around Tish's waist. In his midtwenties, the ski instructor had dark hair, a narrow face and a scraggly goatee. "You guys don't think these carjackers are connected with the murder, do you?"

"How many carjackings have occurred?" Zahad asked.

"Five successful ones and three attempts," Dolly said. "They started about three months ago, targeting the ski area. People carry a lot of cash when they're on vacation."

"The police think it's some gang members from L.A.," added Louanne. Although wrapped in a coat, scarf and short, clunky boots, the widow shivered as a breeze stirred snow flurries. "We never used to have crime around here. I didn't even lock my doors until those men started pestering Jenny."

"Another one showed up yesterday, an ex-con," Jenny said. "Zahad chased him away."

"This is all about you, isn't it?" Tish snapped. "I'm the one who got shoved out of my car and lost my new Honda, and all you can talk about is how tough you have it."

"It's not a competition," Jenny snapped, and then wished she hadn't.

"She's got good reason to be upset," Al reproved.

"I didn't mean to imply otherwise."

"At least the cyber-stalking ought to stop now." Ellen's voice shook. "I mean, whoever's been putting this stuff on the Internet about Jenny, surely they'll quit when they find out about the murder."

"Unless the stalker is the killer and he isn't finished," her mother pointed out.

"Oh." Ellen blanched.

"I can tell you the stalker is still active on the Web. An associate of mine trolled the chat rooms yesterday and was solicited in Jenny's name."

"You're kidding!" Ellen hugged herself against the cold. "How could they…" She let out a short puff of breath. "I'm going to post the news of the murder everywhere. I'll make sure people quit falling for that maniac."

"Thank you," Jenny replied. "I'd be grateful."

"It is an excellent idea," Zahad agreed.

Tish eyed him coldly. "I'd like to know what the number-one suspect is doing hanging around here."

An uncomfortable silence fell over the group. "I don't believe a suspect has been identified," Dolly said after a beat.

"Parker was talking about him last night at the robbery scene," Tish went on. "I heard him grousing about this sheikh getting underfoot."

"This sheikh was in his own country on Monday and has witnesses to prove it." Jenny didn't know why she sprang to Zahad's defense, except that in a way Tish was impugning her, too. And despite her sympathy over the carjacking, she had tired of her neighbor's gratuitous nastiness.

"My brother deserves justice," Zahad added. "If the police are going to waste their time targeting me, it appears I am the one likely to solve this case."

"I can see why Parker doesn't like you," Tish said.

Al shook his head at his wife. "Why don't you cut people a little slack?"

"Because I don't feel like it," she said, and went into the house. Al spread his hands and followed his wife.

"What's with Tish?" Dolly asked.

"Oh, leave her alone. She got robbed and thrown out of her car. How would you feel?" Ellen stamped her feet. "My toes are going numb. Excuse me."

"I've got to go, too," Dolly said. To Zahad, she explained, "My husband, Bill, suffers from fibromyalgia. He's in a lot of pain, and he's absentminded, too. Last week he was going to the store and got on the wrong bus. If Ray hadn't found him wandering around Crystal Point, I don't know what would have happened. But if there's anything I can do to help, please tell me."

"Thank you," he replied.

That left only Louanne. "I'd be happy to help, too, but I'm afraid I don't know anything."

"It is possible you have observed more than you realize. May I accompany you to your house and ask a few questions?"

"I'd be honored." The widow beamed. "I never thought I'd have a sheikh visit me!"

"I will come by later," Zahad told Jenny.

"I'll be there, scrubbing away." Struggling to focus on the chores ahead instead of on the memory of yesterday's unwelcome visitor, Jenny crossed the street to her property. She couldn't keep relying on the sheikh to protect her.

She hoped he would learn something valuable in his questioning and that this whole mess would soon be over. Because she didn't want to go on feeling her breath catch in her throat and her hands grow moist every time she turned up her own driveway.

Chapter Six

If any uncluttered space had dared to present itself in Mrs. Welford's house, its owner would no doubt have hunted it down and stuffed it with bric-a-brac. Zahad had never seen so many figurines, doilies, souvenir plates and stuffed animals. Despite the scent of lemon cleanser, dust clung to the air particles.

The widow herself proved a font of neighborhood chitchat, none of it very helpful. However, Zahad listened politely and filed everything away for future reference.

Over hot tea and crisp cookies, the widow described Cindy Rivas and Beth Sanger as two little dolls. She was glad Jenny had moved into the former home of her great-aunt, who'd been a good friend of Mrs. Welford's.

She also told him about Dolly Blankenship's marital history. "She and Bill were newlyweds when they moved here," the widow confided. "She was married twice before. Her first husband, Ellen's father, died of something—a heart attack, I think. They say her second husband won the Florida lottery after she divorced him. If you ask me, she should have waited!"

"Indeed." Zahad was more interested in learning about Dolly's son-in-law, who might have been the source of the scrap of paper he'd found. "I understand she retired. Why did her daughter's family move here?"

"Ray's a nice fellow but things never seem to work out for him."

His hostess offered him more cookies. He declined. A man who consumed too many sweets grew soft. "What do you mean?" Was Ellen's husband unstable?

"I heard he first wanted to be a pilot, but there was some problem with his eyesight. Nothing serious, but you know how picky the airlines are."

She seemed to require feedback, so the sheikh made an encouraging noise.

"After he moved here, Ray worked as a deliveryman but he hurt his back," she went on. "He started doing repairs, handyman stuff, but he didn't charge enough and he spent too much time chitchatting. I hope that job at the bank pans out for him."

"He must have spent a lot of time in people's houses." That meant Ray might have known where Jenny kept her gun. And a handyman would have had no trouble duplicating a key or rigging a booby trap.

Mrs. Welford nodded. "He's so friendly, you don't mind having him around."

"I must talk with him." With a smile that he hoped didn't betray his impatience, Zahad rose from the depths of his cushioned chair. "Perhaps he has observed something useful."

"He'd have been at work on Monday, when this terrible thing happened," she said, getting up at the same time. "Although I don't think he leaves until after nine. Maybe he passed someone suspicious on the road."

An elementary-school principal probably departed earlier, Zahad thought. Ray would have had time to do his dirty work after Jenny left. He'd had the means and the opportunity. Only the motive remained unclear.

After thanking his hostess, Zahad made his escape. Outside, he sucked in the cold, clear air.

From atop the small rise upon which Mrs. Welford's home was situated, he took in the lay of the land. Mountain peaks rose to the north, emphasizing the alpine quality of Jenny's neighborhood.

Straight across the street lay Ray and Ellen's modest house. There was a carport directly across the driveway and a garage on the far side of the house. The garage faced a rock retaining wall about three feet high.

Farther up the driveway stood a second home. Dolly's, obviously. An irregular line of snow-dusted greenery and rising terrain connected her property with Jenny's.

A man of peace might find it difficult to believe that Fario had been slain in such a picturesque setting. But having seen sunbaked villages smashed by tanks and colorful city markets dynamited, Zahad knew the swiftness and ruthlessness of death.

Once he had taken stock of his surroundings, he descended to the street. Several times he slipped in the snow and, although he avoided a fall, his shoes and pant cuffs became soaked. Zahad made a mental note to buy winter clothing.

He followed Dolly's driveway uphill. In the window of the first house, a little girl with light brown hair held her teddy bear to the glass. They both swiveled solemnly to watch Zahad go by.

He stopped outside the open garage, which was only wide enough for a single vehicle. It housed a classic car with shiny paint and a restored bumper. The occasional clanking noise from within drew his attention.

"Mr. Rivas?" Zahad called.

"You bet!"

The brown-haired man who ducked around the car had a typical American openness to his expression. Only slightly below Zahad's height, he had the kind of pudgy physique that bears testimony to too many pints, most likely consumed in front of televised rugby matches. Make that cans of beer and football, he reminded himself.

"Hey, you must be that sheikh fella my wife mentioned." Ray wiped his hand on a rag and stuck it out. "Sorry about your brother. That's a real shame."

His grip was firm and scented with motor oil. It occurred to Zahad that he might be shaking hands with Fario's killer. Before anger sharpened his tongue, however, he reminded himself that if Ray Rivas was innocent, he could be useful. He'd probably visited most of the neighbors' houses and ought to know who was fixated on Jenny.

"As you may have heard, I am making a few inquiries," Zahad said.

"Inquire away," the fellow replied cheerfully.

"Did you see anything suspicious on Monday morning?" It was a relief to get right to the point. With Mrs. Welford, he'd tried to behave more sociably.

"Afraid not. I already told the police everything, not that there was much to tell. But I've got my theories."

"Theories?" Zahad asked.

"You know, about Jenny. I mean, she's such a babe," Ray told him. "All the guys notice her but the one that might be motivated to go off the deep end is her ex-husband. I watch cop shows and the criminal is almost always somebody like that."

"I see." To forestall any more unhelpful guesses, Zahad said, "Do you know why the lady who was carjacked dislikes her?"

"You bet!" He put one foot up on the bumper. "Tish is just plain jealous. One time her husband said right in front of her that she looks a little like Jenny but Jenny's more glamorous. How's that for a poke in the eye?"

"Is her husband after Jenny?"

"I don't think so." Ray grinned. "Hey, we all like to look at the scenery and Jenny's easy on the eyes. But that's as far as it goes."

"What about Parker Finley? Does he like to inspect the scenery?"

"Sure, and he's single. But would he set Jenny up and harass her? And then fix a gun to kill whoever walked through the door? Man, I don't see it. Whoever did this has to be crazy.''

"Have you met a teacher named Lew Blackwell?'' Zahad might as well run through his list of suspects. "He loaned Jenny his cabin.''

"Naw. My daughter doesn't start kindergarten till next year, so I'm not up on the teachers. I mean, none of it makes sense. Jenny gets along with everybody. Heck, we all get along.''

Perhaps a bit too well. Dolly, for example, had a key to Jenny's house and, apparently, a finger in everybody's pie. Taking an oblique shot, Zahad said, "It can't be easy living next door to your mother-in-law.''

"Aw, she's the salt of the earth,'' Ray replied. "You wouldn't believe how patient she is with Bill. He's getting senile and he's got some kind of muscle disease, too. He's so tightfisted he goes over their credit-card slips with a fine-tooth comb. She says he's always been that way. If you ask me, she should have stayed married to her second husband. He won the Florida lottery.''

"So I heard.'' The topic seemed to fascinate the neighbors.

"You know what? You ought to stick around and protect Jenny. I hate to think about her and Beth being at that house by themselves.''

"You wish me to remain here?'' Ray had surprised him, after all. It began to seem less likely that he was the killer.

"Sure.'' The man scratched his scalp through his short, light brown hair. "The women around here might stop giving Jenny the evil eye and the men could quit tripping over their tongues. Maybe you'll even catch the guy who did it. You seem like the watchful type, if you know what I mean.''

He couldn't resist mimicking the man's phrasing. "You bet.''

They shook hands.

"I'm sorry I don't have one of my cards on me,'' Ray

added. "I saw you at the bank the other day. I'd be glad to assist you any way I can."

"Thank you." Embarrassed to have been caught spying and finding it hard to believe Ray was as guileless as he seemed, Zahad gave him a nod and headed for Jenny's house.

He could feel ice crystals forming in his socks. Time to take himself indoors.

JENNY WAS GLAD she'd turned up the heater when she saw how pale Zahad looked. If she'd needed further proof that he was chilled, it came when he accepted her offer of a pair of oversize sport socks.

"You can borrow my SUV and run into town if you'd like to change into some of your warmer stuff." She'd straightened the house but still wanted to wash the dishes and pots from the cabinets.

"I fear I have no warmer stuff," Zahad replied, his innate dignity unmarred even by the clunky socks. "Also, perhaps I should rent a more suitable vehicle."

"You can buy chains at the hardware store." When he didn't respond, Jenny explained, "You wrap them around the tires to get traction in the snow."

"Ingenious," he said.

From outside came the grumble of a car in the driveway. Zahad grimaced. "I suppose I should put on my shoes in case I have to perform kung fu."

"You know kung fu?"

"I learned a variation in military camp."

She glanced through the window. "Don't bother. It's Parker."

"He will not be pleased to see me." Zahad's mouth twisted.

"He'll love the socks." Jenny went to the door.

When she opened it, the detective was stamping his boots on the mat. "I wanted to make sure you're all right. After you told me that sheikh was hanging around, I got—'' He stopped, having spotted Zahad.

"As you can see, I am still hanging around." Her guest lounged on the couch with his sock-clad feet prominently displayed.

Parker grimaced. "What the hell is he doing here?"

Jenny raised an eyebrow disapprovingly. "Language, please."

"Sorry," the detective muttered. "No, I'm not sorry. I found out a few things about you, Mr. Adran."

"I have a lengthy résumé. Which part has aroused your interest?"

"The part where you were a suspect in a murder-kidnap in Orange County about three years ago."

Jenny's heart flipped into her throat. Zahad certainly hadn't mentioned that.

"Please note the use of the past tense," the sheikh told her. "I am no longer a suspect. The case was solved and my name cleared."

"I talked to a detective down there." The officer braced himself with his feet apart. "He says you may have pulled off a few things they never nailed you for, like breaking and entering."

To Jenny, Zahad said, "My cousin Sharif had a son by a surrogate mother in Orange County. She was murdered and I assisted him in recovering the boy and identifying the perpetrator."

"There was another woman involved," Parker warned. "The victim's sister."

"Her name is Holly and she is now Sharif's wife," Zahad replied. "In addition to Ben, they have a one-year-old daughter and another baby on the way." He didn't mention the breaking and entering, Jenny noticed. But in the course of rescuing a child and catching a killer, something like that seemed minor.

"Well?" she said to Parker. "It sounds as if he was more of a hero than a villain."

The man looked as if he'd bitten into something nasty. "It's a bad idea for people to take the law into their own hands. Innocent people get hurt that way."

"So do guilty ones," the sheikh countered. "You know, Sergeant, your suspicions of me lack logic."

"How so?"

"If I had arranged to kill my brother, why would I come here and risk arrest? You would have had a devil of a time extraditing me from Alqedar."

"Criminals return to the scene of the crime. And here you are."

Parker had a point, Jenny reflected reluctantly.

The sheikh didn't rise to the bait. "Speaking of criminals, do you see a connection to the carjackings?"

"Unlikely," Parker said. "They've all taken place near the ski lodge on the far side of town. We think it's an L.A. gang targeting women, taking their cars and purses, probably shipping the cars down to Mexico or selling them to a chop shop."

"If they're from L.A., why come here?" Jenny queried. It was a two-hour drive.

"Easy pickings. People are more trusting, plus we don't have the resources of an urban police force."

"How many robbery-homicide officers are there in Mountain Lake?" Zahad asked.

"Two," Parker replied. "And usually we're so underutilized we help out with burglaries. Right now, we're a bit overworked, but that doesn't mean we need help."

"I commend you," the sheikh said. "But clearly you do not have time to guard Mrs. Sanger. That is why she has invited me to stay with her until my brother's body is released."

I did not! The protest never made it to Jenny's lips, probably because she dreaded remaining here alone. Besides, she didn't want to embarrass Zahad by contradicting him in front of Parker. Instead, she said simply, "Mr. Adran is a trained security officer."

"He's a trained killer," Parker retorted.

"A revolutionary," Zahad corrected. "One who must adapt to living in civilized society. I admit my manners have rough edges, but who better than a school principal to give me pointers?"

The situation did not call for humor, yet his cheekiness lifted Jenny's spirits. As if the sheikh would accept lessons in comportment from her!

The detective frowned. "I'll check with the medical examiner and see what's holding up your brother's release. Usually he finishes his work within forty-eight hours."

"He mentioned incomplete ancillary studies," the sheikh said.

"What kind of studies? Your brother died from a bullet wound." Jenny had assumed the cause of death was obvious.

"The M.E. has to make sure there isn't something else going on," Parker told her.

"This is a high-profile case," Zahad added. "No doubt the coroner wishes to avoid mistakes."

"By the way, your stepmother was pretty steamed when she called," the detective said. "I gather autopsies violate your customs. But our law requires them in a homicide."

Zahad inclined his head in agreement. He held his silence until Parker, realizing the conversation was over, excused himself and left. Jenny purposely hung back as he went out, to avoid giving him a chance to lecture her again about the sheikh.

One way or the other, she'd given her guest permission to stay. She turned to face him. "Well, what happens now?"

He arose fluidly. "I must go into town for supplies. Thank you for the loan of your vehicle. I will purchase chains."

Jenny hesitated only a moment before making a further decision. "I'd better give you a house key, too, and the alarm code."

"I know the alarm code."

So he *had* memorized it the other day. "I changed it."

A fleeting smile marked his approval. "Very wise. People rarely change their codes."

"How do you know?"

"I have sometimes found their carelessness useful."

Jenny could see why the police in Orange County hadn't caught him breaking and entering. Well, he wasn't going to have to break into her house. Whatever happened now, she would have no one to blame but herself.

IN TOWN, Zahad found that the main roads had been cleared and the stores were open. He was surprised by how many vehicles filled the streets and parking spaces, most of them bearing license frames with the names of other counties. Apparently skiers had arrived en masse to take advantage of the fresh powder.

He ate a late lunch at a café, after which he bought boots, a brown suede coat and groceries. At the hardware store, he purchased a set of chains to fit his rental car and a combination lock for Jenny's toolshed.

Before checking out of the motel, he hooked up his laptop and reviewed his e-mail. There was a message from Sharif, promising to do his best as an advocate, and another from Amy.

In a style sounding like her speech, she wrote:

I've been nosing around. Listen to this! Hashim flew to London about two weeks ago. Supposedly he was partying hearty, but nobody knows the details. It isn't even clear exactly when he got back. I'm looking into it. For all I know, he could have flown from London to California without anyone noticing. Will send more info when I have it.

Zahad wrote back with his list of suspects.

Please advise Numa, if she will listen to you without screaming, that I am doing my best to avenge Fario's death. She would do well to trust me.

He did not, of course, mention he planned to stay with the temptress herself. This would not play well in Alqedar. Thanks to cell phones and e-mail, no one needed to know his address.

He copied the message to Sharif and added a note of thanks. Then he typed up his recollection of that morning's interviews.

As he transferred his suitcase and computer to the SUV, it occurred to Zahad that it would be inconvenient if anyone attempted to carjack Jenny's vehicle at this point. He would be forced to defend it, possibly with lethal results. Sending another body to the M.E. might further delay the release of Fario's remains.

He took a moment to survey the busy sidewalk outside the motel for loiterers or thugs. There was no one of that description, only a steady flow of males and females who appeared almost interchangeable in colorful jackets, knitted caps and ski pants.

From the pharmacy next door emerged a figure oddly out of place among the physically fit masses. Thin and wiry with disheveled white hair peeking from beneath a hunting cap, the man moved with the aid of a cane. Although his coat hung unevenly, it was made of a fine herringbone tweed that matched his cap.

"Mr. Blankenship!" A young woman ran outside, waving a bag. She had thrown a coat over her white smock. "You forgot your medicine."

"Nonsense. I've got it right here." Grumbling, the man reached inside his coat and patted his shirt pocket. "Where the devil did it go?"

"Here it is." The clerk handed it to him. "Isn't there someone who can drive you home?"

"I may be old but I'm not senile." He snatched the bag from her hand. "I'm taking the bus."

"I heard you ended up in Crystal Point last week." The clerk hugged herself against the cold. "Why don't you come inside while I call your wife."

"They changed the durn bus route, that was the problem," the man said. "I'll be fine."

This must be Dolly's husband. Zahad had no interest in playing Good Samaritan to such a disagreeable figure, but he needed to interview each of the neighbors. Getting Mr. Blankenship alone in a car might be the only way to gain his cooperation.

He approached, keeping one eye on his loaded vehicle. "I am driving to Mrs. Sanger's house. I would be happy to give this gentleman a ride."

The clerk surveyed Zahad suspiciously. "Do you know Mrs. Sanger?"

He realized she suspected him of being one of the Internet creeps. "Yes. I am her houseguest. My name is Sheikh Zahad Adran."

"Oh, wow!" Her face lit up as if she were meeting a movie star. "I've heard about you! I mean, I'm sorry about your brother. Bill, this nice man is going to give you a ride home."

"He don't look so nice to me," the old man growled.

"I will ensure that he gets home safely," Zahad told the woman.

"Do you ever wear those robes and that head thing?" she asked.

"On occasion." Only when it was required by custom or suited his purposes, but he saw no reason to explain that.

"Wow!" Reluctantly, she moved back. "Go on, Bill. He'll take care of you."

"That's what I'm afraid of," Bill grumbled as she went in. On the sidewalk, a young couple with a baby approached. He made no attempt to move aside, forcing them to push their stroller around him.

Although the older man's hand shook as he clutched his cane, Zahad felt ambivalent about taking his arm. "Do you require assistance?"

"I don't require any durn thing. Are we going to get in the flipping car or are we going to stand here and freeze to death?"

Why had Dolly married such a snappish person? Zahad wondered. But perhaps he owed his ill temper to his pain.

When they reached the SUV, Bill struggled to ease himself inside but never asked for help. Ray had said his father-in-law used to be a truck driver. It must be difficult for him to accept his disability.

"You've been snooping around," Bill said as they pulled away from the curb.

"I have a duty to my brother," Zahad told him. He expected no sympathy and he received none.

"You sheikhs oughta stay in your own country."

"I will make sure to advise my fellow sheikhs of your opinion." He halted at a red light.

"I got no patience for small talk," Bill said. "Whatever you want to know, be quick about it. Once we get home, I'm heading for the bathroom, and I intend to be there a while."

"Very well. I would like your opinion of the neighbors."

"You want a rundown? Okay." The light changed and they started forward a little too hard, forcing the old man against his shoulder harness. "Hey! How'd you like it if somebody hit *you* across the chest with a board full of nails?"

"I am sorry." Zahad pointed to the bag. "Perhaps you should take one of those pills."

"They're laxatives."

"On second thought, never mind."

Bill cackled. "Naw, they're for pain. But I got to take them with water."

"Then I shall drive quickly. Please, fill me in on the neighbors."

Bill ran through the cast of characters, at least those he remembered. He didn't seem to know much about Tish and Al, who, Zahad recalled, had moved in recently.

According to Bill, Dolly was a decent wife although she snored and left hair in the sink. Ellen suffered from fits of jealousy, possibly because Ray had a wandering eye. "He's a hot-and-cold sort of fella," Bill added. "One minute he's your best friend and the next he won't give you the time of day."

Ray hadn't struck Zahad as volatile. He filed away the information.

"You don't need to know about the children, so I'll skip them," Bill said. "Jenny's a pretty woman. Ought to have a man in her life. Parker Finley, he'd like to be that man but he ain't her type."

"What is her type?" the sheikh asked.

"The kind that leaves her alone."

"How about Mrs. Welford?"

"Who?"

He dredged up her first name. "Louanne. The widow across the street."

"Don't have an opinion on her. Too boring. Now you tell me."

"Tell you what?"

"What they said about me."

The answer came promptly. "That you're tightfisted."

"I'm a retired fella with no pension and a lot of medical bills the government don't cover. You try living on social security. No, don't try it. You ain't entitled because you ain't American. What do they do with old people in your country?"

"Their children take care of them," Zahad said. Elders were respected and honored in Alqedar.

"What if they don't have children?"

He'd never thought about it. "I do not know."

"You're the sheikh. Ain't you got social programs?"

"I am a sheikh of recent vintage. I will look into it." He meant that.

Also, Bill's remark made him wonder about Numa. In her late forties, she didn't have much to look forward to with her only child dead. Of course, if her sole concern was her financial future, she'd have done better to placate the new sheikh than to antagonize him.

Nevertheless, Zahad knew his father would have wanted his widow to live in comfort. He reminded himself to set up a pension for Numa and assess the needs of elderly people who lacked families.

"Ain't you going to ask me anything interesting?" Bill asked.

"Such as?"

"Like whether I got a history as an ax murderer?"

"It is unlikely you would tell the truth on that score." Still, it couldn't hurt to sound him out. "Very well. How much do you know about the Internet?"

"I been on it a few times. My wife's got a computer. Seem to be a lot of dirty pictures on it." He didn't sound unhappy about that.

Zahad turned left into the driveway on Dolly's property. He passed the Rivas house and continued up a slope to the smaller cottage. With the snow melting rapidly, he had no trouble negotiating it.

The Blankenship house, constructed of dark wood with a deck visible in the back, lay in the deep gloom of overgrown pines. "You ought to get Ray to thin these out," he said.

"Didn't know you sheikhs was into that *Better Homes and Gardens* stuff. Wanna come inside and rearrange the furniture?"

"I will forgo the pleasure." Zahad got out and opened the passenger door. Although he didn't offer to help, he stood ready to catch the old man if he slipped.

The front door scraped and Dolly came out. "Bill! You should have told me you wanted to go into town. I'd have taken you."

"Just because I can't drive no more, that don't make me an invalid." The old man wiggled down from his seat, anchoring himself with the cane.

His wife shook her head. "He's going to be sore as heck tonight. I can't believe he walked all the way to the bus stop in the snow. Thanks for bringing him back, Zahad."

"Exercise is good for my heart." Bill regarded the sheikh. "I suppose you'll be expecting some kind of thank-you for the ride."

"It is of no importance."

"Don't encourage him," Dolly said. "His manners are atrocious."

"Who's this 'he' you're talking about?" asked her husband. "It can't be me. I'm standing right here."

"Sorry," said his wife.

To Zahad, Bill said, "Thank you. If my wife can be polite, so can I, I guess. Don't count on it happening again."

"I assure you, I won't." With a wave, Zahad got back into the SUV and traced the short distance to Jenny's house.

The afternoon sun hung low in the sky, casting harsh shadows across the snow. Against the looming darkness, the house glowed from within. And as he emerged from the vehicle, he caught a whiff of coffee. How easily a man could be lulled into a sense of comfort.

Zahad reminded himself that, beneath the snow, blood still soaked the earth. He had learned many things today, but none brought him measurably closer to solving his brother's murder. And, for him, time was running out.

Chapter Seven

In the late afternoon, Jenny and Zahad drove to Lew's cabin, collected her possessions and put chains on the car, although she doubted the sheikh would need them for long. Still, with another storm predicted in a few days, they might come in handy.

She made one last check of the premises and left a thank-you note. Then she locked up and dropped the key through a return slot, as Lew Blackwell had requested.

At home, they ate a quiet dinner of groceries Zahad had brought from town along with his possessions. Afterward he excused himself to set up his laptop in her home office, which doubled as the guest room.

The dishes done, Jenny laid out scraps of fabric on a pad atop the dining-room table. She wanted to keep her hands busy and her mind occupied so she wouldn't dwell on the fact that an edgy and dangerously attractive man was sharing her home.

Flipping through a box of tiny dress patterns, she chose one for Beth's favorite doll. Even though Grant and Shelley usually showered her with expensive toys, her daughter would enjoy the gift. Like any five-year-old, Beth was susceptible to bribery, but only up to a point.

The last time she'd spent a week with them, they'd gone to Disneyland and the beach in Orange County, about a two-hour drive away. At first enthusiastic in her phone calls

Beth had gradually wearied of the excitement. When she finally got home, she'd gone around the house touching the furniture and had stared at her favorite blue-and-white swirled glasses as if reassured to see them safely in their accustomed places. That was one of the reasons Jenny had been so eager to restore everything before tomorrow.

She and Beth both liked order and feminine frills. Simply laying the small pattern pieces along the bits of fabric, lining up the arrows with the grain and imagining how the seams would fit together gave Jenny an almost sensual pleasure. Her father had scorned fashion and disapproved of makeup beyond a bare minimum. She loved being able to indulge her child and the child in herself.

After a few minutes, she glanced through the kitchen to the office where the sheikh sat in profile at the desk. Wearing a loose-knit fisherman's sweater over jeans, he frowned as he typed on his laptop. Was he searching for the cyber-stalker?

In spite of their tentative alliance, Zahad might take the opportunity while living here to go through her computer for signs that she'd been the one who'd e-mailed his brother. She didn't like the idea, but if he did, finding nothing should put an end to any lingering suspicions.

Jenny returned her attention to the dress. She loved the colors and patterns in the fabric scraps, leftovers from a craft project that one of the teachers had saved for her. Minnie, Beth's doll, would look pretty in flowered sleeves, a solid bodice and a striped skirt, all in shades of white, blue and burgundy.

Without looking up, she registered the sound of Zahad rising and approaching across the kitchen linoleum. He moved so lightly that she imagined he could easily slip past someone's guard.

Coming alongside, he regarded her handiwork. "What are you making?"

"Doll clothes," she said.

"Your daughter is fortunate." He watched her hands adjusting the small pieces. Rather than feeling self-conscious, Jenny enjoyed being the object of his attention.

"I suppose women in your country must be good at crafts. Do they mostly stay home with the children?"

"Traditionally, yes," said Zahad. "However, these days most families educate their daughters. We are a small country and cannot afford to waste human resources."

"There's a practical point of view." His nearness made her conscious of the way her hair floated around her neck and her sweater clung to her breasts. If he noticed, however, he gave no indication. "What about your cousin Amy? I presume she's educated."

"She is an economist. I have placed her in charge of economic development for Yazir."

"Is she married? Does she have kids?" she asked.

"Both."

Jenny finished pinning the pieces in place. "Okay, you get points for equal-opportunity employment."

He must have moved closer, she realized when his breath tickled her neck. "I am a great believer in equality."

She made the mistake of looking up. She noted the bristle of fresh beard along Zahad's jawline and the unruly fullness of his thick black hair. His eyes were full of hunger, his scars a vivid reminder of the battles he'd fought. His wildness took her breath away.

Jenny edged around the corner of the table and picked up a pair of scissors. Zahad made no attempt to follow.

"Did you have any luck on the computer?" she asked.

"I was trying to trace the movements of Numa's nephew Hashim, the man who wants to be governor. Amy discovered he was out of the country these past few weeks."

"Do you consider him a suspect? I thought he and your brother were friends."

"Young men may hang about together and share good times. That does not mean they can be trusted when money and power are at stake."

The sheikh remained on the far side of the table. Although she was the one who'd moved away, Jenny missed the frisson of excitement from being close to him.

"What's Hashim like? He didn't grow up the way you did, did he?" She was beginning to get a picture of two very different sets of people among his country's elite, those who had trained in desert camps and fought for freedom, and those who had lolled in the comfort of a European exile.

"Hashim is no warrior, nor is he, in my opinion, to be relied upon. He told everyone he was in England, partying, before Fario died, but tonight I heard from a friend of his in London who says Hashim disappeared for almost a week."

Her mouth went dry. "When, exactly?" Maybe Zahad really had found the murderer. It was almost too much to hope for.

It also would mean the killer was an opportunist, not the stalker. Hashim couldn't have been aware of Jenny's existence until he learned about her from Fario. Her troubles wouldn't be over even if he was caught.

"He was last seen in London twelve days ago," the sheikh said. "He returned to Alqedar last Sunday."

"The day before Fario died." Not guilty, then.

"Yes, if his friends are telling the truth, but that is far from certain." Despite Zahad's level tone, strong emotions strained beneath the surface. "Nor do we know where he went. We cannot rule out Los Angeles."

After cutting the last piece of the garment, Jenny began cleaning away the cloth fragments. "But he got home on Sunday."

"Still, if he was here, he might have made arrangements. Los Angeles is a big city and there are always people ready to sell their souls for money."

There it was again, the chilling scenario of a hired killer. Jenny kept trying to reject that scenario, she realized, because the idea of such a cold-blooded crime seemed all the more repellent. "How can you find out?"

"I will drive into L.A. tomorrow to seek my brother's acquaintances. Fario had been there almost four months and he made friends easily."

A wistful note in his voice caught her attention. "And you don't?" she guessed.

He gave her a crooked smile. "No, indeed. But the ones I make, I keep forever."

A longing enveloped Jenny to be taken into this man's inner circle. But what would it mean if he kept her forever? Obviously he didn't plan to stay in Mountain Lake.

Besides, she suspected that Zahad, if he ever loved, would want to possess a woman completely. And the only kind of man Jenny wanted was the kind who gave her space.

"Tomorrow's a good day for you to go into L.A.," she said. "It's best if Beth has me to herself for a while after Grant brings her back."

"When will that be?"

"The last time I talked to him, he planned to arrive around 3:00 p.m."

"I would like to know more about your ex-husband. Aside from Hashim, he appears to have the most to gain from this situation."

How could she sum up the man she'd been married to for four years? It seemed easiest to start with practical details. "You already know that he's a computer consultant. His wife, Shelley, is an attorney who handles contracts for him. She's twenty-eight."

"And she wants a child."

"That's right." Jenny felt the tension rising inside her. "They've been married maybe a year and a half. A few months ago, Grant told me she has a medical condition that precludes her having children and she wants Beth."

The half-dozen times Jenny had met Shelley, the young woman had seemed self-absorbed and brittle. She was certainly selfish. Just because Shelley couldn't have a child, that didn't give her the right to try to take someone else's.

"It would devastate my daughter to lose me," Jenny went on. "I told him children can't be handed around like possessions."

"What was his response?"

"He said she's as much his as mine and that he and Shelley can offer her a more secure two-parent home." Jenny's hands formed fists. She barely avoided pricking herself with the needle.

"Was this before the stalking started?"

She nodded. "About two months before."

"Has he taken legal action?"

"No. I expected Shelley to file the court papers by now, but maybe they need to hire a California attorney."

"Perhaps he hopes to harass you until you send your daughter away for her own safety."

"If that's his game, he doesn't know me very well," Jenny said. "I swore when I left him that I'd never let him push me around again, and I won't."

"I am surprised you ever tolerated his abuse."

She knew the sheikh well enough to detect the anger simmering just below his self-controlled surface. "Things didn't start out that way." Wanting him to understand that she hadn't been a doormat, Jenny sketched the circumstances of their marriage.

She'd been a teacher in Long Beach when she met Grant at a party. Twelve years older than she, he'd been a welcome contrast to the immature men Jenny usually fended off. Also, after losing her father the year before, she'd felt in need of stability. They'd married shortly after she turned twenty-five.

Given the difference in their ages, she'd fallen easily into letting Grant make the rules. Since he'd been reasonable and considerate at first, that hadn't been a problem. She'd felt they were building a future together.

After several years of teaching, Jenny had taken leave when Beth was born. During her extended leave, she'd completed work on a master's degree.

Slowly their relationship had changed. Looking back, Jenny supposed there were several reasons. Having a child meant not only that her attention was divided but that she assumed a more adult role. Also, after her husband's business suffered a setback, she needed to return to work. Gradually the balance of power between them shifted.

Grant started to drink and stay out late. At home, he became sarcastic and cold. When she was offered a job as assistant principal at a school in Long Beach, they'd needed the extra money but her added responsibilities and prestige had galled him. After that he'd criticized her almost constantly.

One night when he was drunk, he'd struck her. Jenny took Beth and left. Grant had begged her forgiveness and she'd given him a second chance. Things were fine for a few weeks, and then he began to drink again.

They'd had one last fight. There'd been a shocking moment when he'd shoved Jenny and tripped her. Lying helpless on the floor, she'd feared for her life. As soon as she could get away, she fled with their daughter, vowing never again to let a man control or intimidate her.

Although she'd had Grant arrested, she still felt angry that she hadn't been able to hit him back. No matter how much she told herself that it would only have made things worse, she hated feeling like a victim.

After Grant took an anger-management class, the charges against him were reduced to a misdemeanor. He hadn't contested Jenny's demand for custody as long as she agreed to regular visitation.

"If he does file for custody, I'll throw it all in his face," she said. "He's married a much younger woman, just as he did the first time. He's proven before that he can be violent. I won't let him take my child."

"Good for you." High color flushed Zahad's face. He looked ready to do battle for her, Jenny thought with pleasure. "A man who hurts someone under his protection is despicable."

"If you happen to meet him tomorrow, I'd prefer you didn't say that to his face."

"Why not?"

"We have a daughter together." It was a fact she'd reluctantly come to terms with. "I'm going to have to interact with him until she's grown. It's in her best interest for us to stay on good terms, unless he makes that impossible."

"I will exercise restraint," Zahad promised.

Actually, the prospect of facing Grant tomorrow was more daunting than Jenny wanted to admit. She almost wished Zahad wasn't going into L.A.

She wouldn't let her ex-husband pull any power plays. No matter how upset he got about the murder or the cyberstalking, he couldn't keep Beth until and unless he got a court order.

She wrenched her thoughts away from Grant. The sheikh was right in front of her, and they needed to deal with practicalities. "Would you like help making up the couch in the office?" Earlier, she'd set out sheets, blankets and a pillow.

"I will be fine. If I work late on the computer, I hope it will not disturb you."

"It won't." Tonight, Jenny resolved, she was not going to slip into his room, no matter how frightened she became. "I just hope you learn something useful in L.A."

"As do I."

After donning his coat, he went out to make one last patrol of the premises. When he returned, Jenny activated the alarm and gave him the new password.

It was her first night in the house since someone had been killed here. With the sheikh at hand, that fact no longer shook her to the core. She chose not to worry about what would happen after he left.

As REQUESTED, Amy turned up the name and address of one of Fario's Los Angeles friends. It was a tremendous advantage to have her as an inside source at the palace in

Yazir, Zahad reflected as he typed a thank-you for the information.

He no longer remembered why she used to rub him the wrong way. Because they were both bullheaded, he supposed.

After setting the information aside for later, he spent more than an hour incorporating the latest economic data from his province into its development plan. He forwarded a copy to Sharif to show to the president in support of Zahad's leadership.

Thank goodness for his cousins, Zahad thought. Jenny had been correct when she surmised that he didn't make friends easily. Nor did he walk smoothly along the corridors of power. He preferred an enemy he could fight in the open.

It was impossible to place himself in the shoes of a man like Grant, who had violated his wife's safety. The images that had leaped to mind as she'd talked had filled Zahad with fury.

He had never loved a woman the way his cousin Sharif loved his wife and most likely never would. That kind of all-consuming passion made no sense to him. Even so, when the time came to take a wife and father children, Zahad knew he would give his own life for theirs if necessary. If under some unforeseeable circumstance his mate turned against him, no matter if she attacked him herself, he would do no more than was required for self-defense. Even in the face of betrayal, a man must put honor first.

After logging off the computer, Zahad opened the bed and made it up with military precision. Yet he had never felt less like a soldier. The floral scent that wafted from the sheets carried him back to this morning, when he'd awakened next to Jenny.

His body had reacted instinctively and now did so again, tightening and aching as her scent filled his mind with pleasurable images. Jenny's delicacy stirred him, yet she was far from weak. Her beauty, all that glorious blondness and those eyes green as the depths of a hidden pool, were a bonus. What he valued most was her sharp mind and passion for life.

If she came from Alqedar, he would pursue her, but she did not. After Fario's body was released, she would remain in America to fight her own battles against her ex-husband and perhaps another hidden enemy. Zahad would go back to Yazir, where destiny had given him the sheikhdom denied him by his father.

Of course, it might be necessary to return to America if the local police proved unable to find Fario's killer and if Zahad himself could not do so in the time available. But he preferred not to come back. There was too much vital work to do at home.

From another part of the house, he heard a woman's low voice singing a melody he didn't recognize. When he caught the words *teddy bears* and *picnic,* he realized it must be a children's song. Rustling noises indicated Jenny was changing clothes, and then he heard water running in the bathroom.

It appeared she had become so unselfconscious about sharing quarters that she didn't hesitate to sing out loud. For however long he stayed here, he would prove worthy of that trust, Zahad vowed as he stripped off his outer clothing and laid it close at hand.

The silence of the wooded mountains amplified distant sounds. He fell into a warrior's slumber, awakening every few hours as he registered noises without becoming fully alert. Around 1:00 a.m., the eerie cry of an animal rang out, most likely a coyote. An hour later, he heard an ice-covered tree branch crack.

At four-thirty the rumble of a car brought him halfway to wakefulness. Zahad assumed the vehicle would pass by on the highway, but it grew louder, the engine reverberating through the predawn stillness. Close by, it stopped.

Someone had arrived. Someone definitely not expected.

The sheikh dressed and went into the kitchen to fetch one of the knives he'd seen in a rack. He would have preferred a gun, but Jenny's remained in the hands of the police.

As he moved quietly through the darkened house, he listened for any reassuring signs. Voices, for instance, carrying on a conversation. Or simply for the newcomer to walk to the front and ring the bell.

Neither of those things happened.

Instead, he heard shoes scrape on concrete as someone came around the rear of the house from the parking bay. If the new arrival was trying to be stealthy, he failed.

Zahad glided through the kitchen and eased into the doorway between his room and the rear hallway, avoiding the glow of a night-light low on the wall.

The killer had entered through the back, he remembered.

His brain leaped ahead, calculating what might happen. Should the intruder try the door, either he would find it locked and go away or he would turn a key in it.

The killer had a key. He might not know that Jenny had installed an alarm.

The rear door, like the front, set off a chirping tone that allowed the entrant sixty seconds to input the password into a security panel. Had Jenny consulted Zahad prior to installing her system, he would have instructed her to forget convenience and allow only one delayed entry point. Sixty seconds, plus whatever further delay occurred at the monitoring company and the police station, would give an intruder plenty of time to reach her bedroom before help arrived.

Both Jenny and Sergeant Finley had grossly underestimated the danger she was in. Although the detective lived across the street, he might not be able to arrive for as long as five minutes.

Assuming, of course, the detective himself wasn't prowling around the house.

Zahad adjusted the angle of the knife. If someone broke in, the sheikh could count on the element of surprise to buy him a few seconds against whatever weapon the intruder carried.

He tensed as a key rasped at the lock. So much for the possibility that this was a hapless Romeo summoned by the stalker. Whoever was out there had a key and didn't know the locks had been changed.

If Zahad did nothing, the intruder might leave them in peace. But he would lose the chance to find out his identity.

Sooner or later, he would return. Better to take a chance now and catch him in the act.

Moving quietly into the hall, Zahad tensed. He must act swiftly and give as little warning as possible.

The key scratched again. The intruder either hadn't grasped that it no longer fit or believed he could force it.

Zahad took a deep breath and flung himself forward. In a single fluid sequence, he flipped the dead bolt and yanked open the door.

And found himself staring into a gun barrel.

Chapter Eight

Zahad swung his arm hard and felt the gun fly from the man's hand. The intruder was slightly taller and heavier set but slow to respond. Certainly not fast enough to block a kick that landed square in his groin.

With a grunt, the man doubled over on the narrow porch. The sheikh wrenched him around, clamped his arm about the man's neck and pressed his knife to the pulsing throat.

Inside, warning chirps shrilled rhythmically. Everything had happened so fast that the alarm hadn't even begun alerting the security company.

"Zahad?" came Jenny's voice.

"I have him," he replied hoarsely. "Turn on the light."

A painful brilliance breached the hallway and lapped onto the porch. Blinking against it, Jenny came closer. She was pulling her bathrobe around her. "Who…"

The chirping grew into an ear-shattering screech. The man reacted. "What the—?" He broke off as Zahad clamped his arm tighter.

"Please turn off the alarm," he told Jenny. From this position, all Zahad could see of his prisoner was well-trimmed blond hair and a beefy build that, for all its bulk, lacked skill at fighting. With some relief, he realized that this was not Sergeant Finley.

Jenny input the code. The deafening noise stopped.

In the silence, she took a good look at the man he held. "Grant? Good Lord!"

"This is your ex-husband?" Zahad hauled the man into the house and forced him to his knees. "His gun is on the ground. Will you retrieve it, please?"

"Sure." Jenny grabbed a coat from a hook, slid her bare feet into a pair of canvas shoes and went out. A moment later she returned, gingerly holding a pistol. "I can't believe he came here armed."

"Also, he had a key. Obviously he was not expecting a new lock and an alarm. Or me."

Zahad had loosened his grip a little. On the floor, Grant said, "I knew about you. The gun's for protection."

"It seems to me that I'm the one who needed protection." Jenny handed the weapon to Zahad. He stepped back, pointed it at Grant and gestured at him to rise.

The blond man got up shakily. His face was flushed and he appeared to have difficulty swallowing. When he touched his neck, drops of blood speckled his hand. "Damn. He cut me!" As he leaned against the wall, his voice quivered with what Zahad could have sworn was indignation.

"You are fortunate to be alive. Count yourself lucky that your injury is so trifling."

"Where's Beth?" A dusting of freckles stood out against Jenny's pale skin.

"In the car. Don't worry. She's wrapped up," her ex-husband replied. "I know how to take care of my daughter."

"Yes, you're setting a great example of responsible parenthood," Jenny retorted. "Why did you try to break into my house, and where'd you get the key?"

"I have a right to check the premises," Grant blustered. "The detective called me yesterday with some more questions—" he coughed a few times before continuing "—and he said this assassin might be staying here."

"He called me an assassin?" Zahad couldn't believe Finley had been so irresponsible.

"Well, maybe he said revolutionary. Something like that. Anyway, I knew you were dangerous."

"I am not the one who tried to break in here with a gun," Zahad reminded him.

"It's not loaded." Another cough. "Anyway, you already did break in here and wiped out your brother. I wasn't leaving my daughter until I made sure you weren't around."

Zahad's civilized instincts held him in check only by a slim margin. "Jenny, please call the police before I do something I will regret." He examined the barrel of the gun, a small .32-caliber revolver. It was indeed unloaded.

Only a fool carried a gun without bullets. An armed opponent would not have hesitated to shoot him.

To Grant, Zahad said, "Do not make any sudden moves. I can kill you without this."

The man glanced at him warily. Reluctantly, he nodded.

"I'm going to call Parker and get Beth out of the car." When her ex opened his mouth, Jenny said, "Shut up, Grant. Zahad's a security expert and he's here to guard me. If he has to break your neck, I'll support any story he tells."

The beefy man fell silent. Zahad wondered if it was the first time in his life a woman had put him in his place.

He no longer felt quite so angry with Grant Sanger, however. What infuriated him more was that, if the man told the truth, Parker Finley had put them all in danger by warning Jenny's ex-husband of Zahad's presence.

A worthy opponent looked you in the eye. Only a weasel manipulated others into doing his dirty work.

TRYING TO SET ASIDE her fury, Jenny put her exhausted daughter to bed. She wanted Beth to feel secure in her own home, and apparently she did. Worn out from being dragged across the country on a red-eye flight, the little girl fell asleep almost instantly.

Although she could hear Parker in the front room trying to sort out what had happened, Jenny lingered to gaze at this child who owned her heart. The tangle of blond hair and the air of childish innocence filled her with wonder. Jenny wished she could take Beth away from all this darkness and cruelty.

But that wasn't right, she reminded herself. Her job was to raise her daughter in the imperfect world where someday she, too, would live as an adult.

With a sigh, Jenny pulled the covers up and went out to face the furor Grant had created.

He sat handcuffed in the living room, his face still flushed. Parker must have sent Zahad out of the room.

"Am I interrupting at a bad time?" Jenny asked.

"We're done for the moment." Parker clicked off his tape recorder and closed his notebook. She admired his thoroughness in using both. "I've got Mr. Adran's and Mr. Sanger's statements. I still need yours." As he ruffled one hand through his brown hair, she noticed dark circles under his eyes.

"Would coffee help?"

"Yes, thanks." He stifled a yawn. "I was up late with another carjacking. A tourist broke her arm trying to hang on to her purse." From his tone, it was obvious the robbers had escaped. "We're beefing up patrols. We're going to make it so hot around the ski slopes that those creeps will take their business back to L.A."

After reluctantly summoning Zahad to keep an eye on Grant, the sergeant accompanied Jenny into the kitchen. Over coffee, he took notes while she ran over the events of the past hour.

"Did Grant say where he got the key?" she asked when she'd finished.

"Apparently you loaned him one a few years ago in case he brought Beth back early from a visit. He made a copy."

"What an idiot. Under the circumstances, why on earth

would he tip his hand and risk us finding out that he's got it? It makes him an obvious suspect.''

"One thing that's never in short supply on this earth is stupidity,'' the detective replied.

"And the gun?'' It had occurred to Jenny that, thanks to security measures, her ex-husband couldn't have carried it on the plane. He couldn't have bought it after his arrival, either, because California law mandated a waiting period.

"He says he kept it in a storage unit near the airport. It's registered to him but he's not licensed to carry it concealed. He's lucky it was unloaded or he'd be in even more trouble.''

"A storage unit?'' Jenny hadn't heard about this before.

"He claims he makes business trips out here and doesn't like to schlepp his clothes and computer equipment on airplanes,'' Parker said. "Look, I'm sorry I mentioned Mr. Adran to him. I had no idea he'd decide to sneak in to see if the two of you were sleeping together.''

"Is that what he was doing?'' Jenny's temper flared. "And what was he going to do if he caught us?''

"He claims he just wanted to make sure the sheikh didn't shoot *him*.''

"Who I sleep with is none of his business or anyone else's.'' Jenny didn't bother to protest the false assumption. She had a right to do as she pleased. "You were out of line to tell him anything about my household situation.''

"I apologize. I don't know what I was thinking. But I do worry about you, Jenny.'' The darkness beneath Parker's eyes failed to soften their steeliness. "Sheikh Adran shouldn't be staying here. You've got an alarm for protection.''

"If Grant had been determined to shoot me, that wouldn't have stopped him. I feel safer with Zahad here, and it's my decision.''

The detective folded his hands on the table. "You should listen to me, Jenny.''

Frustration wiped away her tact. "Which part of 'it's my decision' don't you understand?"

"What I understand is that—"

He broke off as Zahad entered from the living room. Although they'd been talking quietly during the interview, they'd raised their voices during the last part and Jenny suspected he'd overheard.

Her hunch was confirmed by the glitter in the sheikh's eyes. "I am impressed with your efficiency, Officer," he said icily. "You have inspired a woman beater to attempt to break into his ex-wife's home. You have put a foreign dignitary at risk of being shot. You have also recovered a key and a gun from the prime suspect in a murder case. And on what do you focus your attention? On trying to control the sex life of the pretty woman who lives across the street from you."

Parker got to his feet faster than she would have believed possible. To Jenny's horror, she saw his hand poised above his holstered revolver. "Don't push me, Mr. Adran."

"Anyone would think you wanted Mr. Sanger to burst in here and get rid of me," Sahad said. "Why? Is it jealousy or do you have something to cover up?"

Couldn't he see the detective had no reserves of patience left? Jenny wondered. Glaring, she moved between them and made a time-out T with her fingers.

Zahad ducked his head in acknowledgment and Parker moved his hand away from his gun. She was pleased to see that the signal worked as well on testosterone-infused men as it did with schoolchildren.

"I'm sure Sergeant Finley will take appropriate steps to deal with Grant," she said. "Won't you, Parker?"

His gaze never left Zahad. "I'll arrange to have his home, office and storage unit searched. If he's your stalker, we'll find the evidence." He stretched his shoulders stiffly. "In the meantime, I'm taking him into custody for attempted breaking and entering and illegal possession of a gun. Satisfied, Jenny?"

"As long as you keep him in jail and away from me."
More and more, she believed Grant must be the one who'd
been targeting her on the Internet, although she wasn't convinced he'd killed Fario.

"That'll be up to the district attorney and the judge,"
Parker replied.

A bright spot occurred to her. "I don't think he's going
to make much headway trying to get custody of Beth after
this."

"Let's hope not," said the sergeant. "But right now,
who's watching the prisoner?"

Zahad, who stood close to the door, glanced into the
living room. "He appears unrepentant, but he is not attempting to escape."

"As I told Jenny, I'm sorry about this," Parker explained. "That doesn't change the fact that I think it's a big
mistake letting you stay here. You and Mr. Sanger both
have alibis for the day of the murder but that doesn't rule
out a conspiracy, for either of you."

"There is one important difference between him and
me," the sheikh said.

"I'm listening."

"He had a key to this house. I did not."

"From what I've been told, there isn't a lock in California that could keep you out if you really wanted to get
through it." The sergeant nodded to Jenny. "I'll stay in
touch."

"Thanks for coming," she said. "I know how hard
you're working."

A rare hint of warmth pierced Parker's stony expression.
"Nobody wants this case solved more than I do, Jenny,
believe me."

She walked into the front room with the two men. The
sight of her ex-husband sitting handcuffed threw Jenny back
to the night when he'd attacked her. Although she'd fled
before calling 911, she'd had to go to the police station in

Long Beach to make a statement, and she'd seen Grant in custody.

He wore the same air of offended dignity now as then. Some people never changed, she thought with a surge of anger.

"What about medical attention?" Grant demanded.

"Are you injured?" Parker asked.

"He damn near cut my throat open."

The detective glanced skeptically at the tiny wound. "We'll get someone to look at it. Come on, cowboy. I've had a long night."

"You're taking me in?" Apparently this was news to Grant. Despite the handcuffs, he drew himself up as if he were king of the world.

"That's what we usually do with men who try to break into their ex-wives' homes," the sergeant said. "Do I need to call for backup or are you going to cooperate?"

"I'll come along quietly, Officer." He spoke the line with a note of sarcasm.

After scooting awkwardly to his feet, Grant glowered at Jenny. When he opened his mouth to speak, she said, "If you're going to tell me this is all my fault, I'll slug you. And I don't care if Parker books me for assault."

Her ex-husband blinked. Slowly the aggression wilted from his stance. "I was going to ask you not to tell Beth I've been arrested. It'll upset her."

"I'll use my judgment." It occurred to her that Shelley wouldn't be happy with her husband, either, but that was between the two of them.

The detective called to let the station know he was bringing in a perpetrator and to arrange for someone to collect Grant's rental car. After he escorted his prisoner into the overcast morning, Jenny realized with a start that day had dawned.

She closed the door, swung around and ran straight into Zahad. He felt so solid that Jenny sagged against him, her energy depleted. If he hadn't caught her, she would have collapsed onto the carpet.

With her cheek resting on his shoulder, she felt the thrum of his heartbeat pumping strength into her. Jenny wound her arms around Zahad's neck and simply clung as the full shock of the past few hours rushed over her.

"I could kill him for doing this to you," the sheikh said.

"If you hadn't been here…" The gun hadn't been loaded and the key hadn't worked. But Grant was still larger and stronger than Jenny, and she'd have had to open the door to let Beth in.

"Do not waste time on what-ifs." Zahad steered her gently toward her bedroom. "Remember instead that perhaps the perpetrator has been caught and your troubles may be over."

"I hope it's that simple." Shock had temporarily evaporated all of Jenny's self-reliance. How strange, she reflected, that circumstances had brought a total stranger to protect her when she needed him. It felt right that he should be here, guarding her home, watching over her and Beth.

She knew her overstressed mind was playing tricks on her, but she didn't care. Zahad's company was a gift that she accepted gratefully.

"I appreciate that you defended me to the detective," he said as they entered her room.

"What did I say?" Exhausted, she could scarcely remember her conversation with Parker.

"That you felt safe with me." Zahad lowered her onto the bed.

Jenny thought about removing her robe and decided against it, not from modesty but because she was simply too tired.

"I value your trust."

"You've more than earned it." She struggled to keep her eyes open.

The sheikh pulled the sheet and the quilt over her. "You should sleep as late as you like."

"I'll get up when Beth does."

"I will make sure she is all right."

Jenny wanted to thank him again, but her muscles had gone slack and her tongue felt impossibly heavy. As if from afar, she felt his gentle fingers stroke her hair away from her temple.

Utterly at peace, she slept.

ZAHAD NAPPED FOR a couple of hours. At eleven o'clock, he arose, showered and donned slacks and a pullover. After checking his e-mail and confirming the address of Fario's friend Ronald Wang, he went into the kitchen.

Outside, the morning light filtered through cloud cover revealed a patchy vista of half-melted snow. Inside, it filled the house with soft radiance.

As he waited for the toaster oven to crisp the frozen waffles, he noted the welcoming effect of the red-and-white chairs against off-white linoleum and beige countertops. Jenny's spirit filled this house. Fario had come here to meet a fantasy woman, but the reality was far more complex and, in Zahad's viewpoint, far more desirable.

He had brewed coffee and was removing the waffles when a small voice asked, "Are those for me?"

Surprised that he hadn't heard the child approach, he made a brief examination of the pajama-clad pixie standing a few feet away. Beth was, Zahad saw with a twist of appreciation, a miniature version of Jenny, from the fine drift of blond hair to the assessing way she tilted her head. Only the eyes, blue instead of green, hinted at differences.

"I made them for myself, but I will give you half. Then I will make four more and share them also. Will that be acceptable?"

She nodded, but her forehead puckered. "Who are you?"

He took out another plate and a mug, decided that coffee might not be suitable and replaced it with a glass. "My name is Zahad. I am a friend of your mother's."

"I never saw you before." Beth climbed onto a chair and curled her bare feet beneath her.

Zahad poured milk into the glass. That was what Amy always served her children, who were a few years older than this poppet. "I am visiting."

"Did my daddy leave?"

"Yes." He saw no reason to elaborate.

Beth chewed on her lip as she watched him across the table. At last she transferred her attention to her waffles. "You forgot the syrup."

"A serious omission," Zahad agreed, and went to get it from the refrigerator. He put more waffles in the toaster, as promised. "I am not very familiar with children. Do you pour your own syrup or would you like me to?"

"Me." Beth took the bottle and glopped an outrageous amount on her waffles, pouring it all over the plate as well. "That's how you do it."

"I see," said Zahad, and poured the same outrageous amount on his own waffles and plate.

"You're funny," said the little girl, who had skewered her stack and was sawing raggedly with her knife.

"How so?" He handed her a paper napkin from a basket and took one for himself. On second thought, he gave them each an extra.

"The way you talk. I'm only five. You talk to me like I'm a grown-up."

"This is the way I talk to children," he explained. "Even to my cousin Sharif's son, Ben, who is three."

"I bet he likes you."

"I hope so. Many adults believe I am crunchy. Excuse me, I mean crusty."

Her smile reminded him of sunshine breaking through clouds.

"I want to be crunchy, too."

She scooped a huge dripping piece of waffle into her mouth. For a moment, Zahad feared it was too large and that she would choke, but she chewed mightily and downed the food with a gulp of milk.

It surprised him to discover he found this child interesting. He spent little time with youngsters and then usually in the company of their parents, so there was no need for him to interact. He had always had the impression that those below the age of adult reasoning were best left to their mothers.

As their conversation continued, what impressed him most about Beth was how seriously she took herself and everything in her world. Although she might look helpless, she had a strong sense of personal power and held to firm opinions.

She waxed scornful on the subject of her stepmother who, it seemed, believed that Beth ought to like the same clothes and toys she herself had once preferred. "Shelley's not a mom," the little girl concluded as she mopped the last syrup from her plate. "She thinks she is but she's not."

"You do not get along with your stepmother?" Zahad reflected that he had a similar problem, although on a larger scale. Such clashes were unfortunate but far from inevitable. After the war in Alqedar, he had seen many stepmothers become a blessing to motherless children.

"She's always mad at me," the little girl said. "Like when I painted my face with her lipstick."

"What did she do?"

"She called me a bad name." Beth's lower lip trembled until she got it under control. "I said I was sorry. But I wasn't."

"Sometimes I do things other people don't like, and I am not usually sorry, either."

At this remark, laughter erupted behind him. "Mommy!" cried Beth in delight, and nearly overturned her chair as she ran to Jenny.

Zahad watched with pleasure as the two blondes hugged each other. With a little assistance from Jenny, Beth climbed up her mother like a monkey until they were face-to-face. They played a quick kissing game back and forth on cheeks and noses. Then Jenny lowered her daughter to the floor.

"It's good to have you home," she said.

"Zod and I had breakfast," Beth explained.

"Zahad," her mother corrected.

"Zod likes his waffles the same way I do," her daughter continued.

Jenny eyed their plates. "Drenched?"

"Your daughter has expanded my range of culinary experiences." The sheikh cleared their dishes to the counter. "Now I must leave for the afternoon. It may be late when I return."

"Will you be here tomorrow morning?" Beth asked.

"That is my intention."

"Good," she said.

Hugging her daughter from behind, Jenny smiled at him. "I'm glad you two hit it off."

"We are very much alike, I think," Zahad said gravely.

He wasn't happy about leaving. Many things might go wrong for Jenny today, from Grant being released on bail to another Internet Romeo showing up. To his surprise, he found that he regretted leaving not only because of the danger but also because he was sure to miss a great deal of playing and perhaps some more doses of pint-size wisdom.

However, it could not be helped. He must talk to Fario's friend, whom he hoped to catch off guard. There were many things about his brother that Zahad did not know, including whether he had made enemies locally. And, of course, he must try to gather as much information as possible about Hashim's movements.

"Good luck with your mission." A shadow of anxiety fleeted across Jenny's face. For an instant, he thought she was going to ask him to stay, but she lifted her chin and remained silent.

"You will be careful." He knew better to say more in the child's presence.

"Of course."

He sketched the ladies a bow, the formal kind with one hand behind his back, and retrieved his coat before venturing out into the tingling air. Zahad briefly contemplated buying a gun on the black market but decided it would be too time-consuming and, in view of Detective Finley's suspicions of him, perhaps too risky.

As he got into his car, he hoped he would not regret that decision.

Chapter Nine

Jenny had known Zahad would take good care of her daughter while she slept. What she hadn't expected was to see him addressing Beth as an equal and behaving in a manner that could only be described as charming.

Grant rarely gave the little girl his full attention. He loved her, of course, but even when he played with her, he always seemed distracted.

The sheikh's behavior did not mean he was ready for fatherhood, she reminded herself. Nor did she want him to be. Beth had a father already, deficient though he might be.

She'd expected her daughter to stay happily at home today playing with toys she hadn't seen in two weeks, but the youngster had other ideas. Jenny had barely finished breakfast when Beth announced she wanted to play with Cindy.

"I don't know what her family's doing today." After all, it was Sunday. "I'll call them later."

"Call them now!" The little girl folded her arms and tapped one foot on the linoleum, a pose Jenny hadn't seen before.

"Is that the way Shelley stands?" she asked.

"I guess so." Beth relaxed her arms. "Please call them."

Since it was already afternoon, the Rivases had probably returned from church by now. "Okay, since you asked nicely."

The line was busy. "They're home but they're on the phone," she told her daughter.

"Let's go!" Beth pelted into the rear hallway and pulled down the coat Jenny had hung there last night.

"You haven't finished unpacking." She hated to barge in on her neighbors unannounced. "I'll call them again in a few minutes."

"I want to go now!" The little girl fumbled with her front snaps. Judging by her pout, she was on the verge of a tantrum.

Normally, Jenny didn't tolerate defiance. Today, however, she felt in no mood to fight, not after they'd been apart for so long. Also, Beth must be feeling off-kilter from yesterday's long trip.

The Rivases knew what little girls were like, and Cindy would be happy to see her friend. It wouldn't hurt to tell her neighbors what had happened last night, either.

"I'll tell you what," she said. "We'll walk over and knock on the door. If they're busy, we'll leave and you'll be a good sport about it. All right?"

Beth nodded. "Okay."

Jenny tucked her cell phone in her pocket. As they went out, she set the alarm and explained to her daughter how it worked. "There've been some strange men hanging around and we want to be careful," she added.

"I know." One of the would-be lovers had been waiting on the porch a few weeks ago when they got home from school. Fortunately, he'd backed off quickly when he learned the truth.

"Did your daddy say anything about what happened while you were gone?" She'd been debating with herself whether to mention the murder, but perhaps Grant had already done so.

"He said a man got hurt on the walkway and went to heaven," Beth told her.

"That's right." Silently, she thanked her ex-husband for

his uncharacteristic tact. "We're very sad about it. He was Zahad's brother."

Beth skipped ahead on the pathway that led downhill to the Rivases' house, but the rough terrain soon slowed her and she let her mother catch up. "I like Zod," she said as if the conversation had never been interrupted.

"Me, too," Jenny said.

After last night, no doubts lingered about her decision to let him stay with her. For all his concern, Parker hadn't been there when her ex-husband showed up.

But Zahad wasn't here now. Uneasily, Jenny glanced toward the street, checking for unfamiliar parked cars. She couldn't afford to let down her guard, not even on a quiet Sunday afternoon when the sun peeked through the clouds and Beth swung alongside her.

When they neared Ray and Ellen's house, Jenny heard the clink of china from inside. Although it was nearly two o'clock, they must be eating. She hesitated, but Beth raced ahead.

"Honey!"

Too late. Beth rang the doorbell and was hopping up and down with excitement. Reluctantly, Jenny joined her.

The door opened and Cindy's little face, surrounded by russet hair like her mother's and grandmother's, poked out. "It'th you!" she cried. "Bethy!" The two girls hugged. They were so cute that Jenny wished she had a camera with her.

"Cinders, you're not supposed to answer the door by yourself." Ray ambled into view. "Oh, hi, Jenny, good to see you." He gave her a lazy, welcoming smile. When she'd first met him, she'd thought he was flirting, but although he came over to help with repairs sometimes, he'd never so much as hinted at anything improper. She'd decided that he simply liked women.

"I didn't mean to interrupt," she said. "Your phone was busy and Beth got antsy."

"Sorry. I called my mom." He stood back to let her in. "Come join the neighbors."

Jenny felt a moment's trepidation as she caught sight of the group around the table that occupied one end of the front room. In addition to Dolly, Bill and Ellen, Al and Tish Garroway were drinking coffee and sampling muffins from a basket.

The look on Tish's face appeared far from welcoming. Ellen wore the same guarded expression she'd assumed around Jenny for the past few months.

"Tish brought over these delicious muffins," Dolly said. "Please join us." She, at least, seemed friendly.

"Just for a minute." Fleeing would only make the situation more awkward. Besides, she remembered, she had news for them. "I wanted to let you know that my ex-husband broke into my house last night, carrying a gun. Parker has him in custody."

A flurry of questions erupted. Over coffee and a muffin, Jenny answered them as concisely as possible. Ellen seemed very relieved to hear that the killer had apparently been apprehended.

"It's a good thing the sheikh was there," Ray replied.

Jenny remembered something Zahad had told her. "I'm glad you encouraged him to stay with me. Parker was giving him a lot of flak."

"You suggested he stay?" Ellen regarded her husband in surprise.

"It seemed like a good idea, with everything that's happened," Ray said.

"I don't like him snooping through the neighborhood." Al scratched beneath his scraggly beard. The ski instructor wouldn't be bad-looking without that ratty facial hair, Jenny mused, but perhaps Tish liked it. "Did you ever think that the sheikh might be hanging around to cover his tracks?"

"You sound like one of them gorillas that don't want no competition," Bill said. "One look at that sheikh fella and you started beating on your chest and howling."

Dolly's jaw dropped in dismay. "Oh, Bill!"

Although amused, Jenny couldn't let Al's remark pass. "Zahad's a security expert. In fact, he found a piece of evidence the police missed."

Heads turned. As everyone started talking at once, Jenny felt a pang of doubt. Maybe she shouldn't have revealed so much.

"I'd like to hear what it is," Al said.

"Maybe he planted it himself," Tish put in.

"Did it have anything to do with Grant?" Ellen asked.

Dolly waited attentively. While she focused on Jenny, Bill quietly slathered butter on a lemon muffin he'd sneaked past his wife, who tried to keep them both on a healthy diet.

Too late to back down now. "He moved a wastebasket that the killer must have walked by and found a scrap of paper." Remembering Tish's remark, Jenny added, "He'd just arrived at the house, so he couldn't have planted it."

"Was anything written on it?" Dolly asked.

"No, but there was a crystal watermark in the paper," she replied.

Al shrugged. Tish looked puzzled. Ellen bit her lip.

"Wow," Ray said. "That sounds like the documents at my bank."

"I know." Jenny wished she could read their reactions more clearly, but no one's response stood out as unusual. "Maybe part of a deposit slip."

"Were there fingerprints?" Dolly queried.

"Not as far as I know, but I'm sure Parker will check."

Ray smacked his forehead. "So that's why he was there!"

"Excuse me?" Al said.

"The sheikh. He dropped by the bank the other day," Ray explained. "I guess he wanted to check it out. Not that he could have learned anything just walking into the lobby."

Zahad hadn't mentioned stopping at the bank. Jenny

wondered what he'd hoped to find. Perhaps he'd simply wanted to look around.

"I can't see what good a scrap of paper is unless it has a fingerprint on it," Ellen commented. "Lots of us use that bank."

"We don't," Tish countered.

"It might have stuck to somebody's clothing and dropped off anytime," Jenny said. "Weeks ago, even."

"You never know." Belatedly, Dolly noticed her husband stuffing the muffin into his mouth, but she let it go. "If the police start to focus on a suspect, it might prompt them to look into his account."

"For what?" Al asked.

Ray brightened. He loved watching TV cop shows and had often recounted the plot twists to Jenny. "Suppose there was a hired killer and he put his blood money in an account. I mean, the police might notice that he'd made a large deposit. If it was a check, they could trace it to whoever hired him."

"The police can't look into an account without a subpoena, can they?" Al said.

"That's right," Dolly agreed. "They'd have to have reasonable suspicion."

"Yeah, but I'm not a cop," Ray said. "I could take a quick look at a few people's records, the ones that know Jenny. I wouldn't violate anybody's privacy or anything."

"How would you nose around people's bank accounts without violating their privacy?" Ellen asked.

He shrugged. "I don't know."

"In any case, I hope we're done with those awful men coming by," Ellen added. "I've posted warnings all over the Internet."

"Thanks. I appreciate it," Jenny said.

The phone in her pocket rang. After excusing herself, she moved to the far side of the room and answered, her spirits lifting at the possibility that it might be Zahad.

It was Parker, and she heard a tired edginess in his voice.

"I want to alert you that we're going to release Grant on bail."

"What?" Jenny nearly dropped the phone. "How can you do that?"

"He gave us permission to check his house, his office and his storage locker, so we didn't have to wait for warrants. He gave us his computer passwords."

"You mean for his home in Missouri?"

"Correct. St. Louis P.D. got right on it. So far, we haven't found one bit of evidence tying him to the murder or the cyber-stalking. We had to set bail and his wife's flying out to pay it. Actually, I think she left as soon as she heard he was in jail."

Jenny shivered. "I don't like the idea of him walking around free."

"It isn't up to me. I agree he might be dangerous. Speaking of dangerous people, is the sheikh with you?"

"No."

"Where is he?"

"In L.A." She refused to reveal anything else. In her opinion, Parker wasn't rational about Zahad.

"He'd better not be prying again."

"Oh, for heaven's sake!" Jenny's sympathy for the overworked detective evaporated. "I'm the one whose life is in danger, and I'm glad he's doing it."

"Jenny, you don't understand these matters. The more I look into this, the more suspicious that man becomes."

"Only to you," she snapped. "I'm coming down to the station to find out what's what. I'm not going to sit around my house waiting for Grant to show up."

"I wouldn't advise confronting him. However, I'll be glad to issue you a temporary restraining order. If he does approach you, we'll arrest him again and this time he won't get out so fast."

"I'll be there in fifteen minutes. Thanks for letting me know." After hanging up, she explained to the others what had happened and asked if she could leave Beth there.

"Of course." Ellen sounded friendlier than in a long time. "Cindy's missed her terribly. Don't worry about a thing. I'll even let them play with some of my makeup samples, if you don't mind." She sold cosmetics as a side business.

"Thanks," Jenny said. "I'll be at the police station." Her neighbors had her cell-phone number if they needed her.

Dolly, Ray and Al wished her luck. Bill slipped a blueberry muffin into his napkin and smiled at her like a Cheshire cat.

ZAHAD HAD VISITED his brother's apartment when he first arrived in the area. He'd flown into Los Angeles instead of directly to Mountain Lake so he could examine the premises, which the police had already searched, and ship home his brother's effects. The two-story white-stucco building where Ronald Wang lived lay about two blocks away, tucked into a side street near UCLA.

A two-hour drive—for which he had removed his tire chains—brought him to a different world. Here, palm trees replaced the pines of the mountain village, and instead of snow and a sharp wind, the city basked in filtered sunshine. Zahad parked on the street, fed a meter and headed for the building.

Casually clothed young people ambled past him, some carrying shopping bags. They had the open, comfortable look of Californians for whom a public street was merely an extension of their private space.

He reviewed what he'd learned about Ronald Wang from Amy and an Internet background check. At twenty-seven, he was slightly older than Fario and came from a middle-class family. A graduate of UCLA, he'd worked as a junior insurance executive for a couple of years before returning to get an MBA.

His family appeared to be of Chinese or Taiwanese descent, but the young man himself had been born here. The company with which Zahad contracted to run checks on employees had turned up a misdemeanor arrest years earlier for marijuana possession. Wang had avoided prison by undergoing counseling.

There'd been no mention of him in the initial police report. Amy had learned of his existence from one of Hashim's friends in London. Apparently Ronald had taken Fario and Hashim nightclubbing.

If Hashim had hired a hit man, it might have been this fellow or some connection of his. He was, after all, one of the few contacts Hashim could have made while he was here.

At the front of the building, Zahad found the name Wang and pressed the buzzer. Seconds ticked by and then a voice over the speaker said, "Wazzup?"

"I wish to speak with Ronald Wang."

"That's me. And the way you sound, this had better be— what's your name? Zad, Zan, Zach?—or I'm not letting you in."

"I am Zahad Adran." He hadn't realized that his slight accent and formal manner of address gave away so much, let alone that Fario had discussed him with his friend.

"Just for verification purposes…"

"Why do you require verification?"

"A—You sound foreign. B—Somebody killed Fario who was my buddy, and the consensus on the Internet is that it had to be political, which means one of those wackos might come after me because I know something that I don' know I know. If you watch spy movies, you'll understand."

"I understand." Zahad wondered if Ronald Wang normally carried on such lengthy conversations over the intercom.

"I'm not finished. Let's see, oh, yeah, we're up to C. This isn't exactly in your favor but according to chatter on the Internet, the cops think you did it, only I don't. So, for verification purposes, tell me what Fario liked to drink."

"Champagne. His favorite nonalcoholic beverage was

;oat's milk mixed with Mountain Dew.'' Zahad considered he concoction disgusting, but his brother had enjoyed it.

"Okay, I'm buzzing you in."

Inside, Zahad had no difficulty finding apartment 2C. An Asian-American man of medium height answered the door.

"Man, I gotta shake hands with you." He proceeded to do so. "Fario told me a lot about you."

"Did he?" The sheikh had assumed his brother rarely gave him a thought.

"He made you sound like James Bond." Ronald stepped back to let him inside.

The sunny front room was furnished with a white wicker couch and chairs. The other contents included an array of audiovisual equipment, a desk crammed with a computer and printer, and shelves loaded with video games and DVDs. Zahad noted a couple of textbooks, as well.

"Has anyone else come by to talk about Fario?" he asked.

"No."

"Where did you hear about his death?"

"It was all over campus," Wang said.

"The police haven't talked to you?"

A sideways shake of the head. Well, Zahad was certain he sergeant would consider this visit interfering with a police investigation, but if it weren't for him, the witness would never have been questioned at all.

"I'm really sorry about Fario," Wang said. "He was a great guy."

"Thank you." Zahad rather liked this young man. However, appearances could deceive. "Did he have enemies? Perhaps a rival for a woman?"

"The only woman he ever talked about was that one he met on the Internet. Can I get you a Coke or something?"

Zahad declined. He prowled the room, looking for anything out of place while asking Wang how Fario had come to "meet" Jenny.

"I used to date a woman I met in a chat room," the

young man explained. "I'm afraid I encouraged him.
knew it could be dangerous for women but I never heard
of a guy getting hurt."

"You met his cousin Hashim?"

"Sure. A wild man." He grinned. "You Alqedarians o
whatever you call yourselves sure know how to have a good
time. Well, not you personally, I guess. Fario said you were
kind of serious."

"When did Hashim leave?" Zahad asked.

"Saturday."

That would be two days before Fario's murder. "You are
certain?"

"Fario drove him to the airport," Ronald said. "I went
along for the ride 'cause he has such a cool car. I mean
had. What happened to it, anyway?"

"It is in police custody." Zahad would arrange for a
buyer when the vehicle was released. "Is there anything
else, however insignificant, that you could tell me?"

"Well, there is one thing." From a desk drawer, Wang
removed a stack of papers. When he handed them over
Zahad saw that they were printed-out conversations from a
chat room.

"I was mad about my friend getting killed, so I figured
I'd get the goods on that woman," Ron explained. "I went
online to see if I could find her. I wasn't going to try to
meet her, just learn as much as I could."

"Jenny is not the murderer," Zahad said.

"If you say so. Anyway, look at those papers. Go on."

He flipped through the sheets. The ones on top contained
chats between Jenny S and a writer called TheWiz. The
ones on the bottom were between Jenny S and Arabprince
"Some are your conversations and some are my brother's,"
he guessed.

"Yeah. He made me copies because they were so sexy
Look at the way she wrote to me and the way she wrote to
him."

One discrepancy struck Zahad immediately. "There are

more misspellings in the newer ones." They included "lushous" instead of "luscious" and "freind" instead of "friend."

"The writing's cruder, too," Ronald said. "Shorter sentences and more four-letter words. These were posted by two different women."

Despite his fluency in English, Zahad doubted he would have caught that distinction. Now that it had been pointed out, however, he could see that Wang was right.

"A copycat," he said. It might be someone playing a cruel prank. It might also mean that the original stalker had stopped and someone else had decided to continue the harassment.

"This could be useful," he told Wang. "May I keep these?"

"I'll make you copies." The young man ran them through the printer-copier. "What do you think it means?"

"I do not know."

"Do you have any suspects?"

"My stepmother has proposed Hashim as the next governor of our province," Zahad said. "He stands to gain a great deal by my brother's death."

"Hashim? The killer?"

"It is one possibility."

Ron shook his head. "He warned Fario not to go. He said this Jenny person probably had an incurable disease or was some kind of criminal."

This was a point in Hashim's favor. It didn't necessarily clear him in Zahad's eyes, however.

"For what it's worth, I don't believe you did it, either," Wang added.

"Why not?" Zahad asked.

The young man grinned. "Fario said you were hard-nosed. Man, he was right."

"Hard-nosed?"

"Tough. He was always bragging about you. How brave you were. How smart. Like you were some hero."

"Perhaps you misunderstood," Zahad replied. "My father was his hero."

"Not really." Wang fed more papers into the copier. "He said his dad always took the easy way out, like going into exile, and that you're the only one in the family with guts."

A sadness touched with regret came over Zahad. To receive this knowledge of his brother's admiration from beyond the grave was a rare gift, but also a reminder of what might have been had Fario lived.

"I wish I had known this while he was alive," he said.

"He came here because of you." The young man tapped the copies into a neat pile and handed them over. "He wanted to make something of himself so you'd respect him."

"Thank you for telling me these things."

"I'm glad to help any way I can. I sure hope you catch that woman."

"The person who lured my brother was not Jenny Sanger," Zahad said. "I suspect it was a man."

"No way!"

"Why do you say that?"

"Because he talked to her on the phone."

Stunned, Zahad took a moment to respond. "How did this happen?"

"She asked him to send her his phone number," Ron explained. "He told me she was curious to hear what a sheikh sounded like."

This was amazing news. "Did you hear her voice? Perhaps you would recognize it if you heard it again."

"Sorry, I didn't."

So the stalker had been a woman. Zahad had met four female neighbors, but of course there must be women teachers at Jenny's school who could have also done this.

"You must convey this information to the police," he urged. "Please call them on Monday, but do not mention that you talked to me."

"I don't know if I should," Ronald said. "I had this little marijuana conviction. He'll probably think I'm a suspect, too."

"He needs this information. Both about the second stalker and about the woman on the phone." On a spare pad, he jotted down Parker Finley's name. "It's the Mountain Lake Police Department."

"Yeah, okay," Wang said. "And I won't rat you out. You're doing exactly what Fario would have wanted."

"Thank you." They shook hands.

Zahad had just stepped into the hall when his cell phone rang. Retreating to the stairwell, he answered it.

"It's Jenny." He could tell something was wrong. "They're releasing Grant on bail. Apparently they searched his home and office and didn't find anything, so he's just facing charges from this morning."

"Where are you?"

"I'm at Ellen's, but I'm going to the station," she said.

"I will come as fast as I can."

After hanging up, he took the stairs at a rapid clip. On his way down, it occurred to him that Grant Sanger had a wife who wanted Jenny's child.

Could the voice on Fario's phone have been hers?

Chapter Ten

After calling Zahad, Jenny headed toward town. The day had warmed above freezing, although the weather forecast on the radio predicted lower temperatures tomorrow and a storm after that. She saw hardly any motorists on the way, but that wasn't unusual, since Pine Forest Road didn't connect to any major highways.

Her mind played over the conversation at the Rivases' house. She hoped Ray wouldn't do anything illegal at the bank. It seemed unlikely he could uncover clues simply by poking through people's account records, anyway. And if by any chance the killer really had deposited his hit money there, he might decide to come after Ray.

If Ray was in danger, so were Ellen and Cindy. Jenny shook her head at her own paranoid imaginings. Nobody was going to start killing people en masse in Mountain Lake. The worst thing likely to happen was that Ray might get fired from his job, which would be bad enough.

At least Ellen's hostility had eased. It wasn't hard to guess that she'd been jealous, although heaven knew why. Learning that Ray had encouraged Zahad to stay must have persuaded her he didn't have designs on anyone else.

At the thought of Zahad, Jenny began to smile. Wouldn't people be amazed if they had seen him joking with Beth across the breakfast table.

If only Grant had been so genuine and open. In retrospect, she could see how manipulative he was. Unfortunately, he exuded a superficial affability that she'd been afraid would work on his behalf in a custody case. Well, he'd just shown what kind of man he really was, and he had an arrest record to prove it.

Jenny rounded a curve and snapped back to the present. Ahead, a green sedan blocked her lane. While two guys peered beneath the hood, a third man in a windbreaker stood in the left lane, waving for help and blocking the road.

Normally, she would have stopped. Now uneasy questions nagged at her. Why hadn't the men pulled to the shoulder? Didn't at least one of them have his own mobile phone?

Carjackers.

She might be wrong. But why was that man standing on the left, endangering himself to force her to stop? A stalled vehicle only a few miles from town in clear weather hardly required such measures.

Jenny's stomach clenched. If she stopped, even with the doors locked, they could smash her windows and haul her out, grab her purse and take the SUV. She'd be at their mercy.

Jenny couldn't turn around on the two-lane road and she couldn't pass them to the right on the narrow shoulder. To the left lay a sharp drop into a creek bed.

She'd have to speed by in the left lane and hope no other car approached. And she must do it fast. As she drew closer, she made out a large wrench in the man's hand, plenty big enough to smash her window.

She was never, never going to let another man push her around.

Jenny hit the gas and steered left. A few dozen yards ahead, the man held his ground. He was daring her to hit him and smugly certain that she wouldn't.

He wore a smirk, just like Grant. Or like Oliver when he'd grabbed her arm.

Fury whited out Jenny's constraints. She didn't want to kill anybody. But if she veered off the road into the creek, she herself might be killed.

Her jaw tightened. She braced for the thump.

At the last minute, she made eye contact with the would-be robber. His sneer mutated into alarm.

As if in slow motion, she watched him dive toward his companions. Jenny flashed by inches away, her foot hovering between the brake and the gas. Her SUV slowed for a second until she realized she hadn't struck anyone, and then she floored it.

The men might have guns. They might come after her.

She flew along the road, watching for oncoming cars to warn but did not see any. She couldn't bring herself to pull over and she was going too fast to risk calling the police. She'd be at the station in a few minutes anyway.

Two miles passed with agonizing slowness despite her speed. There was no sign of anyone following, but on such a winding road they might not lag far behind. At last she turned on Lake Avenue and hit green lights all the way to the civic center.

Not until Jenny parked and slid out did she realize she was shaking. Holding on to the vehicle door, she forced herself to breathe evenly.

The realization that she'd won steadied her. She hadn't panicked. She hadn't let the criminals intimidate her.

She was no longer a little girl cowering from her father's anger. She wasn't Grant's wife, either, trying to placate him and save her marriage. She was a school principal and she'd stood up to carjackers.

Jenny marched across the pavement and through the front door of the station. The desk officer, a member of the PTA, recognized her at once. "Hello, Mrs. Sanger. Are you here to see Sergeant Finley?"

"Yes, but first I have to make a report," she said. "Three men tried to carjack me. At least, I think they did."

Her teeth started to chatter. Disgusted with herself, Jenny collapsed into a nearby chair. "I'm sorry."

"You all right?" He was dialing someone as he spoke.

"I could use a stiff shot of rum." She managed a tremulous smile. "Just kidding."

A minute later, a black-haired detective arrived. She'd met the officer, Hank Rygel, during the initial investigation into Fario's murder.

He was taking down the information when Parker joined them. Jenny described the men she'd seen and their car's color and possible make, but she didn't have a clue about the license plate.

After issuing an all points bulletin and assigning someone to warn Jenny's neighbors of the activity in their area, Parker escorted her to his office for further questioning. By the time he finished, Jenny felt as if her brain had been picked clean. Three interviews by Parker Finley in one week seemed more than any human being should have to endure.

The interviews weren't really the problem, she admitted silently. It was the fact that every criminal in California and maybe a few other states seemed to have her name tattooed on his brain.

Parker shook his head. "We thought we were driving the carjackers out of town. Instead, we just chased them into outlying areas where they'll be even harder to catch."

"Maybe they'll stop considering the locals easy prey now," she replied without much conviction.

"We should be so lucky."

"How's Grant?" she asked, getting back to the original reason for her visit.

"Beginning to see the error of his ways, I suspect. Mrs. Sanger—the second Mrs. Sanger—got here a few minutes ago. She stopped by the jail to pay him a visit. Hang on while I finish my notes, would you?"

"Sure." Sitting back, Jenny wished she didn't have to deal with her controlling ex-husband. Thank goodness Zahad was coming. It felt good to have someone backing her up.

She wanted him to stay a little longer. At least until they solved Fario's murder and she could shelve her imitation of Superwoman for next Halloween.

The phone rang. Parker answered, acknowledged the message and hung up. "Sanger's wife posted bail and they're releasing him. Are you sure you want to see them? You've been through one hell of a lot today."

It was tempting, but she wanted to see where Shelley stood on this custody business. In light of Grant's arrest, his wife might have second thoughts about engaging in a lengthy court battle with Jenny.

"How could I miss this?" she said with a lightness she was far from feeling. "It's my own personal soap opera."

"In that case, I'm sorry I left my video camera at home," Parker joked, and escorted her back to the lobby.

The last time she saw Shelley, Grant's wife had worn an expensive business suit and perfectly coiffed hair. This afternoon, as she stood at the front counter, her eyeliner was smudged and the dark roots of her blond mane needed a touch-up.

She addressed Parker edgily. "My husband is willing to plead guilty to misdemeanor trespassing if you'll give him probation."

"The district attorney decides on the charge," Parker replied. "You should know that. And he'll have to enter his plea in court."

"I'm not a criminal attorney." With a clear effort of will, Shelley forced herself to look at Jenny. "You could use your influence. I'm sure the D.A. would listen to you."

"What he did was serious, Shelley. He tried to break into my house with a gun," Jenny said.

"Unloaded."

"It was still a gun. He's fixated on me," Jenny added. "I want him out of my life and this custody business is going to make it worse."

Wearily, Shelley pushed a loose strand behind one ear. "You don't have to worry about that. I changed my mind. Your kid drives me crazy. I can't understand how you put up with her. As far as I'm concerned, the less we have to do with her, the better."

"She's just a normal five-year-old," Jenny said.

"If she's normal, I guess I don't have mothering instincts, after all." Shelley sounded surprisingly vulnerable. "My friends are all having babies and I thought I wanted a kid, too. Boy, was I wrong."

Jenny spared her a moment's sympathy. Beth certainly could get into mischief, but any competent parent would recognize that she'd been acting out because she missed her mother.

An inner door opened. "Oh, great," Shelley said. "Here comes Einstein now."

A rumpled Grant appeared in the company of a poker-faced guard. His gaze traveled uneasily between Shelley and Jenny. "What happens next?" he asked Parker.

"Your wife's posted bail but you need a criminal lawyer," the detective replied. "You'll be arraigned in court within a few days. As for the exact charges, that's up to the district attorney's office."

"We'll find an attorney," Shelley said.

"Because this is a domestic-violence situation, I'm going to give your ex-wife an emergency restraining order," Parker added. "It's good for five days, during which time she can get one that lasts up to three years. If you go anywhere near her or your daughter without a judge's permission, you'll be back in custody, Mr. Sanger, and this time you won't get out so fast."

The last scrap of pomposity wheezed out of Grant. "What I did was stupid. Believe me, I'm not planning to make it worse."

Jenny hoped she could believe him. Since their divorce, it was the first time he'd pulled anything like this. Assuming, of course, that he wasn't her stalker and Fario's murderer.

Through the glass, she saw Zahad striding toward the entrance. It was good to see him. Wonderful, really. She felt as if they'd been apart for much longer than a few hours.

Jenny ached to smooth back that shaggy hair and fasten a button he'd missed on his brown suede coat. And she wanted to tell him everything that had happened so he could help her sort it out and make it right.

The sheikh opened the door. Parker went rigid, like a dog scenting an enemy. Grant merely looked disgruntled.

"I asked him to come," she said. "He's acting as my bodyguard, remember?"

The detective nodded tightly.

Zahad caught sight of Jenny and his eyes lit up. She felt pulled toward him, and only held back by reminding herself where they were and who was watching.

As she greeted him, it saddened her to give him more bad news, but he needed to know about the attempted carjacking. Neither Grant nor Shelley had heard of it, either, and they all listened with varying degrees of dismay.

"I've put out an all points bulletin," Parker added when she finished.

"I hope they are caught quickly." Zahad looked grim.

"This was near your house?" Grant said. "I can't imagine how you can consider this place safe for Beth. Where is she now?"

"With a retired policewoman," Jenny snapped. "I might remind you, I'm not the one who left her alone in a car while I tried to break into someone's house."

Shelley held up one hand to forestall further arguing. "I don't think we're in any position to question Jenny's parenting decisions, Grant. Let's get going. I want to find a motel and take a shower."

Parker directed them to the Mountain Lake Inn down the street. After the couple departed, he said, "I'm going to get

Jenny a restraining order against Mr. Sanger. Then, Mr. Adran, I have to ask you to step into my office.''

"What for?" Jenny inquired.

"This is between the sheikh and myself." The sergeant's eyes never left Zahad's face.

"Of course, Sergeant. I am always ready to cooperate."

Jenny wished she'd never mentioned that Zahad had gone into Los Angeles. It was too late to do anything about that now, though.

THEY'D NO SOONER reached Finley's office than he turned on Zahad. "I told you to stay the hell out of my investigation. What were you doing in L.A?"

"Sight-seeing," Zahad said.

"The hell you were!"

He hated to lie, especially since Ronald Wang might slip tomorrow and admit having talked to him. That is, assuming Wang actually did call. On the other hand, if he told the truth, the detective would likely arrest him for interfering. "There is much to see. Have you visited the La Brea Tar Pits, Sergeant?"

"I know what you're up to," Finley retorted. "One of the neighbors called to complain about you pestering people. I want you to pack your bags and move to Crystal Point until the coroner releases your brother's body. Let me know where you're staying."

Which neighbor had called? Zahad hadn't interviewed the Garroways, but they seemed the most likely to object to his presence. On the other hand, perhaps Ray Rivas had more to hide than he let on.

"Mrs. Sanger has requested that I stay at her home. It appears she is in danger on several fronts and you are unable to guarantee her safety."

"And you are?"

"No one can guarantee safety. But I was there last night and you were not."

"Mr. Sanger would never have gotten into that house if you hadn't opened the door," the detective snarled.

His skin looked sallow this morning, a sign that lack of sleep and pressure were catching up with him. Zahad didn't spare him any sympathy. This man's bullheadedness was endangering Jenny.

"You have lost your objectivity," he told the sergeant. "You dislike me for personal reasons and therefore you seek an excuse to get rid of me."

"Oh, I'm biased, am I?" Finley growled. "I had an interesting telephone conversation this morning with a Mr. Hashim Bin Salem."

This was unexpected. "How did you come to contact him?"

"He said he was calling from Alqedar," the detective told him. "Mr. Bin Salem informs me that your president may appoint him governor instead of you and he's afraid he's next on your hit list."

"Hashim fears me?" Zahad wouldn't mind giving the callow young man a fright, but he suspected an ulterior motive lay behind the phone call. "What else did he say?"

"That's not public information," the sergeant replied.

"He called to stir your suspicion of me," Zahad speculated. "Perhaps he told you that Fario also feared me."

"He sure did." Weariness and resentment loosened the detective's tongue. "He said your brother was going to appoint him chief adviser and kick you out of power entirely. According to Mr. Bin Salem, that's why you killed him."

After talking to Ronald Wang, Zahad knew better than to believe his brother had intended any such thing. "Hashim is playing you. He wants me out of his way. If he fears me, it is because my influence in our country interferes with his ambitions."

This was disturbing news, all the same. Zahad had believed his young rival was simply falling in with Numa's plans. Perhaps that had been the case at first, but Hashim was now apparently determined to seize power even at the cost of lies and machinations. Zahad would indeed give him reason to be frightened once he returned to Alqedar. In the meantime, Hashim could pose more of a threat than anticipated.

"I can't force you to get the hell out of Dodge. But if I were you, I'd think seriously about leaving while I still could," Finley retorted.

Zahad refused to be intimidated. "I did not kill my brother. I am determined that one of us should find out who did. I do not care if it is you or I, Sergeant Finley. But I will not rest until it is done."

"Exactly where does Mrs. Sanger fit into this picture?" the detective asked.

That was a question to which the sheikh no longer had the answer. A few minutes ago, when he'd seen her safe inside the police station, relief had swept over him. He had not felt so happy since the time twelve years ago when he'd learned that Alqedar was free at last.

When she'd described the carjackers, he'd had to fight a near compulsion to race out and hunt them down. How could he leave her unprotected?

"I have pledged to protect Mrs. Sanger," he said in reply to the detective's question. "Her fate has become bound up with the crime against my brother. He would not wish me to abandon her."

"So once we catch this murderer, assuming it isn't you, you're history?"

"There are those in my country who consider me a part of history, and those who wish I would become history. I see you stand with the latter."

"You've got that right."

"Are we finished here?"

"Unless there's something you'd like to tell me about what you did in L.A." Finley waited with feigned patience.

"The Los Angeles County Museum of Art is also fascinating."

Wordlessly, the detective stepped aside and let him leave. He didn't bother to hide his disgust.

Zahad found Jenny alone in the lobby. One look at her pale face and he offered to drive her home. She declined, but at least she agreed that they should pick up dinner on the way.

Caravanning their vehicles, they bought hamburgers en route. Zahad was pleased to see that collecting her daughter and listening to the animated childish chatter helped restore some color to Jenny's cheeks.

After dinner, the three of them played a simple board game, which Beth won. Later, with Jenny's encouragement, Zahad sat on the edge of the little girl's bed and read her a story about small animals facing a moral dilemma. It was not only educational but also entertaining.

"I like the way you do the voices," Beth said as she snuggled under her quilt.

"I was not aware that I was doing voices. I simply spoke them as it seemed they should be spoken."

"You did a good job," Jenny added.

The sheikh was more pleased than he wanted to let on. He had never considered himself to have domestic skills other than basic cooking, a necessity in training camps.

Afterward, they drank decaf coffee at the kitchen table. Jenny explained that a search of Grant's home and office had come up clean. Zahad told her what he had learned from Ronald Wang.

They discussed the second cyber-stalker, debating who it might be without reaching any conclusions. The subject clearly distressed Jenny, as did the information about Fario's telephone conversation with a woman.

"It's easier to understand how a man could stoop to do something so cruel," she said. "I guess I expect more from women."

"I am sorry your experiences with men have made you so cynical." If he reached out to cup her shapely chin, her heart-shaped face would fit perfectly into his hand, Zahad thought. This did not seem to be an appropriate time for intimacies, however.

Jenny's shadowed green eyes met his. "Not all my experiences have been bad. I've had male friends, but never one like you. It's unfortunate…"

"What's unfortunate?" He very much wanted to hear what she'd meant to say.

"We both know how this has to end," she said. "Only the most bizarre circumstances brought us together in the first place. We're from different worlds and neither of us can change, even if we wanted to."

Zahad finger-combed an errant shock of hair from his forehead. He had never had such a personal conversation with a woman or, indeed, with anyone. "I suppose you're right," he replied at last, and regretted that it sounded inadequate.

Jenny went to bed a short time later. At the computer, Zahad found an e-mail waiting from Amy.

Holly, Sharif's wife, had gone into labor and was having difficulties. Her husband could not even think of leaving her to go to the capital.

She wrote:

Hashim must have found out that you're investigating him. He's doing his best to portray you as a threat to anyone who gets in your way. The latest word is that he and Numa want President Dourad to ban you from the country entirely.

Zahad's chest tightened. How could this happen? Surely the president was not so easily stampeded, but how could he be certain? He continued to read Amy's e-mail.

I doubt he'll take any immediate action. You're one of the men who paved the way for him to take office, after all, and he knows you're loyal. But this economic

plan we're putting together may not be enough to show
what a great leader you'll make. You need to plead
your case in person.

He closed his eyes and remembered what Jenny had said.
Unusual events had thrown them together, but it could not
last. Soon they would be torn apart.
What must be, must be. After hitting Reply, he wrote:

Believe me, as soon as Fario's body is released, I will
catch the next plane.

Despite his concern for Jenny, he hoped it would be soon.
Otherwise Zahad might face the unthinkable: a future as a
stateless person. For himself, he would find a way to sur-
vive. But for his people, it would be a disaster.

Chapter Eleven

In Jenny's dream, she drove along a street near the house in Long Beach where she'd lived during her marriage. There was a disabled car by the road and a man in the center, waving at her to stop. Grant.

She tried to steer around him, but he kept shifting in front of her. "I have to get by!" she shouted, but he refused to listen. The next thing she knew, she'd swerved off a cliff and was falling endlessly.

Someone caught her. The solid strength of his grip drew her up through layers of sleep until she lay in a man's arms, drinking in his exotic but now-familiar scent, feeling the scratch of his cheek against her temple as he sat cradling her.

"I am sorry to awaken you, but you called out," said a deep, gentle voice. Raising his head, Zahad gazed down at her. "Do not try to recall the dream. Let it fade away and you will sleep again."

"I'm not sure I want to." The sheikh had thrown on a robe, Jenny saw. Judging by the bare chest revealed in its gap, he wasn't wearing much underneath. She remembered waking up beside him at Lew's cabin and feeling drawn to the powerful, lithe splendor of the man.

"You must rest." His dark eyes reflected sparks of the moonlight flowing through the window.

"I'm too keyed up." With her head lying against his

shoulder, she became aware of the blood surging through her arteries. How much of her excitement was from the nightmare and how much a response to his nearness, she had no idea.

"A massage might help," he said.

"Don't tell me you learned how to do that in military camp!"

"In truth, I did." Zahad lowered her to the pillow. "Along with basic medical skills, we were instructed in techniques to ease muscle stiffness. A cramp can cause a man to miss his shot."

"I wouldn't want to miss my shot," she murmured.

"Turn over and cease disputing," he ordered.

Although she wasn't convinced it was the wisest course of action, Jenny obeyed. When he touched her, she felt a tingle, an almost electric spark.

As his hands roamed over her, she registered the coolness of his skin and the roughness of calluses. His palms were large enough to span her shoulder blades and surprisingly skilled as they probed the knots of tension along her spine.

A delicious ache spread through her. Warmth radiated to her lips, to the points of her breasts and between her legs. Jenny had never known such a sweet awakening, free from the need to defend herself against a man's demands. Beneath Zahad's healing touch, she relished her response.

It intensified as his thumbs found the taut small of her back and searched lower. Pleasure rippled through her, bringing with it a longing to touch this man and arouse him as he was doing for her.

She didn't fear growing close and then losing him. It was inevitable that he would leave. What she feared was never having a chance to know him.

Yet he had issued no invitation to anything beyond a back rub. For the first time, Jenny recognized how a man could act on his own sexual impulse without considering that the woman might not share it. It would be wrong to place Zahad in an awkward situation when he was only being kind.

She closed her eyes and concentrated on the lovely sensations and the longing to surrender. The heat of her blood burned away the helplessness and panic of her nightmare.

Utterly content, she drifted into a new and much more pleasant dream.

ZAHAD DREW the covers over Jenny, careful not to awaken her. He felt glad she'd found temporary peace and grateful that she had no inkling of the passion she aroused.

In his younger days, desire had existed as a simple physical response, a thing apart from the rest of his being. This longing for Jenny was the opposite. It touched his soul.

In her presence, all the disparate parts of him merged. He became a warrior who read bedtime stories to a little girl, a fierce avenger who wanted only to hold one woman close and keep her safe. He became a man he didn't know and, at the same time, his most fundamental self.

He was relieved that he'd restrained his instinct to kiss the nape of her neck. Too many men had tried to exploit Jenny. He would sooner suffer alone than have her think he resembled them.

Zahad sat for a while watching her sleep. When he left, he went to Beth's room and watched her, too. The child was a picture of innocence, her blond hair trailing across her closely held doll.

He thought of Sharif, half a world away, seeing his wife fight for her life and the life of their baby. Zahad had always valued children, but he had assumed it was because of what they might become. Now he felt how precious this little girl was and what a vast abyss would open up if she ever came to harm.

His cousin's pain and worry became his own. It was, he supposed, what people called empathy. Once, he would have believed that it weakened a man. Now he saw that it bridged the distances between him and the people he cared about.

He had Jenny to thank for this knowledge. Also for the restlessness that kept him awake for a long time afterward.

AS SHE GOT READY FOR WORK on Monday, Jenny drifted through her routine with a sense of disconnection. In a way, everything seemed normal. *Fix breakfast, make sure Beth dresses warmly, run through the day ahead.*

But nothing was normal, not really.

One week ago, Fario had died here. On Friday, an ex-con had grabbed her on the front steps. Yesterday, Grant had tried to break in, and three men had attempted to carjack her.

Thank heaven for Zahad. He made everything else tolerable. Sitting at the breakfast table in his robe, he looked thoroughly at home, untroubled by the dark stubble on his jawline and hair so rumpled she doubted a comb would make it halfway through.

"What are you going to do today?" she asked as she fixed a peanut butter sandwich for Beth and a tuna on rye for herself.

The sheikh buttered a couple of slices of toast and handed one to Beth. The two of them seemed to have entered into an unspoken routine of sharing their food.

"I believe I should keep my prying low-key. Detective Finley seems hypersensitive."

"You're sure this Mr. Wang won't make matters worse when he calls?"

"It remains to be seen." He obviously wasn't given to worrying about what-ifs.

"You'll try to find out who the woman is, won't you? The one who called your brother." She'd been trying not to think about the possibilities that came to mind. They were too close for comfort.

"If I can," Zahad said.

"Can we have something good for dinner?" Beth asked the sheikh.

"Would you enjoy a fresh roasted goat?" he inquired.

She made a face.

"Perhaps some stuffed sheep's stomach?"

"Ick!" She giggled. "You can do better than that!"

"Mr. Adran is our guest, not our cook," Jenny chided her.

"I will prepare the evening meal," Zahad replied calmly. "It will be a pleasure."

"No yucky stuff," the little girl said. "No vegetables. I hate them."

The sheikh and Jenny exchanged glances. "I will make it excellent," he promised. "But I do not guarantee the absence of vegetables."

Before she left, Jenny said she'd be home by five-thirty. "I have to pick up Beth at day care on my way home," she explained. Her daughter was one of about a dozen youngsters who rode a private bus to the nearby center after kindergarten let out at noon. "I can get fast food if you want."

He folded his arms. "I am not incompetent in the kitchen."

"No one would accuse you of being incompetent at anything." As she spoke, Jenny flashed back to last night and the expert massage. She turned away to hide a blush.

Zahad frowned. "I am not thinking clearly. Wait one moment while I throw on my clothes."

"Why?"

"I will drive you to town and pick you up later," he said.

Jenny glanced toward her daughter, who waited impatiently at the door. She appreciated his offer, but she couldn't accept it.

"Thanks, but no. You won't be around forever." She had to stand on her own two feet. "Besides, I might need my car at work."

Jenny expected him to argue, as most men would. Instead, Zahad simply regarded her for a moment before saying, "I admire your courage."

He respected her decision. The realization was both heady and disconcerting, because part of Jenny feared what might lie ahead today. She drew herself up. "Thank you."

"Call if you need me."

"I've got your number programmed into my cell phone." Jenny couldn't resist reaching up to cup his prickly cheek with her palm. When he blinked, startled, she quickly hustled her daughter out the door.

Please, she thought, just let us get through this one day without anything terrible happening. It would make such a nice change.

JENNY'S TOUCH LINGERED on Zahad's cheek as he showered. The tenderness in her eyes and her spontaneous gesture had surprised him. In only a few days, they had grown very close.

Yet she was correct: He could not protect her forever, Zahad told himself. It was a good thing Jenny possessed inner strength, because she would likely need it.

As a soldier, he had once doubted women's capacity to endure hardship. That was before he saw Sharif's first wife die in childbirth. Only then had he understood how ignorant men were of the courage required by women's lives.

Remembering the life-and-death struggle that Holly faced, he called Amy's number as soon as he finished shaving and dressing. "How is Sharif's family?" he asked when she answered.

"Holly had a C-section this morning and delivered a healthy girl," his cousin said. "They're naming her Jamila." The name meant "beautiful." "I'd have called you sooner, but I didn't want to wake you."

"How is Holly?"

"Still weak. Sharif wants to make sure there are no complications before he goes to Jeddar.'' That was the capital city, several hours' journey from his provincial capital.

''I understand.'' With Hashim seeking to send Zahad into exile, he could no longer wait. ''I will call President Dourad myself and plead my case.''

''That's a good idea. I'm hoping he won't do anything before you return with Fario's body,'' Amy said. ''But Numa's burning with a sense of injustice and she has plenty of friends in Jeddar. She honestly believes you killed Fario.''

''I will plead my case.''

After ringing off, Zahad put in the call. It was early evening in Alqedar, and he was only able to reach one of the president's aides.

''I'm glad you contacted me,'' the man said. ''President Dourad has scheduled a session on Saturday morning to consider the governing of Yazir Province. He grows tired of the squabbling. I advise you to be present in person.''

''Thank you for your counsel.''

To reach Alqedar by Saturday morning, given the time difference and the possibility of flight delays, Zahad realized he must depart no later than Thursday morning. Ideally, he should go sooner. He hated to leave while matters remained so unsettled here, but Numa and Hashim were forcing his hand.

If Fario's body could not be ready, Zahad would of course have to return for it. Otherwise, he wished to come back anyway for Jenny's sake, but that would depend on the political situation.

He sent an e-mail notifying Amy and Sharif of the new development, then called the coroner's department. A deputy told him the medical examiner still had not released the body.

Although he felt tempted to point out that any competent physician could have harvested tissue samples by now, Zahad knew that insults were likely to backfire. He said a gruff thank-you instead and added that he needed to take the body back to his country for burial as soon as possible.

"Are you aware that the remains will have to be embalmed before any airline will accept them?" the deputy asked.

"No, I was not." Zahad massaged his forehead. Yet another bureaucratic obstacle!

"You should call a funeral home. They'll take care of it for you," the man said.

"I will do that."

In the Yellow Pages, Zahad located the Mountain Lake Funeral Parlor. The woman who answered assured him they would do their best to handle the embalming and assist with shipping arrangements on short notice.

He thanked her and provided information about Fario for later. Afterward, feeling too restless to remain in the house, he decided to talk to Dolly. She was, after all, the witness who had found Fario's body.

Outside, clouds layered a pale sky and the light breeze carried a nip. After setting the alarm, Zahad followed the path toward the Blankenship property. Near the Rivases' carport, he turned right and followed the driveway uphill.

The Blankenship cottage sat in a shaded patch, only a trace of weak sunlight filtering through the overgrowth. Standing on the porch, he heard the chatter of a game show inside. He realized the doorbell must have sounded like one of the chimes on the television, because it failed to catch anyone's attention.

Zahad rapped firmly. Dolly threw the door open as if she'd been expecting him and said, "Come on in."

Leaving him to close the door, she returned to the couch. With her short, reddish-brown hair and flowered blouse tucked into her blue jeans, she presented a sturdy, almost ageless figure. But he guessed she was in her sixties.

The home seemed even darker inside than out. The worn carpet and scuffed paint gave it a shabby air, but it smelled pleasantly of coffee. There was a great deal of overstuffed furniture, mostly oriented toward a large TV.

"Can you figure out what the phrase is?" Dolly indicated the screen, which showed a series of squares with some letters revealed. A clue appeared at the bottom.

"It would be difficult for me." Zahad lowered himself into an armchair. "I am not a native English speaker."

"You speak very well, if you ask me." She picked up a shapeless wad of knitting. In the show, a woman spun a wheel while people clapped encouragement. "She ought to buy a vowel, but people get overexcited and forget."

Zahad wished he could inspect the premises, since he wanted to know who else might be in the house, but it would seem indiscreet. "Does your husband not enjoy this show?"

"Oh, he went out. I practically had to hog-tie him to let me drive him to the senior center this morning," Dolly said. "He loves playing checkers but he always insists on taking the bus himself and he keeps getting lost. I can't tell him anything. You probably noticed how grumpy he is."

"Perhaps it comes from being in pain," Zahad said.

She didn't seem to hear him. "Oh, no!" It took a moment for him to register that the contestant had landed on the bankruptcy slot and lost all her money. "I hate when that happens!"

He had little sympathy for gambling. However, he had come to sound out Dolly, not promote his own opinions. "Perhaps you should apply to appear on the show."

"I wouldn't do well," she replied. "Besides, I don't need the money as much as other people, so it wouldn't be fair."

"A policeman's retirement must be more lucrative than I imagined," he said.

A commercial came on and she muted the sound. "I get a nice pension," she explained. "Plus I bought this property and a few rental units around town."

"You sound like a wise investor. You do not mind that

your second husband won the Florida lottery after you divorced him?''

The woman's laugh rang out. ''I don't begrudge Manley anything. We always got along as friends. Couldn't live together—the man's a slob and spends most of his time fishing—but he bought me this TV when he won because he knew I'd enjoy it. I call that darn decent.''

''Very decent,'' Zahad agreed.

She continued talking, more voluble now that the ice had been broken. As the contestants struggled to solve puzzles, he learned that she baby-sat her granddaughter after lunch each day and that she wished her son-in-law had more self-discipline.

Once the show ended, he steered Dolly to a more serious topic. Discovering Fario's body had been a shock, Zahad saw from the way her voice quavered when she described the scene. He learned nothing that hadn't been in the police report, however.

''Do you think you were in danger yourself?'' he asked.

''You bet. I can't stop thinking about it,'' she said. ''It's just good luck that Cindy was sick that day and kept asking for me, so I only made a quick check of the property. Usually I would have tried the front door.''

''Will you patrol after I leave?''

Dolly reflected briefly. ''Oh, what the heck. Sure I will. Jenny and Beth are my friends.''

Zahad hoped he could trust this woman with confidential information, because he needed her insight. ''Sergeant Finley says one of the neighbors complained about my inquiries. Do you have any idea who that might be?''

''I wouldn't put it past Bill, because he's such a crab. Or Tish Garroway. She's so possessive of her husband that I think she's a bad influence on my daughter. Something about Jenny makes them both insecure. It's nonsense. If a husband's going to cheat, he doesn't need to have a raving beauty next door.''

''What do you think of Parker Finley?''

"He's sweet on Jenny, but that's as far as it goes." Dolly stretched out her legs on the couch. She wore fuzzy blue slippers more suitable for a young girl than a grandmother.

"He would be displeased if he learned I had questioned you," Zahad remarked.

"Then let's not tell him. Parker's a good cop, but he's spread too thin right now. By the time he stumbles across the perp, Jenny could be dead."

"Thank you. If you think of anything later, please call."

"Absolutely," she replied.

Zahad let himself out. As he walked downhill, he reviewed his list of suspects.

If Fario was the intended victim, Hashim had the strongest motive. If the target was Jenny, he had to consider Tish's jealousy as well as Ellen's.

That left Ray and Grant, the most obvious choice. Zahad hoped the police would delve into financial records that might indicate whether he'd hired someone to get rid of his ex-wife.

The sticking point was the bizarre decision to attach a gun to a chair and tie it to the door. A hit man wouldn't take such an indirect route. Zahad had trouble imagining why anyone else would, either.

He was so lost in thought that only the scrape of a side door in the Rivases' garage alerted him to someone's approach. Sneakered footsteps crunched on a gravel path, then Al Garroway came into view.

Surprise and unease showed on his narrow face. No wonder. In his arms, he held a large battery-powered chain saw.

Zahad tensed. Although heavy and awkward to wield, this was a formidable weapon.

"Hey." The ski instructor made no threatening move. "I'm not stealing this, if that's what you think."

The sheikh assumed a casual stance. "Certainly not. I understand people often borrow each other's tools in this neighborhood."

"That's right." Al wedged the saw against his hip for

support. "I'm going over to Louanne's house to cut down some branches."

"You are kind to help an elderly neighbor." Zahad noted Garroway apparently didn't have to be at work at an hour when the neighborhood seemed virtually deserted. Last Monday, he could easily have helped himself to a different set of tools from Jenny's shed.

"I'm not all that kind," Al admitted. "See, being a ski instructor doesn't pay great and the hours are limited. Since Ray started at the bank, people have been saying they could use a handyman. He told me I could borrow his stuff, so I thought I'd try it."

It was a plausible explanation. Zahad tried a different tack. "I hope your wife has recovered from the carjacking."

"She's still pretty freaked out about it. We heard what happened to Jenny yesterday. It's a darn shame."

"Does your wife also work limited hours at the lodge?"

"Yeah, mostly on weekends. She's looking for a second job in town. We both liked the idea of living out in the country, but it's not what we bargained for."

"Your wife seems to dislike Mrs. Sanger." It was a bit off the subject, but Zahad didn't care.

"Oh, she dislikes any woman under forty who doesn't look like a prune. Except maybe Ellen," Al said. "Listen, I've got to get going. A big storm's due and Louanne doesn't want one of those large branches falling through her roof. One of them barely missed her on Friday."

"Please do not let me stop you." Zahad moved aside, a symbolic gesture since he wasn't blocking Al's path.

"Catch you later."

"Sure thing." The casual phrase felt unnatural to him, but it fit the local vernacular.

When Zahad reached higher ground, he turned and surveyed the street. Al was heading toward Mrs. Welford's house, as he'd said.

Inside, Zahad went online and checked a weather site, which did indeed predict a snowstorm for Mountain Lake.

He hoped it wouldn't delay his return to Alqedar. In any case, he needed to firm up his plans. Switching to another site, he checked international plane schedules for Thursday morning.

Chapter Twelve

Thanks to the local radio station, everyone at school had heard about Grant's arrest and the attempted carjacking. Just when the gossip about Fario's death had begun to die down, Jenny was inundated with more questions and expressions of concern.

She spent her lunch hour meeting with a lawyer and signing papers for a restraining order. She didn't put much faith in the power of a sheet of paper to protect her, but at least it assured that Grant would face dire consequences if he so much as showed up on her property.

During the drive home, she watched the road for carjackers. It would be a long time before Jenny made this trip without fear. *Please let us get back to normal,* she thought, and then realized that she hardly remembered what ''normal'' meant.

However, the changes in her life weren't entirely bad. If not for everything that had happened, she wouldn't have met Zahad. Thanks to him, she had learned how to relax around a man and enjoy her own instinctive sexual response without feeling threatened. Even if nothing more passed between them, he had affected her in a good way.

''Mommy, is Zod going to stay with us?'' Beth's line of thinking apparently paralleled her mother's. They were both looking forward to seeing him in a couple of minutes, Jenny thought.

"He's only here for a few days." Her voice caught at the end.

"I want him to stay."

Jenny didn't know what to say. Thank goodness they were almost home.

Yet when she pulled in to the driveway, painful memories assailed her again. She trembled until she cleared some trees and saw the sheikh's car in the parking bay. *I'm turning into a basket case. I have to get over this.*

The trouble was, she couldn't get over it because it wasn't over.

When they entered the house, Jenny noticed the tantalizing smell of baking chicken. Then she heard Frank Sinatra singing "It Was a Very Good Year." The music must be coming from the boom box she kept in the kitchen.

"Hello!" she called as she and Beth hung up their coats.

"Welcome home, Mrs. and Miss Sanger." Zahad emerged from the kitchen, his red apron a cheerful contrast to his dark brown sweater and tan slacks. He carried salad tongs in one hand.

"You promised no yucky stuff!" Beth said.

The sheikh drew himself up to his full height. "I assure you, I have fixed no yucky stuff."

She pointed at the tongs.

"What I have created," he announced, "is Aladdin's Magic Salad." To Jenny, he explained, "My cousin Amy e-mailed me her children's favorite recipes."

"I hope I get a chance to meet Amy someday," she said. "I think I'd like her."

"What's that smell?" Beth asked, adding, "I like it."

"Camel patties," the sheikh replied.

"Camel patties?" Jenny regarded him dubiously.

"It is really oven-baked chicken nuggets, but 'camel patties' sounds more intriguing."

"Is it ready?" the little girl demanded.

"Give me five minutes."

"I'll go wash my hands!" Beth dashed down the hall.

Jenny wanted to tell Zahad how much she appreciated what he'd done but before she could form the words, she realized that she couldn't tell him what she really felt. I would mean revealing that he had given her violated home a new sense of solidity, and that he had brought joy into two lives she hadn't even been aware were lonely.

Even if such candor didn't embarrass him, it might give him the wrong idea. No matter how appealing he looked a he led her into the heart of the kitchen and no matter how much she longed to slip into his arms and tease him with kisses, Jenny knew she must not.

She understood both herself and their situation. During this magic time, while she and Zahad were united by common goal, they had formed their own temporary uni verse. There was no use pretending it could last, even i they both wanted it to.

Jenny had found it impossible to establish a lasting re lationship with any of the men she'd dated or with the one she'd married, even though they shared her culture and background. With Zahad, once the initial impetus ended reason told her there'd soon be nothing left to build on.

She would hate it if this special relationship deteriorate into discomfort and misunderstandings. It seemed far bette to have a radiant memory to cherish.

Zahad clicked off the boom box. "You are very quiet Has it been a difficult day?"

"Better than yesterday," Jenny replied, "although that' not saying much. How about you?"

"Ronald Wang e-mailed me. He assures me he spoke to the detective but revealed nothing of my visit."

"Good." Jenny was glad Parker knew about the woma caller and the fact that there were apparently two cyber stalkers. She wished he was willing to work with Zahad however.

"I hope it will help." The sheikh released a long breath and the two of them stood in the kitchen simply looking a each other

Jenny didn't want to hear anything more about murderers or stalkers or carjackers. "I don't know how you feel, but I'm on investigation overload."

"We both need a respite," Zahad agreed. "During the revolution in Alqedar, sometimes the danger and loss threatened to overwhelm our morale. When that happened, we declared a camp evening. I suggest you and I do the same."

"What's a camp evening?"

"For a few hours, we became youths again." Picking up pot holders, the sheikh went to the oven. "We sang foolish songs, ran three-legged races and told jokes."

As he removed a tray of browned chicken nuggets, Jenny asked, "Is it fair to assume the jokes don't bear repeating in polite society?"

A trace of color appeared on his high-boned cheeks. "Assuredly not." He fetched grape juice from the refrigerator, poured it into three wineglasses and carried them to the front room. He'd already set the table—somewhat unconventionally, with the spoons on the plates and the napkins on the chairs. Perhaps he'd done so deliberately to make the occasion lighthearted.

Jenny picked up her napkin and sank into her seat. "Thanks for doing this."

"It is my pleasure."

When Beth bounded into the room, her eyes fixed on her wineglass. "Mommy won't let me have that. Will you, Mommy?"

"It's grape juice," Jenny said.

"All right!" Handling the glass very carefully, the little girl took a sip.

From the kitchen, Zahad fetched a large bowl containing salad greens strewn with some white flakes and brown bits. Jenny did want her daughter to eat vegetables, but what was this?

"Allow me to present Aladdin's Magic Salad," the sheikh announced.

Beth eyed the concoction suspiciously. After a long moment, she brightened. "It's got chocolate chips!"

"The white shreds are coconut." Zahad placed the bowl in front of her with a flourish. Next to it, he set a small pitcher of yellow dressing. "This is pineapple sauce."

Jenny tried to guess how chocolate chips, coconut and lettuce tasted with pineapple sauce. She decided to simply keep quiet and eat it.

Beth grabbed the tongs and plopped salad onto her plate, showering a fair measure onto the table in the process. She scooped it up and ate heartily. "Wow! Dessert in the salad!" she exclaimed when she came up for air.

"Why didn't I think of that?" Jenny had to admire the recipe's sheer inventiveness.

The sheikh brought in the nuggets on a serving plate and a casserole of scalloped potatoes sticky with cheese. "These are Camel McNuggets and Oasis Chips, according to Amy."

"I've absolutely got to meet this woman. Does she ever come to Southern California?" Jenny asked.

"It has happened. Perhaps someday she will return," Zahad said. To Beth, he added, "My cousin has a seven-year-old daughter. I believe you two would like each other."

"Does she have dolls?"

"Many of them from around the world."

"I'd like that!" The little girl stuffed a forkful of potatoes into her mouth.

Between mouthfuls, Beth told the grown-ups how her friends had welcomed her back after her two-week absence. The class had a new hamster, too, she explained with delight.

Once Beth ran out of steam, Jenny described the school-wide winter decorating project she'd been coordinating. Older children were writing poems and stories to post throughout the building. Some artistic youngsters had been designing a mural to be assembled from many sheets of poster board, which the younger children would paint. The rimary grades and kindergarten were supplementing this rtwork with their own drawings and writings.

She also described seeing Elmer playing with a group of oys. "It looks like he's finally making friends," she said. 'I think the baseball game broke the ice."

"The school is for you as my province is to me." Zahad tudied her across the table. "It gives your life structure nd meaning. Apart from your family, of course."

"Except that you are desperately needed, while I have a apable staff that was already in place when I arrived," enny replied. "I'm just putting on the finishing touches."

"Perhaps you would enjoy a greater challenge."

She'd had the same thought but it had always seemed so mpossible. "At one time, this was everything I could have sked for. But it seems as if the more I do, the more I want o do."

"What is your goal, then?"

Jenny recalled the daydreams in which she'd indulged efore the cyber-stalking and subsequent all-consuming vents. "Someday I want to take on a bigger challenge, naybe work with underprivileged kids. When Beth's rown, I might move to an inner-city area and head up some ind of program there."

"Impressive," the sheikh said.

"It's just a pipe dream," Jenny conceded.

"What did you do today, Zod?" Beth asked.

"Many things. I talked with your neighbors Dolly and l."

"Oh, really?" Jenny was glad to hear he'd been investigating despite Parker's disapproval. "Did you learn anyhing?"

"Perhaps." As he outlined his conversations, the sheikh voided any direct reference to the murder, probably for eth's benefit.

When he finished, Jenny saw from his hesitation that nere was something more. "What is it?"

"I must return to my country Thursday morning. The

president will hold a meeting Saturday morning to conside
who is to run my province. My enemies may have m
banned from the country entirely if I do not present m
point of view."

"That would be terrible." Thursday morning. A hollow
echo rang through her mind like the slamming of a stee
door. Of course she'd known he was going to leave soon
but now that the day had been fixed, she realized she wasn'
ready for him to go.

Amid the turbulence, the three of them had stolen a littl
time to be together. Now that the end loomed, she prize
these family moments even more.

"Will you bring me a camel when you come back?"
Beth asked.

Trust her daughter to come up with the unexpected
Jenny would have laughed if not for a lump in her throat

"He would be most uncomfortable on an airplane," th
sheikh replied solemnly.

The little girl frowned. "He could leave off his se
belt."

That was too much. Shaking with silent laughter, Jenn
gave Zahad a helpless look. She didn't want Beth to thin
she was being mocked.

He managed, heaven knew how, to maintain a straigh
face. "An excellent suggestion, although I am afraid
cannot promise to return. Now, I believe it is time for de
sert."

"Yippee!" Distracted by his last statement, Beth shot t
her feet and cheerfully helped clear the dishes.

Dessert consisted of ice-cream bars coated with chocola
and ground nuts. "Wow, you got the big ones!" the littl
girl said.

"It is a special occasion," the sheikh told her. "Also,
am very fond of ice-cream bars. The bigger the better."

How strange, Jenny reflected as she enjoyed her trea
that in spite of everything that had gone wrong, she didn

recall ever being happier. She refused to allow herself to think about what life would be like without Zahad.

Some things couldn't and perhaps shouldn't be changed. The trick was to let the future take care of itself and concentrate on the moment.

After dinner, they joined Beth in watching a VeggieTales video. The sheikh found the smart-talking vegetables hilarious and announced that he would order one for Amy from the Internet.

"I'm glad your cousin will get something for her children," Jenny remarked. "She's been so helpful to me."

"To me also," Zahad said.

When they put Beth to bed, she insisted on sitting on the sheikh's knee to hear her bedtime story. At first he looked a trifle ill at ease while balancing the sprite, but the respectful warmth in the way he regarded her touched Jenny's heart.

"Tell me about your country," the little girl said.

"It is far, far away."

"Is it in Russia?"

"It is a separate country." Jenny wondered if the sheikh would grow impatient with the child's ignorance, but he simply gathered his thoughts and tried again. "Alqedar is on the Arabian peninsula. Unfortunately, we have no oil and we are not a seaport. The people used to be nomads— that means they traveled around and lived in tents. Now many of them farm and make crafts."

"That sounds like fun."

"Yes, we have a lot of fun," Zahad agreed. "The people wear colorful clothes at the marketplace. They make music and have big families, whom they love very much."

Jenny took a seat on the sturdy toy chest. It amazed her to see how gentle this rough man could be.

"Do you have any children?" she asked.

He shook his head.

"You should." Beth's forehead crinkled with thought. 'Three. Two girls and a boy. Do you live in a palace?"

"Yes, although perhaps it is not as fancy as you might imagine," the sheikh admitted. "It is old and rambling and the plumbing has a bad temper. My stepmother lives there, too."

"What happened to your mother?" Beth asked.

"She died when I was seven. We did not have very good hospitals in our country, although we are building some now. My mother was a proud, brave woman, who taught me to put the good of my country before my own wishes."

"I do that," Beth said eagerly. "I recycle. And I conserve water." Honesty prodded her to add, "Sometimes."

"Good for you."

"Was your mother from a royal family also?" Jenny seized on this opportunity to learn more of Zahad's background.

"Yes. She came from the neighboring province of Bahrim, where she was sister to the sheikh, Sharif's father."

"What about your stepmother?" she asked.

"For his second wife, my father chose a woman from a prominent family in Yazir itself. Unfortunately for me, this makes Numa a local girl supported by many friends and relatives." Noticing Beth's large yawn, Zahad said, "It is time to say good-night, little one."

The girl hugged him. "You can stay with Mommy and me as long as you want to, Zod," she told him.

His dark eyes shone. "I wish it were that simple."

"Some things *are* simple. Like the fact that it's bedtime." Jenny said, lifting Beth into bed. She kissed her daughter and tucked her beneath the covers. The child curled up sleepily, pulling her doll close.

When Jenny and Zahad slipped out, she expected him to retreat to his room to work on the computer. It pleased her that he accompanied her to the living room instead.

"We are having a camp night," he explained as they sank onto the couch. "I am tired of thinking about evil people plotting evil deeds. The world is always full of them, but we need not let them control our minds."

''I couldn't agree more.''

They had so little time together, Jenny reflected as a peaceful silence fell over the room. Only two more days. So little chance to explore each other.

The excitement she'd felt during the massage tantalized her. She wanted more of that, much more. She loved the person she became around him.

The truth struck Jenny with simple inevitability: She wanted to make love to Zahad. It would be the first time since her divorce that she'd slept with a man, but there was, she realized, no reason to hold back.

She didn't need to fear the slow, miserable breakdown of a relationship or the stifling attempts at domination she'd endured with Grant. Because the sheikh was leaving, they could enjoy a beautiful coupling that had at least a chance of remaining untarnished in their memories.

Shyly, Jenny stole a glance at the man beside her. He'd propped his feet on the coffee table, shoes and all, and leaned back his head. In profile, he had a nose strong enough to balance the pronounced cheekbones and firm lips. Her gaze trailed down the length of him and sparkles played through her as she pictured her legs tangling with his.

In his land, she wondered, how did he address himself to a woman? What conventions did they observe, or did they simply get swept away?

His head turned and he met her eyes. Jenny's breath caught as it occurred to her that he knew exactly what she was thinking.

''Many men seek you, but you elude them,'' he said in a resonant, contemplative tone. ''Yet to me you have never seemed coy. Why have you not availed yourself of these lovers?''

''I haven't wanted any of them,'' she answered.

''How would a man know if you did?'' the sheikh asked. ''Forgive me if I am too much of a warrior but when it comes to women, I am not certain I can read the signs.''

Anticipation spread deep inside Jenny. "I guess I'm not the temptress I'm cracked up to be or I wouldn't leave any doubt."

He gave her a rare smile. "Although I have much to learn with regard to reading signs, I am improving my skill at taking hints." His fingers drifted through her hair, parting the strands and lifting their fullness. Her eyelids lowered as she concentrated on the heat and smell of him and on the tug that progressed along her scalp toward the nape of her neck.

Zahad shifted closer. His breath stirred promises along Jenny's jaw and then his lips brushed hers. His mouth lingered for a long moment before letting go.

"I have no further doubts. Have you?"

"I'm the temptress here. I never had any doubts." With the edge of her thumb, she traced the small white scar on his jaw.

Easing onto her knees on the couch, Jenny leaned over and replaced her thumb with her tongue. A groan wrenched from deep within Zahad and he caught her by the hip. Emboldened, she traced his jaw up to his ear and took the lobe between her lips, relishing his shudder.

With a fluid motion, he swung her onto his lap. A little off balance, Jenny rested her cheek against his chest and listened to his heart thundering.

"I've been wondering about your scars," she murmured. "How many do you have?"

"I never counted."

"You have one on your back." She'd seen it at the cabin when he awoke beside her. "Were you attacked from behind?"

His cheek brushed her temple as he nodded. "By a treacherous coward. I dispatched him to a place where he can never betray anyone again."

This was the man who had dumped syrup all over his plate to please a five-year-old, Jenny reminded herself.

"There's a side of you that's so far beyond my experience I can't even imagine it."

"We are not so different. You are a woman of courage and resourcefulness. We have simply operated in different spheres."

She touched the white mark that bisected his left eyebrow. "That must have been a close call."

"Very close. Witnesses claim I was airborne for several seconds after my motorcycle hit a pothole. Alqedar is famous for its bad roads."

"You ride a motorcycle?"

"Sometimes it is the fastest way to get where I want to go." He slid her from his lap and stood, drawing her up with him. "I am accustomed to directness, Jenny." There was a question beneath the statement as he faced her.

He was offering her a chance to retreat. Even now, after she'd initiated the embrace, he didn't press her.

"Good. I like directness," she said.

Zahad gave a slight nod, accepting her decision. "Is your daughter asleep?"

"Let's find out."

They stopped by her bedroom. The little girl's regular breathing and complete relaxation told their own story.

When Zahad released her hand, Jenny glanced at him questioningly. He returned to the living room, from which she heard the beep of the alarm as he set it. On his way back, he switched off the lights.

Did he ever completely lose himself in passion? she wondered, and, with a flutter of excitement, realized she was about to find out.

Chapter Thirteen

When she drew the sheikh into her room, Jenny became aware of the lingering scent of sweet herbs from her drawers. In the intimacy of the boudoir, he loomed large and untamed.

"I wish to see you," Zahad announced. "All of you."

"You want me to strip for you?" She'd never done anything like that for Grant. He'd made her feel a bit self-conscious, and as a result she'd instinctively protected herself.

"You need not make a production of it." Zahad lounged across the flowered coverlet on her bed, forming a brown exclamation point in his sweater and slacks. He had removed his shoes, she noticed. "I want to enjoy the sight of you."

She nearly protested that she felt too shy, until she realized that wasn't true. Not with Zahad. She didn't fear he would find her too bony or too small-breasted or that he would compare her to some airbrushed, men's magazine standard. He always seemed to accept and appreciate the real Jenny.

She wanted to excite him. She wanted to make this tightly leashed man lose control. Jenny smiled. She was going to do it, too.

She replaced the overhead glare with the soft glow of a

table lamp. The golden circle shut out the rest of the world, creating a private realm.

She reached behind her and unzipped the blue dress. The cloth rustled as it slithered to the floor, unveiling a clingy, flesh-colored slip.

On the bed, Zahad swallowed. Jenny dipped her head to let her hair partially obscure her face, then tossed it back as a photographer had once taught her to do when she'd modeled. Then, she'd had to force herself to relax. Tonight, she felt safe enough to play at sexual fantasies with her sheikh.

Her sheikh. It amazed Jenny that this hardened desert warrior was here with her, fascinated by her, longing for her. In so many ways, he still seemed an enigma, and yet she was about to know him intimately.

Slowly, teasingly, she drew the slip up over her hips, her waist, her shoulders. When she tossed it aside, she enjoyed the sensation of his eyes feasting on her. As Jenny pushed her hair atop her head and then shook it free, the sheikh stirred restlessly.

She kicked off her pumps. The first one landed with a satisfying thump near the bed while the other fell onto the carpet nearby. Leaning forward seductively, Jenny eased down the waistband of her panty hose. As she lowered it, the tension in her midsection tightened into a knot of longing.

Zahad shifted to the bed's edge and reached out, his callused hand gentle as it traced Jenny's thigh. His fingers brushed so close to her yearning center that she gasped.

"Let me finish for you," he said, and swung his legs so that he sat straddling her where she stood.

Every brush of his fingers as he rolled down the silky stockings reverberated through Jenny. When he angled forward and kissed her bare navel, she had to catch hold of his shoulders to keep from losing control.

She wanted him more than she had ever dreamed of wanting a man. There was something deliciously liberating about the sensations he aroused, something that made her secure enough to surrender without a second thought.

When he left, Jenny would miss him terribly, but she would still be complete. She could give him everything without losing control.

The pleasure when he unhooked her bra and his hands closed over her breasts felt almost unbearably intense. Jenny shut her eyes but immediately opened them again so she could watch this scarred man radiate joyous desire.

Passion transformed the sheikh, softening his angular features. As his mouth and hands roamed over her, peeling away what little clothing remained, wonder animated his dark eyes.

From where she stood, Jenny bent to nuzzle the unruly length of his hair. She found the rim of his sweater and helped him take it off.

Beneath lay more scars than she had expected, some of them puckered and others crisscrossing savagely. The evidence of his courage stimulated her. Playing her breasts against his hair, Jenny caressed his back.

She could feel Zahad pulling free of his remaining clothes from where he sat on the bed. When they were both naked, he tipped back his head and traced his tongue across her breasts. She stood above his seated figure with nothing to hold them apart.

Their frenzy burned too fiercely to prolong as Zahad's knees separated Jenny's legs. He gripped her waist and lowered her atop him while their mouths claimed each other.

Catching her rounded bottom, he pulled her onto him. Jenny felt the incredible length of him penetrating her, the upward thrust searingly pure. A flame leaped between them, drawing her down, lifting her up again, intensifying until she ignited.

Zahad pulled her onto the bed. Cool fabric met the heat of Jenny's bare back as the sheikh lifted himself over her.

Although it had happened quickly, Jenny was glad to have spent her own desire so she could relish the climax of this amazing man. It thrilled her to see the wild yearning that overcame him.

He poised above, touching her in only one place, the one that joined a man and a woman in a thousand ways. Fiercely intent, he entered her again. His movements slow and deliberate, he drew himself in and out, eyes half-closed, breath rasping as he held himself in place with his powerful arms.

An ache grew inside Jenny. It was only a hint at first, but the incredible fullness of him and the sight of his strength poised above her rekindled the sparks. When he speeded his movements, the embers sizzled into fireworks.

The sheikh possessed an elemental maleness that let him please himself, vibrantly and without hesitation, while drawing Jenny into the brilliance with him. A blast of joy seized her when she felt Zahad's explosive shudders. They flew together, merging until they became a single glorious entity.

Then they were two again, their chests rising and falling rapidly, his arms encircling her on the bed. She felt the coolness of his damp skin against her cheek and inhaled his masculine essence. Inside her, a dozen unseen scars, as profound as the ones marring his body, were reabsorbed.

Zahad might depart on Thursday without a backward glance, but Jenny would regret nothing. He had healed injuries that, until tonight, she hadn't realized existed.

She hoped she had done as much for him.

WHEN HE ALLOWED HIMSELF to yield to temptation, Zahad had been reassured by the knowledge that, as a divorced woman, Jenny knew what she was doing. Also, she had no illusions about their situation, so their encounter would not leave her brokenhearted

He hadn't anticipated his own response. He was still trying to sort it out as he watched her snuggle into a pillow.

Zahad had spent decades building walls around his heart. In a flash, Jenny had torn them down. She had shown him a man who needed to connect with a woman at the most basic level, and who needed her in countless other ways as well.

He saw her eyes large and intense as they had appeared while the two of them talked earlier in the living room. He pictured Beth perched on his knee, assuring him that he was welcome here. He recalled the homey aromas of coffee and maple syrup.

Above all, his mind and body filled with impressions of the last half hour. Inside Jenny, he had felt whole for the first time in more than twenty years. They weren't simply two people who'd chanced to meet. This encounter had been fated, no matter what might come of it.

He rolled onto his stomach, fearing that his restlessness might disturb her but unable to keep still. This was insanity, to imagine bringing home as his bride the siren who some believed had lured Fario to his death. He himself might recognize her innocence, but how could he expect his people to accept her when they barely accepted him?

Zahad released a long breath. He would always cherish the memory of the past few days and especially of tonight. But he could not ask Jenny and her little girl to share the dangers that would confront him in his homeland or to face rejection by people who neither knew them nor wanted to know them.

With regret, Zahad acknowledged that he must begin putting up walls again. It would take a long time and involve more than a little pain, but eventually he would close off this weakness in himself.

Seeking rest, he struggled to clear his mind. At last sleep folded its wings over him.

He was deep within the darkness when a scraping noise reached him. He knew at once, even before fully waking, that it came from outside. Distinctly, he heard the clink of metal on metal.

Zahad bolted from the bed. Due to years of experience, he dressed without light in a matter of seconds.

"What's going on?" Jenny asked sleepily.

"Someone is breaking in to the toolshed," he told her.

"I'll call the police."

"Fine." He headed for the door.

"You can't go out there!" she protested.

It had never occurred to him to cower here. "Of course I will." Zahad put on his shoes. "If it is the murderer, here is my chance to catch him."

"You mean, here's your chance to get killed!"

He let the remark pass. "The flashlight by the back door—are the batteries current?" He should have checked them himself, he reflected.

"Yes." Jenny hesitated with the phone in one hand. "Take anything you need."

"I will." He had not intended to ask for permission.

Zahad grabbed a knife from the kitchen, threw on the coat he'd left in the rear hall and shut down the security system. He chose not to activate the exterior lights because they would give him away.

He took a key, as well. When he went outside, he locked the door behind him.

Cold air chilled his face and hands. Ignoring it, Zahad dodged to avoid becoming an easy target. No gunshot shattered the stillness, however, so he paused to listen for suspicious sounds beside the porch, where he was out of direct view. At the same time, he scanned the backyard for odd shapes and for signs of movement.

He heard only the breeze in the pines. He saw nothing but shadows.

In the faint moonlight, he approached the shed at a zigzag. All the while, his senses sought evidence of the intruder. He spotted no one, but on a cloudy night like this a man could hide only yards away without being detected.

Once he reached the shed, he shone the flashlight on the lock. The shackle was gouged as if someone had tried to sever it with a bolt cutter. Zahad played the beam across the ground, hoping to find a footprint or an object dropped in haste.

Only frozen earth met his gaze.

If the interloper had driven here from elsewhere, he would most likely have parked nearby, yet Zahad had not heard an engine start. Since it was likely the man or woman remained in the vicinity, he decided to concentrate on the nearby area.

Overgrown trees and bushes filled the land behind and to one side of the property. Attempting to search such a large area alone struck Zahad as futile. Sometimes, however, the simplest course also proved the most effective one.

Moving to one corner of the shed, the sheikh stood silently letting the night carry its sounds and scents to him. When he heard someone stirring in the house, the trespasser might have dived for the nearest cover instead of fleeing. If so, how steely were his or her nerves?

Zahad waited. In the house, a light came on in Jenny's room. The thick curtains prevented him from seeing inside.

He jammed his hands into the open front of his coat for warmth. Although he preferred to stand at the ready, it would do no good if his fingers became so cold he fumbled the knife.

As his brain filtered out the murmur of the branches, he began to perceive sounds behind sounds. Nature had its own rhythm: in summer, a living hum of insects and birds; in winter, the subtle shifting and settling of stones and trees.

Attuned to any discrepancy, Zahad tried not to let himself be distracted by speculation. Yet his mind teemed with questions. If the intruder was the killer, why would he want to raid Jenny's shed a second time? Surely tools like hers could be purchased at the hardware store or taken from another neighbor's garage.

Perhaps the goal had been to lure Zahad outside. While he hunted the murderer, he might instead become the prey.

Inside the coat, his hand tightened on the haft. The sheikh braced himself in case he had to dodge an attack and throw the weapon. Even his deadly accuracy, however, might fail to bring down someone clad in heavy clothing.

He was allowing his mind to work against him. Harshly, he refocused his attention.

There's someone here.

He knew it without being able to pinpoint how he'd drawn that conclusion. Perhaps, subliminally, he'd heard a rasp of breath. Now, straining and keyed up, he could have sworn he detected a heartbeat reverberating through the frigid earth.

Was it his own heart? If only he had more experience at tracking in a wintry landscape. If only he understood how vibrations interacted with icy surfaces.

In the overgrowth behind the property, some thirty feet from Zahad, a twig snapped.

He swiveled to face that direction. If the intruder moved again, even slightly, he would have the location. Most people would bolt under such circumstances, thrashing through the brush and making a run for safety.

Any minute now. Any minute…

Down the road, Zahad heard a car approaching. *Let it pass quickly.*

Instead, tires crunched into the driveway. The police had had the good sense to leave off the siren, but whoever was hiding in the brush didn't wait around for the sheikh's re-inforcements. Rustling and a sharp exhalation signaled his rush for deeper cover.

The sheikh raked the scene with the flashlight. He saw movement, too far away for an accurate throw of the knife. But he had the advantage for the moment. He pelted across the flat yard while his target struggled through rougher terrain.

"Police!" A voice rang out behind him. "Stop or I'll shoot!"

Every instinct urged him to keep going. A few dozen more steps and he could nail the person who might have killed Fario.

He could also die at the hands of an overzealous police officer.

Furious, Zahad stopped. "It is I, Sheikh Adran! Our target is escaping!"

"Come out where I can see you," the officer ordered.

Judging by the man's brittle tone, Zahad believed the policeman must be alone. He sounded young, also.

Barely restraining himself from showering the man with curses, Zahad strode into plain view. The officer crouched between the house and the garage, his gun positioned in a double grip.

The sheikh aimed the flashlight at his own face. When the officer failed to respond, Zahad experienced a moment of sheer alarm. If he had mistaken the voice, if this were Finley, he might seize the opportunity and shoot anyway. What better excuse for eliminating a rival?

"You can see it is I," Zahad called.

The patrolman lowered his gun. "Sorry about that." When he moved into the clear, Zahad saw that he was indeed younger than Finley and wore a uniform. "I'm Officer Franklin."

Zahad gave a short nod of acknowledgment. Then, with no further time to waste on ceremony, he gestured toward the terrain beyond the shed. "Whoever tried to break into the shed is out there. I heard him moving."

"We've got to catch him before he gets to the street," Franklin said.

"Or to one of the other houses," the sheikh added.

They spread out, keeping within view of each other as they searched. Either their target had found a well-hidden gully, however, or he or she was long gone.

They had given up by the time Finley trudged around the house, apparently having arrived on foot. When Jenny turned on the outdoor lights, they cast far deeper hollows on the detective's face than on Officer Franklin's.

It occurred to Zahad that perhaps this was their target and that the sergeant had conveniently covered himself by pretending to arrive from home. However, he saw no leaves or burrs clinging to the man's jacket and his pants were smooth and neatly creased.

"Did you find anything?" Jenny asked. Wrapped in a robe, she stood silhouetted in the back door.

"He got away," Zahad replied in disgust.

Finley regarded him wearily. "Tell me what happened."

Zahad and the patrolman ran through the details. When they had finished, the sergeant said, "So you never actually saw anyone?"

"That is true."

"I'll dust the lock for prints, but it's freezing out here. Dollars to doughnuts, if there was an intruder, he wore gloves," the detective said. "I'm not calling out a full-scale search team for what might be a raccoon. My men are stretched thin as it is."

"You have not yet apprehended the carjackers?" Zahad inquired.

"They've got to be staying around here, but we can't pinpoint where," Finley answered. "We're beginning to suspect they've got someone local helping them."

Zahad accepted the decision not to search further. At this point, even if they came across a trespasser, too much time had passed for them to be sure he was their man. If it was a neighbor, he could claim he'd come to learn what the fuss was about.

As it turned out, the only prints on the lock were a few partials too smeared to be readable, and they most likely belonged to Jenny or Zahad. At last the patrolman departed. Finley went inside to get Jenny's version of the evening's events.

"It seems suspicious, but we can't be sure it's linked to anything," he said when she'd finished. Zahad joined them in the living room. "Somebody clearly took a whack at that padlock, but it might have been a transient seeking shelter."

"We don't get many of those around here, but I suppose it's possible," Jenny told him. With hair rioting around her face and the bathrobe gaping at her throat, she looked vulnerable and, in Zahad's eyes, velvet with the aftermath of lovemaking. "Could it have been Grant?"

"He's staying at a motel in Crystal Point," Finley replied. "Obviously we can't take his wife's word for his whereabouts, but I'll check with the motel staff. I'll call now and have a cruiser swing by to make sure his car's where it belongs."

"I hope it's not him," she said. "For Beth's sake."

He shrugged. "He's being arraigned tomorrow, by the way."

"That was quick. Should I be in court?"

"If you are, you'll put him in violation of his restraining order," Finley said. "Also, there's no sense in provoking him. I'll let you know what happens."

"Thank you."

"Just doing my job. I'll talk to you soon." With a farewell nod, he went out.

The sheikh locked up. When he returned to the living room, he asked, "Are you okay?"

"A little nervous," Jenny said. "It's nothing. Parker's probably right about the intruder being a transient."

"Perhaps so." Zahad didn't believe that, but he didn't want to frighten her more than necessary. "I will make up my bed now. For Beth's sake, we should sleep separately."

"I'd rather have you with me."

"I assure you, there is nowhere I would rather be. But it is unwise."

She came and brushed a kiss across his mouth. Her lips felt warm and soft, and as he held her, Zahad longed to lose himself in her again. However, he must remain alert in case the intruder returned. "Good night, Jenny."

"I'm glad you're here, wherever you sleep," she said. "Thank you." After lingering for a moment, she vanished.

As he opened the couch and pulled out the mattress, Zahad wondered again why anyone would bother stealing tools from her shed. Had the killer left something behind that he was trying to reclaim, or had he recalled a particular item he needed?

Needed for what?

The answer, unfortunately, was that if the killer had been out there tonight, it probably meant he planned to strike again. Zahad only wished he knew when and against whom.

He sat up listening until his eyes refused to stay open any longer. If there were truths to be revealed tonight, he failed to find them.

Chapter Fourteen

Someone is going to die today.

Zahad awoke with this thought. Having dreamed of pursuing a shadowy figure through a darkened field, he retained an image of its hooded black robe and of the sword gripped in its hand.

"I shall follow your vehicle to school today. That way, there will be no difficulty if you need your car later," he told Jenny over breakfast. Unlike yesterday, he didn't intend to be dissuaded. "Please call me this afternoon when you are ready to leave and I will escort you home also."

She quirked one eyebrow but, noting Beth's rapt attention, didn't question him. "If you think it's advisable."

"I do."

He was about to suggest that he remain at the school and accompany her on her duties, but her warning glance told him she would refuse. Zahad decided not to press the issue. He needed to do many things today and it seemed unlikely the killer would be bold enough to attack in the middle of town. Whoever was doing this preferred isolation and subterfuge.

Zahad felt even more protective of Jenny this morning, perhaps because they had slept together. He wished they could acknowledge openly that they had become lovers, but, of course, they could not do so in front of the child. At least they had the prospect of two more nights together.

Zahad trailed Jenny's SUV into town beneath a leaden sky. According to the radio, a major storm was expected to move into the area on Thursday. His plane would depart just in time to miss it.

At the school, there were already a few cars in the lot despite the early hour. Zahad walked Jenny to the front. "Who opens the building?" he asked.

"The maintenance crew does, shortly before I get here," she said as they ascended the front steps.

"What do you do with Beth before school?" He wanted a complete picture of the situation.

"She stays with me until the kindergarten teacher arrives." Jenny pushed open the main door. "She sharpens pencils and gets supplies from the cabinet for me, don't you, sweetheart?"

"I'm Mommy's helper," Beth confirmed proudly.

Inside the front office, a balding man Zahad recognized as Lew Blackwell glanced up from filling out paperwork at the counter. "Good morning, Jenny, Beth." He didn't greet the sheikh.

"We had a disturbance at my house last night," she explained. "Nothing serious, but Mr. Adran was kind enough to escort me into town today."

"A disturbance?" Lew frowned. "Was it the carjackers or—"

"We do not know." Although Jenny was capable of answering for herself, Zahad refused to be dismissed by this teacher as if he had no importance.

"You weren't hurt, were you?" Again, Lew addressed Jenny.

"I'm fine." She held herself with confidence now that they had reached her territory. "I'd better get to work. I've got to pick the winners in the PTA art contest." The look she cast toward Zahad contained both her thanks and a strong hint that he should depart.

Surely she didn't expect him to leave her and Beth alone

with this man, he thought. Lew's possessive attitude made it difficult for Zahad to consider him a casual bystander.

"Perhaps I should remain until more people arrive," he said.

"Thank you, but that's not necessary."

Jenny's chin lifted. With her air of authority, she was nothing like the somewhat shaky lady he'd taken under his wing last Friday but a woman one hundred percent in charge.

"She's the boss," Lew said, evidently amused at seeing his rival dismissed.

As the sheikh hesitated, Beth broke the standoff by heading toward an interior hallway. "I have to go potty," she announced.

"I'll come with you." Jenny disappeared with her daughter.

Zahad glanced assessingly at the teacher. He knew it would be politic to make himself scarce before the two females returned, but he didn't share Jenny's apparent trust of this man.

"You seem to be spending a lot of time in Mountain Lake," Lew commented. "Don't you have a country to run?"

"Only a province," Zahad replied.

"Don't they miss you?"

"Perhaps less than I might wish."

Through the outer door came a heavyset woman, her cheeks pink from the cold. When she noticed Zahad, she said politely, "Is there something I can help you with?"

"This is Sheikh Adran," Lew explained. "Mrs. Buffington's the school secretary."

"So you're the one everybody's been talking about!" She surveyed Zahad with open curiosity. "What's it like being a sheikh?"

Her foolish question accomplished what neither Lew Blackwell nor Jenny had. It showed Zahad the wisdom of making a quick exit.

"It is most entertaining," he told her. "Good day to you both."

On a Tuesday morning, the town lay quiet and almost devoid of pedestrians. The small shops across Lake Avenue from the school had not yet opened. No one appeared to be coming or going from the police station down the way or from the lodge where Zahad had stayed until a few days ago.

In his pocket, the cell phone rang. He answered it en route to his car.

Before he could speak, a man said ominously, "There is going to be blood on the sand."

A chill ran through Zahad. His waking thought returned: *Someone is going to die today.* And he had dreamed of Death on the prowl.

Nonsense. He didn't believe in bad omens. "Hello?" he said.

"Sorry. I did not realize you had picked up." This time, he recognized the voice as Sharif's.

"What did you mean about blood?" he asked.

"I did not mean that literally. I was commenting to my aide," his cousin said. "Hashim's latest ploy is demanding that the justices in Yazir hold immediate hearings into the possibility that you killed your brother and are compromising the investigation in California."

In addition to presiding at trials, the justices formed a panel that served as the equivalent of a grand jury. Although they were appointed by the governor, once in office they operated independently.

"Hashim has become crazed with ambition." Perhaps so crazed that he had killed Fario in the first place? Zahad wondered. "Is Numa also seeking this madness?"

"She does not object. She is convinced that you assassinated her son and must be punished."

Zahad leaned against his car, the phone to his ear. "It would help if I could produce a testimonial from the local police detective. Unfortunately, he does not like me and objects to my inquiries.'' Remembering the difficulties Sharif's wife was suffering, he added, ''How is Holly?''

''Much better. I will be able to go in person to represent you on Saturday in Jeddar,'' Sharif said. ''However, I cannot be in two places at once, and it seems there is trouble also in Yazir.''

''Have the justices agreed to hold the hearings?''

''Not yet but, according to Amy, they are nervous. They fear that if Hashim replaces you, he will find a way to exact revenge on anyone who stood against him.''

''I am leaving here Thursday morning. Perhaps it must be sooner.'' He regretted losing one last night with Jenny, but there was too much at stake for him to delay. ''How is Amy taking this?''

''She is furious at Hashim,'' Sharif replied. ''She muttered something about taking matters into her own hands, which is why I fear there may be blood on the sand, figuratively speaking.''

''I will call her. Thank you, Sharif.''

''We shall prevail,'' his cousin said. ''Hopefully, any blood that is spilled will belong to that worm, Hashim.''

He expressed no such dire wishes about Numa. In her grief, she could not be held entirely responsible for her actions, Zahad reflected as he said farewell and dialed Amy's number.

A busy signal echoed in his ear. He waited a minute and tried again, with the same result. He would have to call Amy later.

Debating whether to change his airline reservation reminded him that it would be best if he could fulfill his original mission and return with his brother's body. He looked up the number of the coroner's office in his pocket organizer.

''I was about to call you,'' the deputy said when he came on the line. ''Mr. Adran's body is ready to be released. What would you like us to do?''

"I have made arrangements with the Mountain Lake Funeral Parlor. I will telephone them at once."

"Sounds good to me."

The funeral home promised to embalm the body and ship it to Alqedar as quickly as possible. "I'm not sure how long it will take to obtain the necessary permits," the funeral director said. "We've never transferred anyone to your country before."

"I hope we can travel on the same flight. I have reservations from the local airport on Thursday morning. However, I must change that to Wednesday night."

"I should think so. They've moved up the forecast for that big storm. You'll barely make it out in time." The director offered to have his wife, a travel agent, coordinate their plans, and Zahad agreed.

"If you encounter any difficulties in paperwork, please inform me at once. I have connections in my homeland."

"Of course." The director cleared his throat. "The death of Sheikh Adran is a great loss. We will do our best to make sure he goes quickly—I mean, that the process goes quickly."

"Thank you." While clicking off, Zahad noticed that his fingers had gone stiff. The reference to death in connection with his own name and title—which of course had also been Fario's—was disconcerting.

He tried to dismiss his sense that this was yet another omen. Although many of his people believed in the significance of dreams, signs and portents, Zahad did not. The idea of destiny was another matter, but he didn't see it as something to fear.

If it was his destiny to die today, then so be it. Death held no terrors as long as he met it with honor and dignity. Yet it would be hard on Jenny and Beth, as well as on his cousins.

It would be tragic for his people also, or so he believed. Yet Zahad had reluctantly begun to wonder whether he was beating his head against a brick wall.

In the two years since his father's death, he had worked diligently on his tribe's behalf, keeping a low profile to avoid diminishing his brother. He had declined opportunities to take a position in the country's central government, instead devoting his efforts to building up his province's infrastructure.

Yet now that he was assailed on all sides, he saw no signs of loyalty to him among the common people. Although the cowardice of the justices infuriated him and he resented President Dourad's willingness to consider replacing him in such haste, the deepest cut came from the silence of his own countrymen.

Perhaps they didn't want to modernize. Perhaps they preferred to let themselves be led by his father's second wife and her opportunistic nephew. If they were so easily swayed by rumors, so quick to think the worst of Zahad, how could he count on their support in the years to come?

Troubled, the sheikh drove back to Jenny's house. He had only one more day to clear his name of Fario's murder and must make good use of it.

After parking, he went directly to the toolshed. Although last night's intruder hadn't managed to break in, something inside this building would likely hint at why he had returned.

He input the lock's combination and opened the creaking door. Through a large, low-set window with a warped frame, daylight played over a clutter of equipment and tools.

Nothing had changed from his last inspection five days before, except for the appearance of a few more spiderwebs. Traces of fingerprint powder remained from the initial police investigation.

What had the man been seeking?

The problem wasn't a lack of murder weapons but an abundance of them. Zahad dismissed the possibility of the killer planning to use an inefficient blunt-force weapon such as a shovel, given the lengths to which he'd gone to rig the gun device. Nor was he likely to select something as noisy and clumsy as the lawn mower or Rototiller.

There remained plenty of choices, however. A gasoline can held fuel for the mower and tiller. A row of shelves offered a selection of fertilizers, pesticides and weed killers. Long-handled implements hung from a rack along one wall.

Or had the man sought to erase a clue rather than to steal a weapon? The police had missed that scrap of paper in the house, so they might have overlooked something here as well, and he himself had given the toolshed only a cursory inspection on Thursday. A half hour's search, however, left Zahad with nothing more than dirty hands and a slight cough from the dust.

He emerged into a sharp breeze. After refastening the lock, he stopped at a startling sight.

In the western sky towered a black-edged cloud formation. The shape looked remarkably like a robed figure wielding a sword.

It held steady for only a few seconds. Then the wind shattered the weapon and dismembered the figure.

Zahad continued to stare at the jumbled clouds, disturbed. He had seen this shape last night in his dream. Phrases he had heard that day echoed in his mind. *Blood on the sand…the death of Sheikh Adran…we will make sure he goes quickly.*

Perhaps it was a warning after all. He had always known he might be the killer's next target, but it had made little difference in his investigation.

Now, however, he must consider that someone from Alqedar might wish to get rid of him. There was also the unnamed neighbor who had complained about him to Sergeant Finley. Perhaps his questions were hitting too close to home.

Sternly, he reminded himself of his training. The greatest enemy was one's own imagination. He must take all reasonable precautions and proceed with his probe. Above all, he must not allow emotion to rule his judgment.

Nevertheless, when Zahad unlocked the back door and eased it open, the warning chirp of the alarm gave him a start. Tautly, he entered the code.

Inside, he sat down to run background checks on the neighbors through his Internet service. That, he decided, was the logical next step, and he was determined to spend the rest of the day being very logical indeed.

ALTHOUGH CRISTMAS VACATION was two weeks away, the school took on a holiday air as students and teachers posted winter-theme artwork and poems in the hallways. Laughter and cheerful conversations created a music more pleasing to Jenny's ears than any choral concert.

Shortly after the children left for the day, Parker phoned from the municipal courthouse to tell her Grant had pleaded guilty at his arraignment on charges of attempted breaking and entering and carrying a weapon. He'd accepted a sentence of six months in county jail followed by three years' probation, which he could serve in St. Louis. While on probation, he would be allowed to return to Mountain Lake once a month for court-supervised visits with Beth.

"Judging by the way his wife was haranguing him afterward, she wants to keep him as far away from you and Beth as possible," Parker said. "It sounds like they may pass on those visits."

Jenny had mixed feelings. The less contact with her ex-husband, the better for her, but Beth needed a father. "That's up to them. I'm not going to stand between my daughter and Grant if he wants to maintain their relationship."

"Are you all right?" the detective inquired. "You've had a lot on your plate this past week."

"It hasn't all hit me yet," Jenny admitted. "I'm trying to take things one step at a time."

As if he'd just thought of it, Parker asked, "By the way, when is Mr. Adran leaving? I heard they released his brother's body."

"They did?" Jenny tried to tell herself that it made no difference, because Zahad had already scheduled his departure. But subconsciously, she realized, she'd been hoping he might delay. "He made reservations for Thursday morning."

"If you like, you and Beth can stay at my house until we get this thing cleared up. I'll lend you my room. I don't mind sleeping on the couch."

Jenny felt she should refuse. But was that sensible? She still hadn't spent a night alone at her house since the murder and she didn't look forward to it. And, after all, Parker had a live-in housekeeper, so there'd be another adult on the premises. "I'll think about it. Thank you. It's a very kind offer."

"Sure thing," he said, and rang off.

Jenny tried to concentrate on some paperwork, but her thoughts kept returning to what had happened between her and Zahad last night. It gave her a thrill to remember the pressure of his mouth and the glide of his skin over hers.

If only they had days or weeks to explore all the magical things that could develop between them. Not years or even months; she wasn't that unrealistic. Well, at least they had another two nights.

A knock at the open office door roused her from these musings. She glanced up and saw Lew Blackwell. "Come on in."

When he crossed toward her, she noticed a new energy to his stride. His smile seemed broader than usual, too, although she also caught a hint of regret in his expression.

He handed Jenny an envelope and took a seat facing her. "I'll save you the trouble of opening it. It's my resignation."

She blinked, taken aback. "You're leaving us? Lew, if it's anything I did…"

"No, no." He seemed completely at ease. "As a matter of fact, I want to thank you."

"For what?" She'd declined his romantic interest and

trumped him for the job as school principal. He'd responde
with unexpected generosity in loaning her his cabin. Sh
was the one who ought to be thanking him.

"For lighting a fire under me," the teacher said. "I'
completed the coursework for my Ph.D. but never finishe
my dissertation. I figured I didn't really need it, until yo
knocked me for a loop. Getting beaten by you was the bes
thing that ever happened to me."

She leaned back in her chair. "You're actually glad yo
lost the job?"

"Ironic, isn't it? If you hadn't come to Mountain Lak
I'd probably be right where you are now. And I'd still b
there next year and the year after that and so on until what'
left of my hair falls out and I'm ready for retirement."

Jenny chuckled. "What a grim picture!"

"Absolutely right. Instead, I finished the dissertation."

After receiving his doctorate, he explained, he'd applie
for an opening as assistant superintendent of a school dis
trict near San Diego. He'd just learned he got the job, an
would start after the late-January winter break. "It'll b
good for me to move to an urban area, meet new peopl
and face new challenges. I got lazy here."

"Congratulations." She was genuinely pleased for hir
but also sorry to see him go. And, in a way she couldn
put her finger on, a bit envious, as well.

After he left, Jenny sat trying to figure out why his de
parture left her so unsettled. Although she was going t
miss Lew, this had more to do with her own feelings abou
her career, she decided.

Until the last few days, she'd never realized how muc
she wanted a broader scope for her efforts. Much as sh
enjoyed her job here, she longed for a chance to help
larger number of students with greater needs. As a singl
mother, however, she knew it would be many years befor
she was in a position to work on a doctorate.

Seeing Zahad's concern for his people had opened he

eyes. Now Lew, too, had whetted her appetite for a greater challenge.

It was, she feared, going to be a long time coming.

DURING DINNER, Zahad listened for sounds from the yard. He found it hard to concentrate on Beth's and Jenny's account of their day at school and to make casual conversation suitable for a child's company. He mentioned running background checks but, catching a warning look from Jenny, postponed giving her the details.

Halfway through the meal, it occurred to him he'd forgotten to call Amy again. Since it was now the middle of the night in Alqedar, that would have to wait.

After dinner, the doorbell rang. Motioning to his two companions to stay in the kitchen, he answered it himself.

It was Dolly, Ellen and Cindy, going for a walk. They'd come to invite Beth to accompany them, they explained when she and Jenny appeared.

"Ellen has some cosmetics to drop off at Tish's house," the older woman said. For Zahad's benefit, she added, "She sells them on the side. Anyway, it's nice brisk weather and we all decided to take a walk. Then we'll go back to Ellen's and have some hot chocolate."

"Please, please, can I go?" Beth begged.

Jenny looked to Zahad. "Do you think it's a good idea?"

"I believe it will be fine." He couldn't keep the child locked up and, in fact, since the killer was most likely targeting either him or Jenny, Beth might be safer away from the house.

"All right," Jenny told the women. "Give me a call when you return to the house, okay? I want to pick her up before it gets too late."

"We will," Ellen promised.

Bundled up and hopping with excitement, the little girl went off with them. Jenny made decaf coffee, and she and Zahad settled in the living room to catch up on the day's more serious events.

He took pleasure in the graceful way her hands curved around the coffee cup as she described Grant's plea bargain and told him of Lew's imminent departure for greener pastures. It seemed that Parker had also informed her about Fario's release.

"The funeral director believes his body can be shipped tomorrow night. With the storm forecast, I have changed my reservation."

"You're leaving on Wednesday?"

"A little after 9:00 p.m."

"I'm sorry." Green depths glinted in her eyes and she stared into her cup.

Zahad felt his own eyes sting. "I am, also."

He felt that there should be something more to say or do, an acknowledgment of what had passed between them and of the bond that had grown. There must be conventions to help a man and woman deal with such moments, facing a separation that might be permanent. Should he promise to write—but if so, what good would it do? Should he invite her to visit, when he knew she never would?

It was beyond him to put a good face on the need to say goodbye. He did not have the temperament or the social graces to smooth over this painful end to something precious. Having spent most of his adult life preparing for war and dealing with its aftermath, he had never learned how to deal with the subtler sorrows of peacetime.

And so, when he saw Jenny's lips tremble, he didn't offer comfort. Indeed, he had none to give her.

Outside, the wind picked up. Tree branches lashed the air. From the direction of the Rivases' house, Zahad heard someone gunning an engine. As a precaution, he went to the window, but he could see nothing in the deepening darkness.

"That must be Ray. He's always working on that car." Jenny came to stand beside him.

"I assume it is a hobby, since they have two operational vehicles." Zahad fingered the silken lightness of her hair.

Jenny caught her breath but made no move to return the caress. "It's a classic. He swears it will be worth a lot of money when he gets done."

Zahad could not resist touching her again. He laid his arm lightly around her waist, hoping she would not mind.

To his satisfaction, she swayed toward him. A slight shift and she was in his arms, her face upturned, her lips parting. Savoring the moment, he lowered his mouth to hers.

She kissed him fully, her tongue exploring his teeth and her arms winding about his neck. At once he was ready for her, but, unwilling to hurry their tenderness, he ran his hands along her hips as he nuzzled her cheek and neck.

A loud crunch resounding from outside startled them both. Instinctively, he released her and turned. Still he could make out nothing through the glass.

"I hope he didn't hit the retaining wall again," Jenny said.

"You mean Ray?"

She nodded. "One time the brakes failed while he was backing out and he hit that low wall. He spent a fortune for a new bumper on eBay."

"A fortune?" Zahad said. "I wonder if he truly cares whether he turns a profit or whether he simply enjoys the process. It seems to me there are more worthwhile ways to use one's spare time. In fact, we have hit upon one ourselves, have we not?"

"I..." Jenny wavered indecisively. Zahad hoped she would ease back into his arms, but instead she retreated. "We'll have to go get Beth soon."

"Yes, of course." He swallowed his disappointment. "Tell me what you learned today. You said you ran background checks."

"There was nothing definitive. My service filled in a few interesting details, that is all."

From a police standpoint, the neighbors were a relatively clean bunch, Zahad explained. Bill had a drunk-driving conviction from six years ago, and the police in Big Bear had arrested, but later released, both Tish and Al eight months earlier for engaging in mutual combat during a squabble at a restaurant. In addition, their credit reports were a mess, although they'd paid off quite a few bills recently.

"I'm sorry to hear they fight so much," Jenny said. "That doesn't bode well for their marriage."

"They do not strike me as a happy couple," Zahad agreed. "It might help if they had a large family nearby, as we do in Alqedar. The older men would counsel the husband, and the women would heap advice upon the wife. They might make peace simply to avoid being inundated with tender concern."

She smiled, but her smile faded quickly. Outside, a branch hit the side of the house as the wind stirred again.

Jenny checked her watch. "I hope Beth's on her way back. She needed to let off steam but…"

From the direction of the Rivases' house, a woman's scream tore through the air. The heart-stopping cry came again, filled with anguish.

"Beth!" Jenny cried. "Oh, please don't let anything have happened to her."

The two of them ran for their coats. Why had he been so fixated on himself? Zahad wondered in disgust. Why had he let the little girl go outside when all day portents had signaled that someone was going to die?

He barely remembered to switch on the alarm and lock the door as they exited. Jenny was already racing ahead of him along the path, desperately calling her daughter's name.

Chapter Fifteen

The night was pitch-dark, with only faint illumination from overhead, and the flashlight in Jenny's hand revealed little as she raced up the path. The cold air burned her lungs and she stumbled twice before slowing.

Zahad's long strides devoured the ground, and he caught up with her quickly. Although she didn't spare the time to acknowledge him, she was grateful for his presence.

As they hurried along side by side, she struggled against panic. Surely Beth wasn't injured. No one would want to hurt her. Something else must have happened.

Whatever it was, it must have been terrible. That scream had made the hair on Jenny's arms stand on end.

They rounded the carport and got their first clear view of the driveway. In the glare of exterior lights, she saw Ray's old car sitting outside the garage. There was no one in sight.

"Ray?" she called. "Is anyone here?" Maybe he'd gone in search of the woman who'd screamed.

The sheikh extended one arm to halt her close to the carport. "Do not put yourself in danger by rushing in," he said in a low voice.

"I have to find out…"

"It may be a trap."

A trap. In Jenny's mind this phrase triggered a terrifying image of the gun as it must have looked rigged in her living room. In her anxiety over Beth, she never would have thought of that. Had the killer lured them here by screaming? If not for Zahad, she'd have rushed forward heedlessly.

But where was Beth? And Ray and everyone else?

Motioning to her to stay put, Zahad eased toward the classic car, which looked odd to Jenny sitting right out in the open. It didn't appear damaged, however, at least not the part that she could see. So apparently Ray hadn't backed it into the retaining wall.

In advancing, the sheikh wove from side to side as if expecting to be shot at. Jenny scanned the area. It was eerie how threatening a familiar setting could seem, she thought, and shivered.

From the direction of the street, she heard girlish voices heading her way. Ellen entered the diffused brightness first, blinking as she called out, "Mom? Where are you?"

"Grandma!" Cindy seconded.

"Mrs. Blankenship!" Beth trailed her friend into the light.

Relief washed through Jenny. Her little girl was safe! For that instant, she didn't care what danger might lurk. She flew across the driveway and gathered Beth close.

The child giggled and hugged her back. "Hi, Mommy."

Cutting short his advance, the sheikh turned to them and positioned himself in front of the women. To Ellen, he said, "We heard a scream. We must make certain it is not a trap."

"We heard it, too. It sounded like Mom," she replied worriedly.

"Why isn't she with you?" Jenny asked.

"She decided to go home to check on Bill. He wasn't feeling well. The girls and I were just leaving Tish's when we heard her." Ellen stared past them. "Why's the car sitting there?"

"Get back!" Zahad grabbed Beth and hauled her to the side of the house, behind cover. "There's someone in the garage."

"Of course there is," Ellen said, following slowly. "It's Ray. Why are you acting like this?"

"We're taking precautions," Jenny answered. "Welcome to my world. This is how it's been for the past week."

"It's Mom." Ellen pointed to the woman coming out of the garage. She moved stiffly as if in shock.

"Don't go in there," she told Ellen.

"Is Ray all right?" her daughter demanded.

There was no answer.

"Mom! Tell me Ray's okay."

Dolly shook her head. Tear tracks stained her ruddy cheeks.

"What happened?" Ellen started to cry, too. "Come on, Mom."

Her mother released a long breath. "I was crossing the street when I heard a crash. The car must have shifted into gear while he was working on it. It…" She swallowed hard. "It pinned him. I backed it out, but I was too late."

That must have been the source of the crash, Jenny thought in dismay. The car had struck the inside of the garage. Ray must have been crushed.

"Call the paramedics," Ellen said shakily.

"I already did," Dolly replied. "I'm sure the police will come, too. Jenny, would you please take the children inside?"

"Of course." She shepherded the youngsters in from the cold. Her relief at finding her daughter safe had been replaced by wrenching sympathy for Ellen.

Despite the turmoil in their marriage, Jenny knew Ellen and Ray had loved each other. She couldn't imagine building a life with a man and losing him so abruptly.

In the distance, sirens wailed. Jenny was becoming sick of that sound.

"Let's have hot chocolate," she told the girls. "I'll put marshmallows in it if I can find some."

They needed a distraction. Cindy would need much more than that in the days ahead, but it was all Jenny had to offer right now.

ZAHAD WAS RELIEVED that Jenny didn't have to see Ray's shattered body where the car had smashed him against the back of the garage, and Dolly resolutely kept her daughter away from the scene, as well. There was no hope of saving him. The paramedics called ahead to the coroner to meet them at the hospital.

Despite the possibility that it had been an accident, Sergeant Finley brought in his crime-scene technicians and secured the area. Although no one had heard a car start on the street or seen anyone else nearby, he sent patrolmen to comb the neighborhood.

Finley ordered Jenny and the girls out of the house so it could be searched. He seemed inclined to take everyone to the police station for questioning, but Ellen was sobbing uncontrollably and Cindy was becoming more upset by the minute. After talking to another detective, a fellow named Rygel, he relented and allowed the witnesses to be questioned in the police cars and at Dolly's house.

As the night wore on, each of them submitted to a separate interview. Since she had found the body, Dolly underwent two interviews, before and after the others. By the time she emerged from Finley's car the second time, she was fuming.

"I don't understand why you keep asking me all that stuff about Ellen," she told the detective as they stood in her driveway. Zahad, who'd come outside to check out the source of some mechanical noise, was staring downhill toward the Rivases' house, where a tow truck had hoisted the classic car onto a flatbed. "She was at Tish's house when this happened. She'd never have hurt Ray, anyway."

"Dolly, you know she was jealous," Finley said. "It can't be any secret to you that she suspected Ray of having an affair."

"She has an alibi for tonight and you know it!"

"I grant you that, but his death isn't the only case I'm working on. Hank and I were on our way here to serve a search warrant when we heard your call."

"What?" Dolly shook her head as if she must have misheard. "A search warrant for what?"

"You know I can't discuss my investigation. I've already said more than I should."

"Parker Finley, she's my daughter!"

"Which is why you shouldn't hear this," he told her. "By the way, she needs to find somewhere else to sleep tonight. She might be able to get back in the house tomorrow, but the garage will still be off limits."

"They can spend the night at my place," Dolly said. "May I at least pack some of Cindy's clothes and her favorite doll?"

"I'm afraid I can't let anyone in the house yet."

She regarded him with distinct displeasure, Zahad saw when he glanced their way. "Well, all right. But whatever you're looking for, remember that Ellen just lost her husband. Cut her some slack."

"I have to follow procedure," Finley replied doggedly. "I'll give you a list of whatever we take. We'll need her computer."

"She uses that to earn a living!"

"I have to do what I have to do." He obviously didn't like being in this position. "Speaking of which, you'll have to excuse me. I've got a search to conduct."

"Go ahead," Dolly said. "The sooner you start, the sooner you'll finish."

Zahad registered the fact that the search warrant involved the computer. That might mean they believed Ellen to be the cyber-stalker. They must have had some fairly credible evidence to persuade a judge.

Mentally, he connected the dots. Yesterday, Ronald Wang had informed the detective about Fario's phone conversation with a woman. Finley must have searched the phone records of any woman known to dislike Jenny. Tish and Ellen both fit that description.

A call from this house to Fario's number would provide enough evidence to justify a warrant. Still, even if Ellen was the stalker, that didn't make her his brother's killer. And she obviously hadn't killed Ray.

Zahad wished he could figure out how everything fit together. He had the sense that either he was missing some key point or they might be dealing with more than one murderer.

The door opened and Jenny came down the steps from Dolly's house, her coat only half-buttoned. "I need to talk to Parker."

"He's down there." Zahad indicated the Rivases' house.

"I just thought of something I forgot to mention in my interview." She looked so cold with the wind whipping her hair that Zahad wanted to draw her against him to warm her up. Such a public gesture would be inappropriate, however.

"Who's watching the girls?" Dolly asked. "Don't tell me it's Ellen. She's in no shape to take care of anyone."

"They're sleeping and Bill's keeping an eye on things," Jenny replied. "He's trying to help in his curmudgeonly way. He does seem weak, though."

"Well, he's no Hercules, but he could roust everyone if an earthquake hit," Dolly said. "What did you remember?"

"It's cold out here," she said. "I want to go explain it to Parker."

The three of them trooped down the hill. The sergeant didn't look pleased to see them until Jenny explained the reason she'd come.

"On Sunday at Ellen's house, I mentioned the slip of paper Zahad found, the one with the logo from the Crystal Point bank," she said. "Ray suggested he snoop through people's accounts and see if anything funny was going on. I think he regarded it as kind of a game."

"That's right," Dolly said. "He was speculating about a hired killer, that he might have deposited his payoff in one lump sum."

Zahad hadn't heard this before, and judging by the way Finley's eyes narrowed, it was news to him, also. "Who else was there?" the detective asked.

"Ellen, Dolly, Bill, me and the Garroways," Jenny said.

Dolly wrapped her arms around herself. "What a stupid thing. He'd never have really done it. Please don't tell me he got killed over that!"

Finley made notes on a pad. "You're sure no one else was present?"

"Just the two girls," Jenny answered.

He tucked the notebook in his pocket. "Thanks. This could be useful."

"Do you require our presence any further?" Zahad asked.

He gave a sideways shake of the head. "I'd suggest you people get some rest."

Zahad didn't argue. He went with Jenny to collect Beth, who nestled against his shoulder on the walk home. When he lowered her into bed, she immediately fell asleep.

"Thank you," Jenny said as they went into the hall.

"It was no trouble."

"I didn't mean for carrying her." She tipped her forehead against his chest. "For being here. For being you. For keeping me sane."

When Zahad enfolded her against his heart, a warmth stole through him. He allowed himself to luxuriate in an unfamiliar sense of peace and wholeness.

"A part of myself exists only with you," he murmured. "The happy part."

Jenny gazed up at him. "I feel like we're living in a magic bubble with evil all around. What will I do when you leave?" She stepped back and with her hands made a little gesture of frustration. "Don't mind me. It's late."

"I am accustomed to death. You are not." But that

wasn't the point, he thought as he took her hand. The point was that he belonged here.

The impossible had happened. He'd fallen in love, and Jenny loved him back. Yet she was right: They *were* living in a bubble, and it was bound to break. He could even name the day and time: tomorrow, Wednesday, at 9:12 p.m., when his flight took off from Crystal Point Airport.

Zahad didn't like to think about what lay ahead for him in Alqedar or the cloudy future he would face if he were removed as head of Yazir Province. Yet if that happened, he would eventually find some other battle to fight, some other cause to live or die for. But he would never again find someone to love this deeply.

Jenny gave him a rueful smile. "It's hard to believe I've got to be at work in just a few hours. I'd better get some sleep."

"Indeed," he said.

Slowly she removed her hand from his. There was no need for additional words. .

Once she had retreated, the sheikh sat in his room reviewing everything that had happened, beginning with Fario's murder. He kept trying to put the pieces together, hoping everything would fit into a pattern.

Something nagged at the back of his mind but he couldn't pinpoint it. Was it something from tonight or from his background checks on the neighbors? Or was it something Ron Wang had said?

The answer eluded him. Perhaps his thoughts tomorrow would become clearer. Zahad hoped so, because tomorrow was all he had left.

ON WEDNESDAY MORNING, he followed Jenny and Beth to school. Zahad had just pulled out of the parking lot when the point he'd been seeking popped into his head.

According to their credit reports, Al and Tish Garroway had paid off a number of bills during the past three months.

Yet Al had complained that neither of them was earning as much in Mountain Lake as they'd expected.

Where had the money come from?

At the next light, Zahad made a U-turn and headed back toward the police station, debating with himself the whole way. Three months ago seemed rather early for anyone to have received a payoff to commit murder. The cyber-stalking hadn't even started until six weeks later.

However, the timing corresponded with the onset of the carjackings. Until the patrols grew heavier, the perpetrators had targeted the ski area where the Garroways worked. They'd certainly been aware that tourists with bulging wallets frequented the area. On the other hand, Tish herself had fallen victim.

At the station, Zahad learned that Finley was out, so he spoke with Detective Rygel. The black-haired man, whom he judged to be in his early thirties, listened intently. "Why did you run a credit check on Al and Tish Garroway?" the detective inquired after taking notes.

"In my country, being a sheikh involves functioning somewhat like a CEO," Zahad said. "I subscribe to an Internet service to run background checks on prospective employees."

"The Garroways want to work for you?"

"I ran checks on all the neighbors. Someone killed my brother. If there are clues in their backgrounds, I wished to find them."

"Parker told me you'd been poking around." The detective regarded him with reluctant approval. "I have to admit, I didn't much like the idea, but this information is worth looking into."

They parted on amicable terms. Although he hadn't shed any light on Fario's death, Zahad mused as he drove home, if he had helped the police to crack the carjacking ring, at least they would have more time to devote to the murders.

But that didn't mean they would solve them in time to protect Jenny.

Uneasily, he recalled the nocturnal break-in attempt at her shed. Whatever the killer had been seeking, it didn't appear to have figured into Ray's death. Had he simply changed his plans and seized the opportunity to use Ray's car as a murder weapon or was he planning an additional crime?

The original target of the slaying might have been Jenny. If so, the killer wasn't likely to stop until he got her.

Zahad couldn't bear to think of her and Beth alone in the house. He might have asked Dolly to stay with them, but she had her hands full with a grieving daughter and grand-daughter.

As he drove along Pine Forest Road, he found himself considering something he once would have dismissed out of hand. He could delay his return and simply let matters fall where they might in Alqedar. If Amy and Sharif were able to stave off the attacks on him, fine. If not, perhaps it was time he set his sights elsewhere.

Zahad didn't delude himself into assuming he and Jenny could build a future together. It might be possible, but even if he were to remain in the United States, it might not. They both had independent natures and vastly different back-grounds.

But he wanted very much to keep her safe. As for the people of Yazir, he'd risked his life to free them and had struggled for the past two years to serve them, and what was their response? Indifference, at best.

At the house, after a quick security check, Zahad entered through the rear door. Warm air redolent of coffee and baby powder triggered delicious memories of Jenny and Beth. Their scents and smiles and voices overlaid the emptiness of the house and filled the void inside him.

He would stay and protect them, no matter what it cost.

Opening his cell phone, he dialed Amy's number. He had intended to call her today in any event, and she had a right to know of his change of heart. He hoped she would not take it hard.

She answered on the first ring. The instant she heard his voice, she said excitedly, "You should see this! You're not going to believe it."

"What?"

"I'm looking out my office window." Located on the upper floor of the palace, it had a view that extended past a freestanding perimeter wall and all the way to the market square. "Half the province is marching in the streets. You'd need a bulldozer to get into the town center."

"What do they want?" Zahad asked in alarm. If Numa and Hashim had brought civil war to Yazir, they would set back his public-works plans and devastate the economy.

"Didn't Sharif tell you?"

"Evidently not."

"I organized a little protest," Amy explained.

"A little protest?"

"Well, maybe not so little."

"You did this?" he asked, unsure how to react. "Amy, what's going on?"

"I figured the people have a right to decide what happens to their province."

There had never been a widespread protest in Yazir before. Zahad hoped she hadn't started something that would careen out of control. "Perhaps Hashim stirred them up."

"No way," she told him. "I run the Web site. And then there's Radio Yazir. They gave me fifteen minutes this morning for my spiel." One of Zahad's first actions had been to restore a long-neglected radio station and staff it with energetic young residents. It broadcast local programming for two hours daily.

"Tell me what you said." He sank into the desk chair, trying to absorb this turn of events.

"I reminded them of everything you've done and told them about your plans for the future. I made it clear that Hashim doesn't care about them, he just wants power. I said that if they don't make their opinions known, they can expect more of the same neglect they've endured in the past.''

"You did not speak ill of my father or brother, I hope.'' Much as he appreciated her support, Zahad wouldn't be party to blackening their names.

"I didn't mention them or Numa, either,'' Amy said. "People can draw their own conclusions. The citizens aren't stupid. They understand what's going on. Well, at least they do now.''

"Now that you've leveled with them.'' He should have done so himself, Zahad thought. He'd assumed they would follow the lead of the foremost families, as they always had, but he'd been wrong. His cousin, who wasn't even a native of Yazir, had trusted them more than he had.

"Well, you should see them now,'' Amy crowed. "The market's pulsing with people waving signs and chanting. Hashim went out a while ago to try to talk to them, and they shook their fists in his face and chased him back to the palace.''

"What do the signs say?'' Zahad was starting to grin.

"I don't want to give you a swelled head.'' She clicked her tongue. "Oh, all right. One of them says, Zahad! Rightful Leader. Then there's, Zahad, Yes! Hashim, Never! And We Will Fight to Keep Our Sheikh. I didn't write that slogan.''

"You wrote the others?'' He chuckled at her audacity.

"Well, sure. Oh, wait, there's a new one. Our Hearts Belong to Zahad. I swear, that one isn't mine.''

"Are you certain you are not exaggerating for my sake? Did you pay any of them?''

"Certainly not! And Radio Yazir just estimated the crowd at ten thousand. It's broadcasting overtime. I can't see them all from here. Apparently they're spilling in from the countryside.''

"Ten thousand?''

"You bet!''

It was unheard of. The province's entire population did

not surpass thirty thousand. Even allowing for wishful thinking on the part of the broadcasters, this was an impressive showing.

Over the years, without realizing it, Zahad had developed an outsider's mentality. Accustomed to struggling in the background with little recognition, he'd never expected to be popular. His spirits soared.

"You have done a wonderful thing," he said.

"You're the star of the show. Everyone wants to see you," Amy said. "When are you getting back?"

"By Friday," he replied. It would take that long, factoring in the international flight and the time difference. "Amy, I can never thank you enough."

"I just lit the fuse. You're the one who built the bomb. Wait. I didn't put that very well."

"I got the point. Thank you."

"You're going to knock 'em dead," his cousin told him. "I'll bet Hashim's packing his suitcase now."

"Let us hope so." As they said farewell, he was already eager to return.

Hashim would never be able to govern the province now. Neither, Zahad suspected, would anyone chosen by Numa.

Never had he imagined his soul could feel so torn, joyful and anxiety-filled at the same time. Yet his path was clear. He must not put personal happiness before his duty to his countrymen. Other warriors, including his cousin Sharif, had lost people they loved while engaged in battle. Zahad hoped it would not come to that for Jenny, but beyond any question, he must return to Alqedar.

He had a suitcase to pack.

Chapter Sixteen

Jenny usually ate in the school cafeteria. However, as Wednesday was her last chance to be alone with Zahad, she took off for a longer-than-normal lunch break after calling to inform him that she was on her way home.

When she came through the door, he gathered her close. They scarcely needed to speak. What she craved was the feel of his hair beneath her fingers, his mouth covering hers, and more…

They left a trail of clothes en route to her room. By the time they reached the bed, they were naked. They barely stopped to use the protection Zahad produced.

He made love to her with all the fierceness of a desert warrior and the tenderness of a man who adored her. But Jenny didn't wish to think about emotions. There was a comfort in the reality of his body entering hers and the intense physical connection they forged.

She knew her future was not meant to include him. So she wanted as much as she could get in the present. And the present had condensed into a few stolen minutes of pleasure so keen it verged on pain.

As she writhed against Zahad, Jenny tried to imprint in her consciousness every detail of him. She relished the way his muscles shifted and his hands caressed her hips. She absorbed his scent and the deep groans issuing from his throat.

She let his fire roar through her. And when the flames began to die, she rolled on top in a sheen of sweat and aroused him all over again.

Zahad reached up and kissed her, completing the circuit. Exquisite sensations arced through Jenny at his thrusting. They rode each other in a white sizzle of electric longing until it blazed to an end. Breathing fast and in counterpoint, they sank into a damp tangle of sheets.

This man, a stranger less than a week ago, now seemed as familiar as her own image in the mirror, Jenny mused as she gazed at him. His scars, his broad shoulders, his angular face filled her days and played through her dreams until she felt she must have known him for years.

She wished they could stretch time. But already the clock on the headboard insistently returned her to reality.

"I have to go back to work." She sat up, fighting the languor of her body.

"I know." He traced the swollen tip of her nipple. "I wish I could stay here longer."

She wasn't about to dwell on impossible hopes. "We both knew we'd have to say goodbye. I hope you can win your battles at home, Zahad."

"Perhaps I already have." He told her about the protests spreading through Yazir.

"I'm pleased for you," Jenny said. "And I'm glad for your people. It must be marvelous to know they appreciate you."

"More than I realized."

She washed up and dressed. As she was leaving, Jenny paused in the bedroom doorway. Zahad lay uncovered except for a sheet thrown over his midsection. When he saw her, his smile lit up the room.

"I'll see you at dinner." It seemed inadequate after what had passed between them, but Jenny couldn't linger.

"I will buy some ice cream for Beth," he offered.

"She'll like that."

Her skin tingled in the cold air as she hurried to her SUV.

She felt alive and full of hope, although she wasn't sure what she hoped for.

It sobered her to remember that last night Ellen had lost her husband. Jenny wished she could find a way to prepare for what life had in store, but she knew better than to ask for the impossible. Who could have predicted the shape events had taken these past ten days, for any of them?

Only the killer.

Yet, as she drove back to town, she discovered that she didn't feel nearly as afraid as she once had. The discovery that she could love a man more profoundly than she'd ever imagined possible and yet find the strength to face the future without him had somehow armored her.

Since childhood, Jenny had battled the instinct to quail before a man's anger. After her marriage ended, she'd withdrawn from men as a defense against their attempts to dominate her.

What she'd also been fighting, she saw now, was her need for intimacy and her fear of rejection. The freedom to give love and receive Zahad's love without strings had liberated her.

Jenny realized her physical safety might be at risk in the days ahead. Yet her old wounds had healed, and she'd heard that scars were stronger than the bare skin they replaced.

She drove back to school and, despite her lack of sleep the night before, finished the day with her head held high.

ALTHOUGH ZAHAD HAD FACED death many times during the war of liberation, at least he had been driven by a single, unified purpose. Preparing to leave that night, he felt torn in two directions. In some ways, leaving was the hardest thing he had ever done.

Together, he and Jenny prepared oven-fried fish for dinner, served with sesame noodles and French bread. Beth helped make a salad. Gleefully, she tossed in handfuls of chocolate chips and coconut.

There was a homespun magic in the way the three of

them moved comfortably around each other in the kitchen. At one point, Jenny gave Beth a little hug, and a few minutes later the child repaid the favor to Zahad. He swung her up and, after a mischievous exchange of looks, he and Jenny kissed the little girl on opposite cheeks at the same time. Beth giggled and wiggled until they did it again.

They were becoming a family. How ironic that he had found these two special people in the wrong place and at the wrong time.

During dessert, Dolly stopped by. The stress of the past twenty-four hours had given her eyes a puffed look and her determinedly upbeat tone revealed a frayed edge. Nevertheless, she seemed under control.

After Jenny invited her inside, Dolly closed the door quickly behind her, shutting out a swirl of snowflakes. "Man, it's getting thick out there and the wind's nasty. I hear we're in for a real blizzard."

"It is moving in more quickly than expected." Troubled, Zahad checked his watch. Almost six-thirty. "I must leave by seven. Perhaps I should go now."

"You're flying out of Crystal Point? The roads won't fill up in the next half hour, but I wouldn't wait any longer than that." Dolly didn't seem surprised to hear that he was leaving. Word traveled quickly around here, Zahad mused.

"How's Ellen?" Gesturing to her neighbor to sit down, Jenny offered her one of the ice-cream bars.

Dolly declined with a polite shake of the head. "She's taking it hard. She blames herself in a way, although I don't know why. Mostly I think she regrets all the energy she wasted being jealous of Ray without cause."

Beth, who'd been squirming in her seat, lost patience with the adult chatter. "May I go play?"

"Sure, honey. Go ahead."

Although he hated to see Beth go, Zahad felt relieved as well. They could talk more freely now.

"Anyway, I came to tell you some news." Dolly rested

her elbows on the dining table. "The police arrested Al Garroway this afternoon."

"For what?" Jenny asked. Zahad hadn't had a chance to tell her about his meeting with Detective Rygel, he realized. "You're not saying he killed Ray!"

"We don't know yet," Dolly replied. "He was arrested in conjunction with the carjackings. It seems the perpetrators were paying him a percentage of the take."

"What was his involvement?" Zahad asked.

"Apparently he tipped off some men he knew from his old job about the easy pickings up here," Dolly explained. "I guess he figured it was a way to make some money. The idiot even rented them a cabin in his own name."

"But they robbed Tish!" Jenny said.

"Yes, the idiots. Her own husband was responsible for the men who attacked her, and she's furious." Dolly arched her neck to release tension. "She stormed over to my house a little while ago asking if I know a good divorce lawyer. Unfortunately, I don't."

"What happened to the carjackers?" Zahad asked.

"According to the radio, the police have surrounded their cabin up near the ski lodge. Parker hasn't had time to check whether there's any connection between Al and Ray's death."

If Al had put his stolen money in the Crystal Point bank, he might have been afraid Ray would figure it out. But he'd had no obvious motive to kill either Jenny or Fario. "We must assume the killer is still free," Zahad said.

"Agreed." Dolly stretched her shoulders. "Which, in a way, brings me to my other reason for coming here."

"Yes?" Jenny said.

"Ellen got permission to move back into her house tonight. I don't think it's a good idea, but she wants to start cleaning and she'd like Cindy to sleep in her own bed."

"I can understand," Jenny replied. "I felt the same way."

"Bill's being a good sport about my sleeping over with

them,'' Dolly explained. ''He even suggested I invite you two to join us. Beth would keep Cindy distracted and you and I could keep Ellen's spirits up.''

Zahad nearly seconded the suggestion. What better way to safeguard Jenny and Beth than for them to stay with the other women?

Before he could say so, Jenny spoke. ''It's a good idea but frankly, I'm exhausted, and we're all under stress. Having us around might make matters worse instead of better. Besides, with all the snow we're supposed to get, I'd feel more comfortable in my own home.''

''You're sure?'' Dolly asked.

Jenny nodded firmly.

Their guest stood up. ''Well, then, I'd better go back. Oh, we'll probably schedule Ray's funeral for Saturday, but that depends on the coroner. I'll let you know.'' She thrust out her hand to Zahad. ''Have a safe trip.''

''Thank you.''

After she left, Jenny said, ''I hope I didn't sound unsympathetic. It's just that I don't have enough emotional reserves right now to provide much support.''

''A wise choice.'' Zahad felt glad he hadn't encouraged her to comply. ''Now, I, too, must depart.''

''I know.'' Jenny swallowed hard.

He retrieved his suitcase and put on the coat he'd bought in town. On the way back, he stopped to look into Beth's room. In a bright disk of lamplight, she sat on the floor talking to her doll and doing a simple jigsaw puzzle.

''Not that piece, Minnie,'' the little girl said solemnly, as if the doll were helping with the puzzle. ''That one won't fit.''

''Your doll is not as smart as you,'' Zahad said.

Beth looked up. Her blond hair formed a golden halo. ''Of course not. I'm her teacher.''

''Is that what you're going to be when you grow up?''

''Yes,'' she replied. ''Or I might decide to be a principal like Mommy.''

"I must go." Zahad's chest squeezed. "I have enjoyed my visit very much."

Girl and doll came hurtling across the room. When Beth flung her arms around his waist, Minnie smacked him in the rear end.

The sheikh lifted them both for a proper hug. Reluctantly, he set them down again.

"I'll see you next time," Beth said.

Perhaps Beth was thinking that he would visit regularly, as her father had done. How could he explain to this tiny tyke that forces on the other side of the world might not allow him to come back?

"Goodbye," he said simply.

"Bye, Zod."

Jenny put on a coat and walked him to the car. Snow flurried around them, obscuring their view of the road, and gusts of wind tossed her hair. "Dolly was right—it's getting bad. I'm glad you put the chains on."

Zahad strove for lightness. "I will make a great racket going down the highway."

"I doubt there'll be many people around to hear you."

With all the padding on them, they embraced like two teddy bears. In a sense, they had said their farewells at midday, he thought. He much preferred the way they had done it then.

"Drive carefully." She didn't cry or urge him to return. He almost wished she would.

Jenny Sanger, the fragile-looking beauty in the photograph, had turned out to be as strong as Zahad himself. Perhaps, at this moment, stronger.

He cupped her chin in his hand. "I will e-mail to let you know when I arrive."

He was about to kiss her, when she said, "I just have one request."

"Whatever it is, I will be honored to do it."

Jenny stuffed her hands in her pockets. "When you face

those people who're trying to get rid of you, kick some good old Yazirian butt for me, will you?"

"I beg your pardon?" The earthy phrasing surprised him, coming from such a sweet-faced creature.

"I know you're not American, but that's the way we think," she said, stepping back. "Give 'em hell. Only don't tell Beth I used that word."

"I promise." Zahad admired her spirit.

"In a way, I envy you," Jenny told him. "You get to slay dragons. It'll be years before I have a chance to do that. In my work, I mean. But I'll get there."

"Of that I have no doubt."

And so he drove off, with the storm blowing and Jenny watching after him. Once she disappeared behind the trees, Zahad turned his attention to negotiating the road amid rapidly diminishing visibility.

He wondered if he would ever see her again.

JENNY DELIBERATELY hadn't kissed him goodbye. If she had, she'd have started to cry.

There was no point. Their paths had converged for less than a week, and now they were both continuing on their rightful courses. It was nothing to weep over, not like the deaths of Ray or Zahad's brother.

That was what she tried to tell herself. Yet the house echoed with Zahad's absence and rattled from gusts of wind hitting the windows.

Uneasily, Jenny checked to make sure the doors were locked. Then, quietly, so as not to call attention to her presence, she looked in on her daughter.

Holding Minnie on her lap, Beth sat on her bed in the midst of an array of stuffed animals. "We're all going to sing a song," she told them. "That way you won't be sad."

Tears filled Jenny's eyes. She felt proud of her little girl's courage and heartbroken at the same time that Beth had to endure so much.

When the tiny voice started singing a tune from *Sesame*

Street, Jenny tiptoed away. Much as she wanted to give comfort, she respected her daughter's attempt to take control of her own feelings.

In the living room, Jenny turned on the radio to listen for a weather report. The local station was playing music, but there'd be an update soon. To keep busy, she took out her sewing kit, chose a pattern for a doll's jacket and began sorting through fabric scraps.

The music trailed to an end. "In case you haven't noticed, it's snowing out there, folks, and we're clocking gusts up to forty-five miles per hour," the announcer said. "The weather bureau recommends you stay off the streets if at all possible."

After predicting more snow overnight and gradual clearing the next day, he segued into a commercial for snow-blowers from the local hardware store. The news followed.

"We've had a report of shots fired at a cabin on Duck Hollow Road," the announcer said. "Police have cornered three suspects in that rash of carjackings. One local resident is already in custody but officers haven't released his name. Now back to the music."

As the radio played "Let It Snow," Jenny pictured her dark-haired neighbor with his thin face and unkempt beard. Al hadn't become a friend, but she'd never felt threatened by him, either. Of course, since he was responsible for bringing the carjackers who'd tried to halt her car, she'd been mistaken about that.

What would make an otherwise law-abiding citizen prey on his fellow humans? Greed, she thought. And selfishness and an incredible insensitivity to how upsetting it was to be the victim of a crime. She wondered how Al had felt when his own wife was attacked.

Her mind veered back to the sheikh. He would give his life rather than expose innocent people to danger, Jenny thought.

She forced herself to concentrate on aligning the pattern pieces along the fabric. She admired Zahad. More than that, she cherished him, but she couldn't ignore the vast differences separating them. Better that he'd left now, before Beth grew accustomed to him and Jenny started relying on him for things she could do herself.

After she finished cutting out the pattern, she put everything away and went to check on Beth again. The little girl lay beneath the covers, fast asleep amid her furry friends.

Jenny rearranged the stuffed animals to make sure none were in a position to block Beth's breathing. Then she turned the lights out.

In the front, she set the alarm for the night and peered out the window toward the street. Snow fell so thickly she couldn't see past the first few trees along the driveway. A dusting had accumulated on the ground.

The wind, which had quieted briefly, was picking up again. It battered the tree branches, raising an eerie, unsettling moan.

After drawing the curtains, Jenny tuned the TV to an old movie. Caught up in the mystery plot, she lost track of time until a loud thud caught her attention. Jenny muted the volume and listened.

For a moment, she heard only the groaning of the trees. Then another *wham!* echoed from behind the house. She could have sworn the noise had a metallic ring to it.

Dread rooted Jenny to the couch. Maybe the wind had blown something into the garage, she told herself.

Or maybe someone was trying to break into the toolshed again.

She was so angry she wanted to end this nightmare once and for all, even if it meant storming out there and confronting the intruder. For the first time, she wished she had her gun back.

No, she didn't mean that. She would never expose herself to danger that way or leave Beth in the house unprotected.

She went to the kitchen and picked up the phone. There was no dial tone. Puzzled, she tapped the cradle in vain until the truth hit her.

Someone had cut the line.

Jenny's chest tightened with fear. She forced herself to think clearly. The phones went dead and the power blacked out around here with annoying regularity, especially during bad weather. The wind might have knocked down the aboveground wire leading to the house.

Thank heavens for her cell phone.

Her hand trembled so hard she had to make two stabs before she pressed the On button. To Jenny's relief, she got a dial tone. She rapid-dialed the police.

"911 emergency." The dispatcher sounded a bit strained.

Jenny identified herself. "I think someone's trying to break into my toolshed. I heard a thud."

"Is anyone in immediate danger?" the woman asked.

"Not exactly." Her tight throat made it hard for Jenny to speak clearly. "It could be whoever killed the sheikh at my house. He took tools from my shed."

"Yes, Mrs. Sanger, I'm aware of that. I'm sorry but unless there's an immediate threat, I can't send anyone right now. I'd have to pull them off an emergency."

"I know about the carjackers," Jenny conceded. "But…"

"We just had a three-car pileup south of town with people trapped in their vehicles," the dispatcher said. "Everyone we can spare is at the scene. Is someone trying to get into your house?"

"No. At least, not yet."

"I promise to send an officer as soon as I have someone free. I'm really sorry… My other line just lit up."

"Thank you," Jenny said. "Send someone as quickly as you can." She clicked off and put the phone in her pocket.

Maybe she should have mentioned that her regular line had gone dead, she thought. On the other hand, that didn't prove anything, either.

She had to find out what was happening in the backyard. The dispatcher was right. Unless someone was actually trying to harm her, the other incidents took priority.

Despite knees that felt like gelatin, Jenny made her way down the hall and activated the exterior lights. As she went into her office, Zahad's lingering scent gave her strength.

Through the glass, she saw loose branches and unidentifiable bits of debris flying across the yard, but nothing that looked human size. Unfortunately, the shed door faced away from the house, so she couldn't tell whether the lock remained in place.

She was taking the phone from her pocket to call Dolly for advice, when it rang, startling her. Her hand jerked, and it was a moment before she managed to open it. "Hello?"

"Jenny?" The thin, quavery voice had a breathless quality. "It's me, Bill. I just woke up. I think Dolly slipped me a sleeping pill."

"Are you all right?" She remembered that he'd been left alone while his wife spent the night with Ellen.

"I heard them talking a while ago," the old man said dazedly. "Something about a fire. Jenny, you gotta get outta there. Take your little girl and go. Far away as you can."

"I don't understand." She could hardly hear through the pounding of her pulse.

"They're gonna kill you. Tonight, Jenny. They're both crazy, that's what, especially Dolly. Crazy with jealousy and I guess some kinda delusions. Been poisoning me all along. Now I know what her other two husbands musta died of."

"I have to call the police." Her thoughts were too jumbled to make much sense of what he had revealed, except to recognize with horror that she'd been about to turn to the very person who wanted to kill her.

"I'll do it." Bill wheezed a couple of times. "You get outta that house before they set it on fire. Better hurry. I don't want you to end up like Ray and that sheikh fella."

"Thank you," she said. "Are you all right?"

"She thinks I'm sleepin'. Don't worry about me. Just go." He hung up.

Fire! An image of a roaring inferno filled Jenny's mind.

The house of one of her students had caught fire last winter from a wood-burning stove and gone up in flames. Thanks to their smoke detector, the family had escaped, but they'd lost everything. And that fire hadn't been deliberately set to trap them.

Now Jenny knew what the intruder had wanted in the toolshed. Gasoline.

She ran to get her daughter.

Chapter Seventeen

Jenny had to get Beth away from here. Even the police couldn't save them if Dolly turned the house into an inferno.

She could hardly believe it. She'd been grateful for her neighbor's offer to watch the house and had trusted her without question.

It made sense now. She'd given Dolly a key. Her neighbor had seemed genuinely upset about finding Fario's body, but that was probably because she'd expected it to be Jenny's. Dolly had admittedly backed out Ray's car, a perfect cover for any DNA evidence inside it, although Jenny still didn't understand why she'd wanted to kill her son-in-law.

And Ellen. In retrospect, she had to be the cyber-stalker. She'd been wildly jealous of any attention Ray paid to Jenny and hostile to Jenny herself, and she knew the Internet inside and out. But she'd seemed so distraught about her husband's death.

None of that mattered now. Jenny had to focus on bundling a sleepy little girl into a coat and wrapping herself warmly. After grabbing her purse and Beth's favorite doll, Jenny peered out the front window to make sure the coast was clear.

Impossible to see anything through the thick, swirling snow. She had to take her chances.

When she thrust open the door, the alarm began to chirp. With her hands full, she couldn't shut it off. Besides, Jenny realized, the alert would add emphasis to Bill's call to the dispatcher.

Icy wind and snow scoured their faces. "Mommy, it's cold!" Beth protested.

"I told you, honey, we have to go." Jenny hadn't explained why.

"But where?"

"To a motel. I'm sorry, sweetie, but we can't wait."

Jenny was glad she'd parked by the front walk instead of in the garage. Because the structure was set far back, she hadn't wanted to face digging out an extra length of driveway. She'd been meaning to put in a carport as her neighbors had done.

Her neighbors. She shuddered. They weren't going to be her neighbors after this.

Struggling to move through the blustery darkness, she felt as if she weighed a thousand pounds. And at any moment, she expected to see Dolly loom into view, her face distorted by madness.

With agonizing slowness, Jenny unlocked the car and strapped Beth into her booster seat in back. "Minnie's scared." The little girl clutched her doll.

"She'll be fine," Jenny said.

The house alarm let loose with a screech. Beth clapped her hands over her ears.

"It'll stop in a minute," Jenny told her.

She clambered into the driver's seat. As she inserted the key into the ignition, another thought struck her.

Cars can burn, too.

Had Dolly rigged a bomb? Maybe the metallic noise she'd heard had come from the front, not the rear of the house. The way sound bounced off the hilly terrain, directions could be deceiving.

Jenny halted with her hand on the key. It was too risky

o try to drive. Maybe she should take her daughter and flee across the street to Parker's house.

With him at work, there'd be no one home but the housekeeper and his little boy. Would she be putting more innocent people at risk? Jenny didn't know. She simply couldn't think of what else to do.

The alarm was still screaming so loudly she could hardly hear herself shout to Beth, "We can't take the car!"

"Why not?"

Oh, heavens, she didn't want to terrify the little girl. Struggling to hide her fear, Jenny said, "There's something wrong with it. Let's go over to Ralph's house."

"I want to go to Cindy's!"

Jenny was searching for a plausible excuse, when a fierce gust jolted them. The SUV rocked and Beth uttered a shriek.

Nearby, trees swayed wildly. One large pine twisted as if alive, swayed to one side and, picking up speed, crashed across the driveway. The boom shook the car windows so hard Jenny feared they might shatter.

Mercifully, the house alarm shut off. Silence fell, or at least it seemed like silence, although after a moment Jenny realized the wind was still stirring.

She commanded herself to breathe. A quick look around indicated that the SUV wasn't damaged and neither was the house.

Scant comfort. Even if she'd dared to drive, she couldn't do it now with the fallen tree blocking their escape route.

"Mommy, I want to go inside!" Beth said.

Jenny found the strength to speak calmly. "We're going to have to walk. We're just going across the street."

She got Beth out of the car. The storm appeared to be worsening, although a few minutes ago that hadn't seemed possible.

"It's not far," she said. "Let's go fast!"

"We don't have to walk," Beth replied. "Somebody's coming."

Jenny heard it now, too: the mutter of an engine heading up her driveway. She couldn't see the vehicle through the tree branches and snow.

She had to take cover. They couldn't stand here waiting to be confronted. "We have to hide."

"But it's cold!"

Why did her usually cooperative daughter pick this time to get stubborn? "We'll just duck around the side of the house. Come on, sweetheart." She bent to pick up the child. "It'll be all right."

Jenny heard the other car come to a stop. Whoever was driving could easily walk around the fallen pine. If it was Dolly, she'd surely be armed.

Half pulling and half carrying Beth, Jenny struggled through the snow. Beyond the tree, a car door shut. Why had gravity suddenly doubled its grip and the wind turned against her?

"Jenny!" A wonderfully familiar baritone voice roared above the wind and the thundering of her heart. "Are you there?"

"It's Zod!" Beth wriggled with joy. "Mommy, it's Zod!"

Tears misted Jenny's eyes and threatened to freeze on her lashes. He'd come back. Her sheikh had returned to protect her.

She didn't want to need him or anyone. But right now she did, desperately.

"We're here." Her voice caught, and she had to repeat the words louder.

"Are you hurt?" He was moving toward them.

"No," she called. "But we've got to get out of here."

He made his way around the tree, his strong, solid shape a refuge in the midst of chaos. Jenny and Beth headed toward him.

"I tried to call you from the airport." Reaching them, Zahad wrapped them in his arms. Jenny pressed close, her heart lifting. "The line kept ringing with no answer," he said. "When your cell phone was busy, I began to fear something might be wrong."

"The regular phone's dead. I was calling the police because I heard someone outside," Jenny explained. "But they're tied up with emergencies." She remembered suddenly how urgently he needed to make his flight. "How could you come back? You might not get home before Saturday."

"I will take my chances." Zahad's dark eyes shone with worry. "Why are you outside?"

"We must leave. I'll tell you on the way."

"Let's go, then." He didn't question her, she noted gratefully.

En route to his car, she outlined what Bill had said. She tried to soften the words for Beth's sake, but she had to share this information with Zahad.

"It is fortunate that I returned." He fitted the booster seat, which he'd taken from her SUV, into the back of his car. "I am only sorry I did not become suspicious of the right person sooner. She fooled me, also."

When they were all inside, the sheikh eased the car toward the street. Although they weren't yet out of danger, Jenny's anxiety lessened. As it did, the events of the past half hour began to replay through her mind.

The metallic thud outside. Her futile attempt to summon the police. The warning call that had saved her life. That reminded her of a point she hadn't mentioned.

"Dolly may be poisoning Bill," Jenny said. "He believes she might have poisoned her first two husbands as well."

"I was told she had divorced the second one. No one mentioned that he had died." Zahad stared through the windshield into the snow falling so thickly he had difficulty making out where to turn onto the road.

"Don't cut too sharply," Jenny advised. "There's a drainage ditch."

"I am aware of that, but thank you," he replied, and

pulled cautiously onto the street. "She told me her second husband bought her a television set when he won the lottery. It seems they were on good terms."

"That's strange." The discrepancy troubled Jenny. Perhaps it simply underlined Bill's increasingly confused mental state.

"What is that?" Zahad indicated a flare of reds and yellows coming into view off to their right. Blurred by the storm, it billowed upward with a surreal, hellish quality.

"It looks like a fire," Jenny said, puzzled.

"It is a fire." Zahad's nostrils flared as if smelling smoke. "It is a house burning."

"It's Ellen's house!" What on earth was going on? Had the women accidentally lit the gasoline in the wrong place?

"It burns very intensely." Zahad halted in the entrance to Dolly's driveway. "This is no accident. There is a ring of fire around the house."

"It looks pretty," Beth remarked innocently.

"Oh, honey!" Anyone inside would be trapped, Jenny realized. "Cindy! She might be in there."

She and Zahad exchanged looks. It took him less than a second to respond. "I will get her out." He left the key in the ignition. "Lock the doors after me. Call the fire department."

"Yes," she said. "Be careful." She didn't know what had happened except that they couldn't save themselves at the expense of a little girl.

He brushed a kiss across Jenny's mouth, his lips cool but his breath warm with promise. She wanted more but there was no time. He had to go.

There might be a world of differences between them, but she and her sheikh had one thing in common. Neither of them would risk leaving a child in a blazing building even to save themselves.

"If I do not come back quickly, drive away," he advised. Before she could respond, he opened the door and vanished into the white fury of the storm.

Jenny tried to imagine what had happened at Ellen's house. Had Dolly gone so insane that she'd tried to kill her own daughter and granddaughter? Had the women entered into some kind of suicide pact?

None of it made sense. The only thing she could deal with right now was the fact that Zahad was risking his life. Taking out her cell phone, she dialed 911, and this time she wouldn't take no for an answer.

THE SHEIKH FOUGHT his way up the driveway through the driving snow. The flames hadn't yet engulfed the house, he saw as he neared it. They were following the lines of some accelerant—gasoline, by the smell of it—poured around the foundation. The fire must have started only moments earlier or it would have spread.

He heard no screech of a smoke alarm from within. Perhaps it had been deactivated, or maybe they didn't have one. Whoever was inside might be sleeping, oblivious to the peril.

He saw no sign of a rampaging Dolly. But she would hardly stand here waiting for him, would she?

In a planter box, he spotted a loose brick. Seizing it, Zahad circled into the unfenced backyard. To rouse the occupants, he needed to target one of the bedroom windows.

Fire licked up the wooden siding, hindered slightly by the patches of stonework that decorated the exterior. In only a matter of minutes, however, it would reach the eaves and explode through the house.

Anyone who'd set a blaze like this wouldn't leave without seeing it to its conclusion. Again, Zahad looked around, but still saw no sign of the madwoman.

At the far end of the house, two windows flanked a smaller, rippled one that denoted a bathroom. Guessing that the corner room belonged to Ellen, he braced himself and heaved the brick.

It crashed into the glass. Through the gale, he heard the

pane break, but no one responded. Were the people inside unconscious or had they left?

Zahad considered it unlikely that this was a setup. Dolly wouldn't expect Jenny to rush into a burning building and she hadn't known of his return.

He had to brave the flames. Zahad crouched, meaning to roll in the snow to armor himself against the heat. As he did, a loud crack reverberated in his ears and a hot streak seared his right shoulder.

Startled, he lost his balance and jolted to his knees. When he put his hand down for support, pain wrenched through him.

He'd been shot. He knew that searing sensation all too well.

Out of the blizzard, a thin form materialized. Riveted by the gun pointed at him, Zahad took a moment to realize that the person behind it wasn't Dolly.

A hunting cap and a shock of white hair topped a narrow face contorted by fury. "If it wasn't for you, it'd be over by now!" Bill didn't look fragile now. He looked maniacal. "You're too damn nosey. You can thank yourself for getting Ray killed!"

"I don't understand," the sheikh said. "Why did you kill him? What about my brother?" He gauged the distance between them and the possibility of dodging the next bullet. The odds weren't close to zero.

"Your damn brother came sniffing around looking for sex. He shoulda minded his own business." Despite his rambling, the man kept one finger firmly on the trigger. "You think I married that witch so I could end up with nothing? More than two million dollars, that's what I got and I ain't giving it up. Goodbye, Mr. Sheikh."

A sudden movement registered on the edge of Zahad's consciousness and he began to turn. So did Bill just as a hard white ball smacked into his temple. His hand flew up and the gun roared into the air. A few yards away, Jenny ducked for cover.

Zahad launched himself onto the old man, his hand closing around the bony wrist. Bill held on, apparently powered by a combination of adrenaline and rage. Twisting harder than the sheikh would have thought possible, he brought up his legs and kicked out.

Battered full in the midsection, Zahad loosened his grip. In that instant, the gun swung back toward him. He barely had time to thrust at Bill's wrist with the heel of one hand before a blast slammed into him.

He landed on his back on the frozen earth, the breath knocked out of him and his ears throbbing. He knew he had to get up. He had to stop this viperish old man from killing anyone else. But his muscles refused to respond.

At last the ringing in his head diminished enough for him to hear sirens in the driveway. Help had arrived. He hoped it wasn't too late to save Jenny, because he had failed her.

"TWO MILLION DOLLARS," Dolly said hours later as they sat in the lobby of the police station. "I can't believe he sacrificed two lives out of pure greed. Heck, I'd have given him the money just to save Ray. Or Fario, either."

It was nearly daylight. Mrs. Welford had taken Cindy and Beth to her home, but no one else had slept. At least the storm had passed more quickly than expected, allowing the police to conduct their searches.

"You didn't even know your ex-husband was dead, let alone that he'd left you his lottery winnings. You couldn't have done anything." Jenny stretched her cramped legs. Except for giving her statement, she'd spent most of the night waiting, first in the hospital while Zahad's wound was treated, then here at Parker's request in case he needed more information. They'd nearly emptied the coffeepot provided for them and had consumed half a box of doughnuts.

Surreptitiously, she studied the sheikh, who'd refused to stay in the hospital for observation. Across the room, he sat talking on his cell phone, his sweater bulging over the bandage on his shoulder.

Mercifully, the bullet wound was superficial. He didn't appear to have suffered a head injury when the gun's recoil knocked him flat. Even so, he'd retreated into his own world.

He'd scarcely reacted on learning that Bill had died in the gun blast or that the brick he'd thrown had awakened Dolly, Ellen and Cindy just in time. Although he seemed relieved by the outcome, she sensed that in his mind he was already halfway back to Alqedar.

"I feel like an idiot," Dolly said. "I married a man who only wanted my money. I got suspicious a couple of years ago when he kept wanting me to put the property and my savings in both our names. When I announced that I was leaving everything to Ellen, we had a big fight. I told him I wanted a divorce."

"What changed your mind?"

"He got sick. I figured he was just playing on my sympathy until the doctor diagnosed fibromyalgia. I guess I'm a soft touch, because I hated to kick him out."

Judging by Bill's conduct last night, he must have been exaggerating the symptoms, Jenny thought. If she hadn't distracted him with that snowball, he'd have killed Zahad.

"About a year ago, he started acting nicer," Dolly continued. "I figured it was a sign I'd made the right choice. I had no idea Manley had died and Bill had intercepted the lawyer's letter."

A police search of Dolly's house in the past few hours had turned up papers forged with her name, claiming the inheritance. There was also a bankbook with a very large balance in the First National Bank of Crystal Point.

Apparently Bill had then set out to get rid of Dolly in a way that wouldn't cast suspicion on him. He'd played on Ellen's jealousy to turn her into a cyber-stalker and tried to take advantage of the situation to make it appear that Dolly had died as an innocent bystander.

Fario had simply wandered onto the scene at the wrong time. If he hadn't showed up, Dolly would have taken that bullet. Bill must have assumed the police would blame Jenny for rigging the gun as a form of protection.

Now Ellen was in jail facing stalking charges. After evidence turned up on her computer, she'd admitted that Bill claimed to have seen Ray and Jenny embracing. He'd talked her into the cyber-stalking, making it sound like justifiable revenge. She'd agreed—until Fario got killed.

Ray had died because Bill feared he'd come across the large amount of money in his account, although he'd already invested some of his ill-gotten funds in stocks and bonds. Jenny doubted they'd ever learn who had dropped that slip of paper with the bank logo in her house. However it had landed there, it had set off a lethal chain of events.

Based on what the police had found in Dolly's computer, Bill had continued the cyber-stalking for a few days, still hoping to set up some kind of smoke screen. When that didn't pan out, he'd made another attempt to kill his wife and frame Jenny. He'd spooked her into fleeing to make her look guilty, or at least, that was what she surmised, and a gasoline can stolen from her shed had been discovered at the scene.

Despite all that she'd been through, Jenny hoped Ellen would get off with probation. Losing her husband and her home seemed like more than enough punishment, and Cindy needed her mother.

Zahad flipped his phone shut and looked up. "My flight was canceled because of the weather. I can catch the same plane that will carry Fario's remains this morning if Sergeant Finley allows me to go."

"I suggested he write a letter of commendation for use in your homeland," Dolly said. "If it weren't for you, my family and I would have died."

"Thank you," the sheikh replied. "I am glad you escaped safely."

When Finley joined them a few minutes later, it turned out he had followed Dolly's advice. Producing an envelope, he told Zahad, "It's addressed To Whom It May Concern and says you aren't a suspect in your brother's death and have cooperated in my investigation. I hope that helps you.''

"Thank you. I would shake your hand if it were not too painful.''

"Understood.'' The sergeant looked a trifle sheepish but Jenny had to admire his good sportsmanship.

"I know there are many loose ends, but I must leave now,'' the sheikh told him. "If it is acceptable to you, I will catch a flight this morning.''

As Parker weighed his request, Jenny noticed pronounced pouches under his eyes. "Ordinarily, I'd ask you to stick around,'' he said at last. "However, I know you've got your brother's body to bury. And I understand there are some serious issues at stake in your homeland.''

"Very serious,'' Zahad agreed. "You have my phone number and e-mail address. I will be happy to answer any further questions.''

"Good luck to you,'' Parker told him. "As for everybody else, you can all go home. We're done for tonight. I mean, this morning.''

"I'd like to see my daughter,'' Dolly said.

"Her lawyer just showed up. You can talk to her when he leaves,'' Parker replied.

She nodded. "I'll be here.''

Zahad couldn't drive in his condition, Jenny realized. "I'll take you to the airport,'' she offered. "I can turn your rental in and catch a cab home.''

"Thank you.'' To Parker, the sheikh said, "Please have the bomb squad check out Jenny's SUV, just in case.''

"We already did. It's clean,'' the sergeant explained. "We removed the tree, too, so we could access the tool-shed.''

The men regarded each other with grudging appreciation. "Perhaps we are more alike than either of us wished to believe,'' Zahad said.

"I'll grant you that." With a rueful smile, the detective held the door. "Have a safe trip."

Outside, dawn light was breaking over a storybook scene of snow-laden buildings and cars. The mounds of white added an authentic note to the Christmas decorations.

Jenny appreciated the chance to spend a little more time with the sheikh. But despite his affability at the police station, he made no move to touch her as they walked to his car.

His thoughts must be flying ahead to what awaited him in Alqedar. Jenny wished they could hold on a little while longer to the magic they'd created amid tragedy this past week. Unfortunately, the bright light of day was dissolving the dream along with the nightmare.

HE HAD NEARLY FAILED Jenny. Lying powerless on the snow after the gun went off, Zahad had realized that nothing in his life mattered as much as keeping her safe.

He had never felt so helpless. Because once he admitted to himself that he loved her, he also had to face the fact that he desperately feared losing her to fate.

While fighting a revolution, the sheikh had never worried about danger. If he lost a battle, he could always regroup and fight again another day. If he died in a just cause, he would go to heaven.

Love was different. It made him vulnerable. A man could not always be there to protect the woman and child without whom his existence had no meaning.

Riding in the car as Jenny negotiated the freshly cleared road around the lake, Zahad collected his thoughts. For hours, he had been stunned by the shock of his wound, by the sudden turn of events at the Rivases' house and by being rendered defenseless, before he discovered the deflected shot had killed Bill.

His cousin Sharif had loved this deeply and his first wife had died. Years later, Sharif had been fortunate enough to love again, but Zahad knew that he would not. He did not form attachments as easily as his cousin. Jenny was his first love and she would be the last.

How much did he have the right to ask of her? Was she not better off staying here, now that her enemies had been routed, rather than coming to a land where his own rivals still flourished?

Beside him, she broke the silence. "I never thought I'd be so grateful that my father made me play softball. You probably didn't notice what good aim I had when I smacked Bill with my snowball."

"I did notice. It is too bad the students at your school could not witness your prowess."

"There's no need for sarcasm."

"I was not joking."

"Then you're forgiven."

She grew quiet again. Morning light danced through her golden hair.

In a few minutes, they would reach the airport and say goodbye. The bond between them, however, would not break. It seemed so strong to Zahad that he imagined it tethering the airplane and bringing it crashing down on takeoff.

Of course that would not really happen. He must take matters into his own hands.

"Come with me," he said.

Jenny blinked. "I'm sorry?"

"I do not mean this instant," he clarified. "I know you have obligations and you must make arrangements to bring your daughter. I am asking that you come to Alqedar and be my wife."

In the pause that followed, he recalled that a man was supposed to stage a production of asking a woman to marry him. He supposed he should have provided gifts and flowery promises, perhaps to the accompaniment of music.

Such affectations lay beyond Zahad's grasp. Simplicity and directness were all he knew.

"I can't," Jenny said with a sigh. "Zahad, I'm sorry.

You mean more to me than any man I've ever known. But I have my own dreams and plans. I can't give them up for anyone, not even you."

"I understand," he replied.

There, it was done. He had taken the risk he must take, and she had given the answer she must give.

Was this truly the end? The end for now, in any case.

They drove for a while longer without speaking. Jenny pulled to the curb in front of the small terminal. When their eyes met, he saw sadness but no uncertainty.

"I will keep you informed of what happens in my country," he said.

"I'll let you know what the police turn up." She swallowed. "Zahad, thank you for everything."

How should he respond? Pat answers evaded him even under the best of circumstances.

What he wanted to say was that someday he would return, that he would find a way to change her mind and that he would shower her with treasure if that was what it took. But to say such things would be an insult. He respected her decision.

"No thanks are due," the sheikh replied. "We have both accomplished our aims. It has been a successful alliance."

Jenny smiled tremulously. "Only you would say something like that at a time like this."

"There is one thing I can promise you if we meet again," he said.

"Yes?"

"I will have an interesting new scar to show you." Zahad nodded toward his shoulder and winced as it throbbed. He made no objection when Jenny came around to open his door. He might be proud but he was no fool.

Outside, they stood awkwardly facing each other. Jenny seemed too beautiful and too delicate to belong to a ruffian like him, but even so, he luxuriated in the sight of her.

"I don't want to hurt your arm, so I guess I can't hug you." Jenny reached to ruffle the ragged edges of his hair.

"You might want to get that cut. After all, you're a very important person."

"I will attend to it," Zahad said, and promptly put it out of his mind.

After a last regretful look, Jenny turned away. He started to reach for her and nearly cried out with pain. Perhaps he should have accepted the doctor's medication after all, he reflected.

In any case, he had lost the chance to touch her.

However, it wasn't his arm that hurt most as Zahad approached the security checkpoint a few minutes later. An ache formed deep in his chest, or perhaps his stomach. It grew more agonizing with every step he took away from Jenny.

By the time he reached the aircraft, it had grown into a fiery corona around a hard black lump. As he thought of what he was leaving behind, Zahad realized this must be what people meant when they spoke of a broken heart. Already, it began to seem familiar, like something he would have to live with for a very long time.

Chapter Eighteen

On a Friday in mid-January, Jenny gave a farewell party for Lew Blackwell during lunchtime. It was just cake and punch in the teachers' lounge, but she knew he treasured the heartfelt good wishes of his co-workers.

"I'm a little envious," Jenny admitted when the other teachers had returned to their classrooms.

"You're ambitious," Lew noted. "There are people who'll hold that against you, but you'll leave them in the dust."

"I guess so." She began cleaning up the paper plates. "We'll miss you around here."

"Don't stay in Mountain Lake too long. You might lose your fire, and that would be a shame."

His words rang in her mind for the rest of the afternoon. What she felt wasn't so much a longing for more money or prestige as a desire to help a large number of students who really needed assistance. Perhaps she could find a way to combine this with raising her daughter, but Jenny had been too busy during the past month even to think about her career path.

Since Zahad left, the days had sped by, although the nights seemed almost unbearably long. Even though they'd known each other for only a short time, she found it hard to believe he was gone. She kept imagining she heard his voice in the other room, or that at any moment she would roll over and see a smile light his scarred face.

Life went on, however. After Jenny spoke on Ellen's behalf at a hearing, she'd been granted probation. Dolly had put her property up for sale so the two of them and Cindy could move to a new community away from bitter memories.

At least they would never want for money. A paper trail had turned up a little more than two million dollars that belonged to Dolly.

The police had definitively linked Bill to both murders. They'd also learned that his description fit that of a man who, years earlier, had romanced then fleeced single women in towns that Bill had once passed through as a truck driver.

Pieces of the puzzle kept falling into place. Jenny remembered the time when Bill got on the wrong bus and landed in Crystal Point. In retrospect, she realized he'd gone there to conduct his banking and pretended to be lost when Ray spotted him.

Bill had been an instinctive liar and a devious plotter. Not all of his schemes worked, but he'd nearly gotten away with them.

As for Al Garroway and the carjackers, all faced trials and potential long sentences. Tish had filed for divorce.

That Friday afternoon, the teachers cleared out quickly at day's end. The following week was midwinter break and many of them planned trips.

Jenny left a little after five to collect Beth. They stopped for pizza at an Italian diner.

"Are you sure you don't want a party?" she asked her daughter while they ate. Today was the little girl's sixth birthday. They could still schedule a get-together for Saturday or Sunday.

Beth shook her head. "It won't be any fun without Cindy."

"I know. I'm sorry." Ellen had already moved away

with her mother and daughter. Although Beth had other friends at school, they weren't the same.

Grant couldn't be here, either. He'd even declined Jenny's offer to visit him at Christmas, saying he didn't want his daughter to see him in jail. The two of them had flown to Connecticut instead to celebrate with Jenny's mother.

"Can Zod come?" Beth asked over a slice of pizza. "I want him to have some of my cake."

Beth was always delighted when the sheikh asked about her in his e-mails. She'd also received one directly from Amy's seven-year-old daughter, Farhanna, and had gleefully dictated a response to Jenny.

"He's very far away," Jenny explained. "But I'm sure he's thinking about you."

"Maybe he can come next week. For school break." It wasn't a question, so Jenny didn't answer.

After dinner and an animated movie, it was nearly eight o'clock when they arrived home. Jenny felt the usual quiver of apprehension as she turned into the driveway. She wondered if her dark memories would ever fade.

"We can have some cake now and open presents," she said as they entered through the back.

"Okay." Beth didn't sound enthusiastic. Most likely she was just tired.

Jenny disarmed the security device and, for an instant, indulged in a fantasy that Zahad was waiting in the other room. He still knew the code, after all. Maybe she and Beth wouldn't have to celebrate alone, ever again.

Of course she found no sign of him when they went in. She'd been as blindly optimistic as her daughter.

The sheikh had asked her to marry him and she'd turned him down. She felt certain she had made the best decision, but sometimes it didn't feel right.

The phone rang. Beth flew by. "I'll get it!"

Who was the child expecting? "Honey, maybe I should—"

"Sanger residence," Beth said into the mouthpiece. "Hi, Zod! I knew you'd call!" The little girl beamed.

Zahad had phoned once before, several weeks earlier, to say that he'd been formally appointed governor of the province. Hashim, humiliated by the people's rejection, had left the country. After learning from news accounts how diligently her stepson had worked to solve her son's murder, Numa had apologized for her accusations. She'd accepted his offer of a pension and gone to live with her sister's family.

"Mommy!" Beth called. "Zod's sending me a doll! Farhanna picked it."

"That's sweet." Jenny was amazed that the sheikh had thought of sending a gift or even remembered her daughter's birthday.

"He wants to talk to you." Beth held out the receiver.

Jenny's hand tingled as she took it. He was right there, on the other end of the line, waiting to talk to her. "Beth's thrilled," she said. "It was kind of you to call."

Grinning, her daughter trotted out of the room. A moment later, Jenny heard her announcing to her doll, "You're going to have a sister!"

"I have often wanted to phone." Zahad's voice vibrated through her deliciously. "However, I know you are busy with your many plans."

Not so busy that she hadn't missed him every waking minute, she thought. "How are you? How are things going?"

"Matters are progressing. A Belgian company intends to build a carpet factory here. Also, a large charitable group will finance a new school, which we need."

"It sounds exciting." Jenny reminded herself to check Yazir's Web site to learn more about those developments.

"What about Mountain Lake?" he asked. "Are you still happy there?"

She didn't know how to answer. "There've been…many adjustments," she said at last.

"My offer has not changed."

Her eyelids stung. In a way, Jenny had wanted to hear that, but she still couldn't accept. As she'd said, she had to plan her own future. "Zahad…"

He must have heard the regret in her tone. "I apologize. I should not have mentioned it."

"It's all right. I'm really glad you called. Beth's been asking about you."

"Farhanna wishes to meet her," he replied. "Perhaps someday Beth can visit here. It would be educational."

What was it like, this palace of Zahad's? Jenny tried to picture the scenes and the people he'd spoken of, Amy and Sharif and their families, and realized she would love to see them, too. "Maybe when she's older."

"Of course."

Their goodbyes were muted. She hung up feeling as if the conversation was unfinished.

At the entrance to her daughter's room, Jenny saw that Beth had arrayed her stuffed animals and Minnie on the floor and was serving them with her miniature tea set. The little girl was holding her own birthday party.

The tears Jenny had held back earlier slid down her cheeks. She wanted more than this for Beth and for herself, as well. But she didn't know where to find it.

She retreated to her office and switched on the computer. In seconds, she made her way to Yazir's site.

She found the news about the carpet factory at the top of the page. Jenny skipped it to read about the new school. It was part of a major overhaul of the educational system, the article stated and provided a link to a job notice for minister of education.

She clicked on the link.

The ad referred to "long hours, tremendous challenges and a modest salary. Knowledge of Arabic not required." Qualifications included a master's degree and experience as an education administrator.

Jenny stared at the screen for a long time.

ON MONDAY, a delegation of German businessmen pelted Zahad with questions during a luncheon at the city's newest restaurant, which was, ironically, French. They seemed impressed both by his blunt answers and by the full sheikh regalia that he had donned for the occasion. This included a long white robe and a red-and-white checked headdress, held in place with a black band.

Zahad hoped no one noticed that he was wearing jeans and a T-shirt underneath. Preoccupied with going over the plans for a new sewer system, he'd hurriedly thrown on his formal wear right before the meeting.

Back at his office, Zahad drummed his fingers on his broad desk. Where was Amy? He'd expected her to hasten into his office to discuss the results of the luncheon, which she had also attended, but she'd disappeared immediately afterward.

Swiveling, he surveyed the busy market scene beyond the palace wall. Even through the glass, he imagined he could smell the spices, perfumes and coffee. Jewelry glimmered in the sunlight and brightly colored clothing hung from kiosks.

A dusty four-wheel-drive vehicle wended its way between two camels burdened with market goods. While two ladies in European dress examined tooled-leather purses, a woman in a long cloak and black head scarf strolled past, talking intently on her cell phone. His land combined the old and the new, the high-tech and the traditional, and Zahad loved it.

After a tap at the door, his secretary entered. The young man had come to him the previous year at Sharif's recommendation. "There is a candidate here for the post of education minister."

"I was not aware I had an appointment," he replied.

"Mrs. Haroun set it up." His secretary knew better than to interfere in the sometimes tempestuous but mutually respectful relationship between the sheikh and his director of economic development.

"Very well. Show him in," Zahad said.

"It is a female."

A woman wished to move to this remote province and assume the job of education minister? He hadn't anticipated this. Indeed, the recruiters he'd contacted before posting the job had informed him it was unlikely he would find any qualified candidate willing to relocate to such a backward community.

"Show *her* in."

"Yes, sir."

On his computer, Zahad reviewed the job notice. When the door opened, he spoke without looking up. "Please sit down."

"That robe is fantastic," said the dearest voice in all the world. "Is that how you usually dress around here?"

He jumped to his feet so fast he banged his thigh on the desk's kneehole. "Jenny!"

Her green eyes looked luminous, as if lit from within. Distractedly, Zahad noticed that she'd tucked her blond hair into a businesslike twist and wore a powder-blue suit.

"I'm here about the job."

"Excuse me?" He stopped in midstride.

"I understand you need a minister of education." Jenny stated the fact calmly, as if it were the most natural thing in the world for her to appear in his palace. "I happened to have a week off so I decided to bring Beth on a little trip."

A little trip halfway around the world? "Where is she now?"

"Playing with Farhanna."

Although he wanted to sweep her into his arms and kiss her senseless, he stayed where he was. "You talked to Amy about the job?"

"I got her number from the Web site and called her Friday night. She thought you might be willing to interview me." Jenny gave him a *Mona Lisa* smile. "The job sounds like what I'm looking for and I'm sure we could get along, although I have to say, if you're going to dress like that, I might get sidetracked.''

He glanced down at his white robe. ''Ah, this was to impress the Germans.'' Feeling a bit overdressed, he removed the headdress and set it aside.

''I'm sure they were very impressed,'' she said.

''Did you really come about the job?'' He finger-combed his shaggy hair, no doubt the worse for wear. ''Because if you did, you are hired.''

''Just like that?''

''I have observed your empathy for children and I know of your experience in the field,'' Zahad replied. ''When can you start?''

''I...soon. How's your shoulder?''

He flexed it. ''Almost well.''

''You promised me an interesting scar.''

The air between them vibrated with unspoken longings. Jenny hadn't come simply to apply for a job or she would not make a personal reference to his body, the sheikh reflected.

This must be one of those occasions when a man was supposed to read between the lines. He felt grateful that this insight had occurred to him. Before he met Jenny, it would not have.

''I cannot show you my scar just now. However, I have something else for you.''

From the desk drawer, he removed a carved wooden box and handed it over. Her face alive with curiosity, Jenny opened it.

He heard a sharp intake of breath as she stared down at the filigree-gold necklace and earrings. ''I saw those in the marketplace,'' Zahad continued. ''I meant to bring them to you one day soon.''

When she raised her eyes, he saw love shining there. At least, he hoped it was, because he knew love was radiating from his own face and he didn't want to look foolish.

''They're exquisite. Zahad...''

His heart nearly stopped beating. He prayed she would not refuse him again. "Yes?"

"After we get married, you're really going to have to get a haircut," Jenny said.

If she had meant to add anything, she never got the chance. Catching her in his arms, the sheikh pulled her into an embrace that lasted for a very long time.

He was glad she had dreams and plans. He was even happier that from now on, he was going to be part of them. "I love you, Jenny," he said.

"It's wonderful to be home," she answered, and kissed him again.

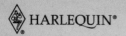

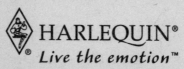

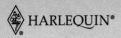

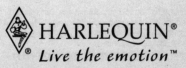

If you enjoyed what you just read,
then we've got an offer you can't resist!

Take 2 bestselling love stories FREE!

Plus get a FREE surprise gift!

National Bestselling Author

brenda novak

COLD FEET

Despite the cloud of suspicion that followed her father to his grave, Madison Lieberman maintained his innocence...*until* crime writer Caleb Trovato forces her to confront the past once again.

"Readers will quickly be drawn into this well-written, multi-faceted story that is an engrossing, compelling read."
—*Library Journal*

Available February 2004.

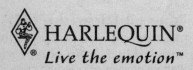

HARLEQUIN®
® *Live the emotion*™

Visit us at www.eHarlequin.com

PHCF

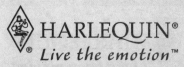

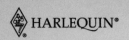

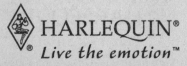